Praise for Bill Myers

Angel of Wrath

"Bill Myers is a genius. Not only is *Angel of Wrath* full of engaging characters and heartstopping suspense, but underneath it explores thoughts and truths that will keep you pondering long after the book is closed."

—Lee Stanley, producer, *Gridiron Gang*

The Voice

"A crisp, express-train read featuring 3D characters, cinematic settings and action, and, as usual, a premise I wish I'd thought of. Succeeds splendidly! Two thumbs up!"

—Frank E. Peretti, author

"Nonstop action and a brilliantly crafted young heroine will keep readers engaged as this adventure spins to its thought-provoking conclusion." —Kris Wilson, *CBA Magazine*

"It's a real 'what if?' book with plenty of thrills . . . that will definitely create questions all the way to its thought-provoking finale. The success of Myers's stories is a sweet combination of a believable storyline, intense action, and brilliantly crafted, yet flawed characters." —Dale Lewis, TitleTrakk.com

The Face of God

"Strong writing, edgy . . . replete with action."

—*Publishers Weekly*

Fire of Heaven

"I couldn't put *Fire of Heaven* down. Bill Myers's writing is crisp, fast-paced, provocative . . . A very compelling story."

—Francine Rivers Siddons, author

continued . . .

Blood of Heaven

"With the chill of a Robin Cook techno-thriller and the spiritual depth of a C. S. Lewis allegory, this book is a fast-paced, action-packed thriller."   —Angela Ewell Hunt, author

"Now this is innovative. Bill Myers has played a great game of 'what if?'—creating a compelling story of grace triumphing over judgment . . . A bold new twist on an age-old theme. *Blood of Heaven* is an enjoyable and provocative read. I wish I'd thought of it!"   —Frank Peretti, author

Eli

"The always surprising Myers has written another clever and provocative tale."   —*Booklist*

"With this thrilling and ominous tale, Myers continues to shine brightly in speculative fiction based upon biblical truth. Highly recommended."   —*Library Journal*

"Myers weaves a deft, affecting tale."   —*Publishers Weekly*

Soul Tracker

"*Soul Tracker* provides a treat for previous fans of the author, but also a fitting introduction to those unfamiliar with his work. I'd recommend the book to anyone, initiated or not. But be careful to check your expectations at the door . . . it's not what you think it is."   —Brian Reaves, *Fuse Magazine*

"Thought-provoking and touching, this imaginative tale blends elements of science fiction with Christian theology."
                    —*Library Journal*

"Myers strikes deep into the heart of eternal truth with this imaginative first book of the Soul Tracker series. Readers will be eager for more." —*Romantic Times Magazine*

The Seeing

"Bill Myers's novel . . . compels the reader to burn through the pages. Cliff-hangers abound and the stakes are raised higher and higher as the story progresses—intense, action-shocking twists!" —TitleTrakk.com

"An entertaining novel, Bill Myers's *The Seeing* is a great reminder of spiritual warfare and the impact of choice and is reminiscent of Frank Peretti's *This Present Darkness*." —IDealinHope.com

When the Last Leaf Falls

"A wonderful novella . . . Any parent will warm to the humorous reminiscences and the loving exasperation of this father for his strong-willed daughter . . . Compelling characters and fresh, vibrant anecdotes of one family's faith journey." —*Publishers Weekly*

ANGEL *of* WRATH

A Novel

BILL MYERS

New York   Boston   Nashville

FaithWords
Hachette Book Group
237 Park Avenue
New York, NY 10017

Visit our Web site at www.faithwords.com.

Printed in the United States of America

First Edition: April 2009
10 9 8 7 6 5 4 3 2 1

FaithWords is a division of Hachette Book Group, Inc.
The FaithWords name and logo are trademarks of Hachette Book Group, Inc.

Library of Congress Cataloging-in-Publication Data
Myers, Bill
  Angel of wrath / Bill Myers.—1st ed.
    p. cm.
  ISBN 978-0-446-69800-9
  1. Clergy—Fiction. 2. Attempted assassination—Fiction. 3. Satanism—Fiction. I. Title.
  PS3563.Y36A83 2009
  813'.54—dc22   2008023673

Book design by Charles Sutherland

To my ISI guys: Thanks for the sharpening!

AUTHOR'S NOTE

Although this is a sequel to *The Voice*, there's no need to go out and buy the first (unless you like the characters or want to help get my kids through college). I've tried to drop in important facts relating to *The Voice* throughout *Angel of Wrath* without giving too much away. In any case, here's a brief background of the three main characters:

Charlie Madison gave up a promising career in Special Ops when he and his wife found God. He even planned on attending a seminary until his wife and daughter were murdered by terrorists seeking revenge. As a result he became a burned-out recluse.

Jazmin is a thirteen-year-old who invaded Charlie's quiet life when her father and her mother, Charlie's sister, were kidnapped by foreign agents. The agents wanted the computer program her parents had discovered that could play back the Voice of God.

Lisa Harmon broke too many FBI rules and was thrown out of the Bureau in her efforts to help Charlie and Jazmin find the computer program. Despite Lisa's emotional baggage, Charlie found himself opening up to her and feeling things he had not felt since he lost his family.

And now it's a year later. . . .

As always, I appreciate your support and hope you find this both entertaining and a little thought-provoking.

Thanks again.

Bill Myers

www.Billmyers.com

"Not by might nor by power, but by my Spirit," says the LORD Almighty.

Zechariah 4:6

ANGEL *of* WRATH

Chapter One

"Molly? Where's my Molly?"

Dr. Norman Gibson chuckled as he stepped back into his daughter's bedroom. "Right. What was I thinking?" He headed across the tan Berber carpet to her dresser. "One Molly Dolly coming up."

He knew it was a ploy to get him to stay longer—after the glass of water, after the prayers, after filling him in on every imaginable detail of her day. Yes, even at four, little Katie knew how to play him. And he loved it. These were the times that calmed and relaxed him, especially on days like today—a hemorrhage that had been nearly impossible to stop, a third-trimester abortion, which always left him just a little bit unnerved, and the fan mail. . . .

"We got another one," the receptionist had said as he passed her desk.

"Another?"

She handed him a church bulletin. It contained the usual announcements and meetings. What was not usual were the four words highlighted:

MISSION CRUISE Sign up today. Enjoy the comforts of a Baja cruise and build a local church in Encinitas. Even though you may not have any building experience, come for the fellowship and enjoy God's blessings as you bless others!

KARATE FOR CHRIST will hold a potluck this Sunday night at the home of Marsha Lane. Check church Web site for directions.

MEN'S BREAKFAST Every Saturday in the Banquet Hall, 8:00 AM. Great fellowship. Great food. Be sure not to miss it.

JUNIOR HIGHERS Prove your warrior skills at the Video Game Marathon this Friday night, 7:00 PM in the Recreation Hall.

The clinic was used to receiving threats. It came with the territory. But this one struck closer to home. The bulletin was from his own church. It had set him on edge more than he cared to admit. Even now, here in Katie's room, he could feel his heart pounding. He knew much of it came from the *grande* mocha that a new cashier at the Coffee Kiosk had insisted he try. It was his nightly routine to swing by the drive-in hut and pick up a small decaf latte on his way home. But the way the young man went on and on about some new blend, and the fact that it was a free sample (and a *grande* at that)—well, he'd had little choice in the matter. To be honest, he couldn't tell that much difference—except for the caffeine. It was supposed to be decaf, but the jolt it packed made it pretty clear they'd made a mistake. And, given his history of heart problems, he would never have taken it had he known.

Norman picked up the porcelain doll from Katie's dresser. Molly was her favorite, at least this month. To his surprise, he noticed a red dot of light glowing on its face. He frowned and turned to his daughter. She must have gotten hold of the laser pointer they used for playing with the cat.

But both of her hands were free. He looked back at Molly. His frown deepened. If the light wasn't coming from Katie, then where—

Suddenly, the doll's head exploded in his hands. He turned away, shielding his face, as Katie screamed. He'd seen his share of cop and spy movies and spun toward the window, expecting it to be shattered by a sniper's bullet.

It wasn't.

"Daddy!"

Realizing danger but not understanding it, he raced to his daughter. "Get down!" He threw himself on top of her and she let out a muffled scream. He scooped her tightly into his arms and rolled onto the floor.

"Daddy!"

"It's okay, it's okay." He raised his head, searching the room, his heart hammering. "Don't worry, everything's—"

He spotted the red dot and froze. It was moving up the wall to the shelf of ceramic dolls above Katie's bed. It stopped on the first doll, a ballerina. He watched breathlessly as it hovered, until the doll's head exploded, spraying pieces of ceramic throughout the room. Katie screamed and he covered her head as the splinters and dust rained down upon them.

Norman spun back to the window. It was *still* intact. He twirled to the shelf as the dot found the next doll and blew its head apart.

"Daddy!"

"Shh, shh." Trying to catch his breath, he turned to the open door. Holding Katie close, he half-crawled, half-squirmed toward it, always protecting her body with his.

The next doll exploded.

Katie's screams turned hysterical.

And the next.

"*Daddy!*"

And the next.

"It's okay," he gasped, fighting for breath. "It's okay." He looked over his shoulder to the dolls' shelf. Printed on the wall behind where they once sat, he now saw the words:

THOU SHALT NOT KILL

His left shoulder flared in pain. He'd been shot! No, that wasn't possible. He spun to the window. It was still there!

"Norm?" He heard Jan running toward the stairs from the kitchen. "Norman!"

At last he reached the bedroom door. The pain spread down his arm, excruciating. Still holding Katie and still crawling, he made it to the safety of the hallway, out of the window's view.

"*Norm!*" Jan stood in the entry hall down at the bottom of the stairs.

He pressed Katie's face to his chest and struggled to stand. He could barely shout through the pain. "Get away from the windows!"

She started up the steps. "What's going on? What—"

"Get down!" he gasped. "Go back!"

The first stair shifted under his feet and he lunged for the railing.

"Norm!"

"Mommy!"

He clung to the railing as Jan ran toward them. "What happened?" she cried. Arriving, she took the sobbing child into her arms.

He grabbed the banister with both hands, forcing out the word. "Down!"

"What happened?"

He could no longer answer.

She took his arm and started helping him down the steps. "You're soaked."

He nodded, barely able to think through the pain. At least they were away from the window. At least they were safe.

"What's going on?" she demanded.

They arrived in the entry hall just in time for him to see the red dot appear in the antique mirror.

"Loo—" he wheezed but could no longer talk. He motioned with his head.

She followed his gaze. "What?"

Was she blind? It was right there in the mirror! "Lll . . ."

"What?"

The room began to spin, growing white. He struggled to hang on and watched in horror as the dot crawled across the mirror toward their own reflection. It caught the top of Jan's shoulder, then came to rest on the center of Katie's forehead.

Unable to breathe, unable to scream, he dragged his legs forward, clinging to Jan for support, until he stood between his family and the light, allowing the dot to hit his chest . . . until his strength gave way and he collapsed into Jan's arms.

"*Norman!*"

He was facing the front door now, and the little half-moon of glass at its top that allowed a pencil-thin beam to shine in. That was the last thing Dr. Norman Gibson saw before he crumpled to the entryway floor—not from a sniper's bullet, but from a destroyed heart.

✝

Getting drunk was a lot easier than Will thought.

He remembered some family reunion where he was a little kid being dared to steal a sip of his uncle's drink. Stealing the sip was easy. Trying to swallow it was not. It burned and made him gag so bad he thought he was going to die. 'Course, everybody thought it was cute, seeing little seven-year-old Willie get his first taste of booze. Everybody but his dad. Sure, he smiled and laughed like everyone else, which Will didn't exactly appreciate, but then again he always smiled and laughed like everyone else . . . at least 'til they got home.

Then it was sermon time.

"Don't you know what people will say? Don't you know how it reflects on God, how it reflects on the church, how it reflects on blah-blah-blah. . . ?"

Life in the fishbowl. It wasn't the first time he'd heard it, and it wouldn't be the last. But times change. And so do people. . . .

Fast-forward nine years. Boys' lavatory. Arlington High School.

"Not so fast, man, save some for us."

Will nodded but continued to gulp. The half bottle of Jack Daniels the three of them had already put down was definitely high-octane—he could still feel its fire in his throat and gut. But this other stuff, it was more soda pop than booze. In fact it even had the word "lemonade" on the label. Talk about user-friendly. No wonder the girls liked it.

"Come on, man," the second kid said. Will didn't even know his name. He was just some tatted Goth, a follower of Jason Ballard. With only a few more minutes of lunch period left, Will passed the "lemonade" back to him. You didn't make new friends by being a pig. And that's what the new-and-improved Will Harmon was all about: making new friends.

The first wave of dizziness hit him hard. The second, harder.

The other kid, a bald and brooding senior, snickered. "I told you it had a kick, man."

Will tried to grin, but wasn't sure he pulled it off. He reached back for the bottle.

"You're wasted, dude. On an empty stomach, you've had way too—"

"I had breakfast." Will's tongue felt thick, but it was true; he'd had breakfast. Waffles and eggs, cooked to perfection by dear ol' Mom. Dear ol' Mom, who did everything to perfection.

He reached for the bottle but misjudged the distance.

More snickers as they put it in his hand.

Another grin. Another guzzle.

"Whoa, whoa, whoa. . . ."

But he didn't listen. If he was going to shed his old rep

for a new one, he was going to do it in style. Besides, the stuff barely had any effect.

"It's Muller!" Someone shouted from the door. "Muller's coming!"

Will's friends became a blur of movement. One minute they were cussing their luck, the next they had literally evaporated, along with the bottle.

"Hey, wai' a min—" His tongue was numb, fallen asleep, like at the dentist's.

He tried again. "Guyss?"

No one answered.

He looked around the lavatory and noticed the mirror moving. He closed his eyes to make it stop. When he reopened them, he had to grab the washbasin and steady himself.

"Heey!"

No answers.

"Whar's evewybuey. . . ." His tongue was lead. Lips turned to rubber. He swallowed. The spinning was making him nauseous.

"Guyss?" He turned his head. Not a good idea. He swallowed hard to keep from retching.

He heard the door open, a voice booming behind him. "Mr. Harmon?"

"Pressent." He giggled. It was pretty funny, when you thought about it.

"Mr. Harmon." Footsteps approached.

Will reached out for the washbasin but forgot where he put it.

"Mr. Harmon, have you been drinking?"

He wanted to answer, but first he had to swallow.

"Look at me when I'm talking to you, young man."

Using all his powers of concentration, Will turned. The combined movement was more than he could handle. Like Mount Vesuvius, he erupted, spewing waffle and eggs all over the man's crisp white shirt.

The first time.

The second, he sprayed his slacks . . . saving whatever was left for Vice Principal Muller's Italian loafers.

✝

"Picture it: ads on every shopping cart in every major food chain. We'll reach an entirely different demographic than our current TV and radio spots." Aaron Buchanan, the jowly outreach pastor, looked at each of the men sitting around the highly polished boardroom table. "And, according to the Lay Media Committee, with the right leveraging we could bring the ad company's rates down 30 percent."

Senior Pastor Thomas Harmon, mid-forties, good-looking with just a trace of a paunch, pretended to take notes on his legal pad. This was important. You didn't become one of the fastest-growing churches in western Washington without aggressive, outside-the-box marketing. But, try as he might, his heart just wasn't in it. He was still back with Jan and little Katie Gibson.

"Heart attack," the sheriff had told him on the porch of the house. "But definitely provoked. Someone broke into the place earlier and attached explosive charges with light sensors to each of the kid's dolls. Detonated them by a low-power laser from across the street."

Thomas shook his head. "Who would do such a thing?"

"We have an idea," the sheriff said. "The guy was a pro, and a trained marksman. That kind of narrows the field."

"And you think it's because of Dr. Gibson's work at the clinic?"

"According to the church bulletin—*your* church bulletin—yes."

Thomas stared down at the doodles he'd been drawing on his pad. Such brutality. And right there in front of the man's wife and daughter. He took a breath and quietly exhaled. Fortunately, the sheriff assured him they'd keep the church's connection out of the media.

"I'm not so certain." Roy White, the administrative pastor, was speaking. "With tithes and offerings flatlining, this may not be the time for any new expenditures. In fact—"

Buchanan interrupted, "This is *exactly* the time. With revenue and attendance plateauing, this is when we should be pressing ahead." He looked around the table with the same dramatics he'd used on the congregation during his times behind the pulpit. "Gentlemen, like Joshua, like Caleb, I say now is the time to move forward and take our community for the Lord. Let's not be afraid of the giants in the land."

For the second time in as many minutes, Thomas felt the PDA in his pocket vibrate. Only a handful of people in the world had the number—just top staffers and his family. It wasn't like the old days, when his dad was at the helm. Back then everyone had access to the pastor. Today, that just wasn't possible. When you're running a church of over four thousand people, you needed as much insulation as you could get. Of course, Thomas hated it. He'd always fancied himself the people's pastor. But turning this once-ruined church around to become the largest in three counties had its drawbacks. Having to shift from pastor to CEO was one of them.

"I suppose we could transfer some funds from our print outreach," Jesse Hawkins, the communications pastor and the youngest of the group, said. "Latest stats indicate fewer than ever read the newspapers."

"Precisely," Buchanan agreed. "Young mothers today don't have the time. But thirty, forty, sixty minutes of the name 'Calvary Cathedral' in front of them, week in and week out—"

Once again Thomas's phone vibrated. He pulled it from his pocket and saw it was his wife, Sharon. "Excuse me, gentlemen." He cleared his throat. "I'm sorry, I need to take this."

They nodded as he rose to exit the room. It was the first break he'd had in ninety minutes, and it felt good to stretch his legs. He waited until he stepped through the conference room's double doors before answering:

"Hi, hon. What's up?"

"I know you're in meetings. I'm sorry to bother you, but—"

"No, that's okay. Is everything all right?"

"Yes. I mean no, I— the school called."

He closed his eyes.

"About Will."

He nodded and took a long, slow breath. "What is it this time?"

Chapter Two

It had been another twelve-hour day for Preston Ander-son. Once again the *Wall Street Journal* folded on the car seat beside him went unread. Maybe he'd have time the next day. Then again, with so many fires for the new VP to put out, maybe not. And what was with the note on embossed church stationery he'd just found on his windshield? A prank? For what purpose?

He rolled his neck, stretching out the day's tension, while he pressed the remote on his steering wheel to change stations. Not that he didn't like Pink Floyd's "Money," or even the irony of hearing its lyrics at this particular milestone in his life, but he needed something a bit more relaxing.

To his surprise, the breezy jazz station he turned to was also playing the song. How strange. With a shrug, he selected the classical station.

It was also playing the tune.

He scowled and reached over to manually change the radio. To what, he wasn't sure. It made no difference, because the song was still playing. How was that possible? The digital readout clearly indicated he'd changed stations.

He tried something at the opposite end of the dial. The song *still* played. Obviously, the stereo was fried—pretty frustrating, considering this top-of-the-line Lexus was less than a week old.

Angrily he reached over and snapped it off. But the silence lasted only a moment before the song returned, louder. He swore and shut it off again . . . only to have it come on again, even louder.

He was about to try a third time when the engine shuddered once, twice, then went dead altogether. The gas gauge showed he still had three-quarters of a tank. If Preston was angry before, he was downright livid now. *One hundred and twenty grand for this piece of garbage?*

He reached down and turned the key in the ignition, but it didn't respond as the car coasted and the music blared.

His headlights caught the railroad crossing just ahead. He tried the ignition again with equal failure as the car gradually slowed. He would pull over to the side once he crossed the tracks. But he had barely reached them when the barrier on the other side dropped down in front of him, its red lights flashing. He hit the brakes and slid to a stop directly over the rails.

He glanced at the rearview mirror. The barrier behind him was also lowering.

Suddenly, white light glared through his side window. He turned to see a train rounding the bend, 150 yards away. He tried the ignition again. Nothing.

The train spotted him and blasted its horn. He could hear it over the song.

Enough was enough. He grabbed his briefcase. No way was he going down with the ship. He'd definitely get a new car out of the deal, and a little extra for mental duress. But as he reached for the door, the lock dropped down. Swearing, he tried the handle. It remained locked. He pressed the lock release. Frozen. He reached up and tried to manually pull it up. It would not budge.

The train's headlight bore down on him, its horn shrieking over the radio. He tried the release again. Then the handle. Then the lock. The horn continued to scream, the music blared. He reached for the ignition and noticed the digital readout on the radio. Instead of listing the song that had played or even the station, the crimson display showed a Bible verse. The same one he'd read on the church stationery:

THOU SHALT NOT STEAL

He turned to the window, blinded by the train's light.

"Dear God!" He slammed the lock release, yanked at the door handle.

The horn wailed.

"Dear God! Dear God!"

There was nothing but light.

"Dear—"

At last the train struck. If there was a God, Preston Anderson would finish his prayer in person.

The night was eerily still. A thick blanket of fog had rolled in from the Pacific, swallowing up much of the sound in the park overlooking Santa Monica. Lisa sat on a bench in the cool dampness, searching for words. "Charlie, I don't . . . what I mean is. . . ."

The good news was, the man had not lowered himself to one knee when asking her to marry him. The bad news was . . . well, just about everything else.

Yes, they'd been dating a full year since they had returned to the States, since they tracked down and destroyed the computer program containing the Voice of God. And, yes, she enjoyed his quiet strength and sensitivity, not to mention his standing beside her through the OPR review, the "lack of candor" charges, and her subsequent dismissal from the FBI. (Seems the government wasn't fond of her breaking the dozen or so rules necessary to accomplish their mission.)

But love him?

"I'm—" He cleared his throat. "Sorry, I didn't mean to put you on the spot. I just thought. . . ." He closed the ring case, unsure what to do with it.

"Oh, Charlie." She could feel his embarrassment. "I'm sorry."

"No apology necessary." He shrugged. "Just misread the situation, that's all."

But it wasn't all. Despite his efforts, she could see the hurt. She set a hand on his knee. "It's not you, it's me. I'm just, you know, not—"

"Forget it. I understand."

But he didn't understand, which made her pain for him all the greater. "Look, if I ever was, you know, ready, you'd be the one. There's no finer man I know than you, Charles Madison. I mean that."

He glanced down, uncomfortable with the compliment.

She wanted to touch his face, even give him a kiss. But

he would take that as sympathy. And sympathy was the other thing he was not good at receiving. So, instead, she simply asked, "You okay?"

He stuffed the case into his Dockers. "Faulty intel, that's all." He looked to her with a slight twinkle. "It'll take more than that to make me concede defeat."

"I hope so." She felt the burn of moisture in her eyes. "I sincerely hope—"

"Nice rock, dude."

They turned to see three Latino gangbangers emerge from the foggy shadows. The biggest wore a wifebeater tank top and held a .22.

Charlie sighed in what Lisa knew was self-contempt. He'd been trained to always be aware of his surroundings.

"Let's have it." The kid motioned with his gun.

"Have?" Charlie asked.

"Don't mess with me." The kid pulled back the hammer. "The ring. Hand over the ring."

"All right, all right." Was it Lisa's imagination or was Charlie's voice trembling? He stuck his hand into his pocket. "Don't shoot. Just don't shoot."

Emboldened by what he thought was Charlie's fear, the kid stepped closer.

"Please, we'll give you whatever you want," Charlie said.

Lisa frowned. "Charlie—"

The kid spun the gun on her—"Shut up!"—then back to Charlie, who dug the ring case out of his pocket with shaking hands. "Here, take it. Take whatever you want. Just don't—"

"Shut up!"

The case slipped from Charlie's fingers and fell to the grass. The kid exchanged smirks with the others as Charlie leaned forward to retrieve it, apologizing. "I'm sorry, I—"

He lunged off the bench, his forearm smashing into the boy's chest, then flying up. Not only did this force the gun skyward, but there was the added advantage of catching the kid's chin and snapping back his head. The evening had not gone well for Charlie and he was a bit out of sorts, so instead of letting the boy stagger backward to the ground and disarming him, he sealed the deal by grabbing the kid's head and bringing it down hard into his rising knee.

The boy was out before he hit the ground.

"Charlie, watch it!"

He spun around to see one of the two remaining kids pulling a knife—a four-inch Ti-Lite. An impressive blade for the streets, but the kid was no pro. His eyes were wild and his hands shook.

Charlie sighed. Feeling bad for overreacting, he held out his hand to the boy and said, "*Todos seria mejor si tu das el puñal a mi.*"

The kid looked to his fallen companion, then to Charlie, then back to his friend— obviously giving the request for the knife serious thought.

"*Picálo!*" the other boy shouted. "*Picálo!*"

The kid regripped the blade, considering the advice.

"Stick him!" his friend repeated. "Stick him!"

"Excuse me." Lisa approached the shouting boy from behind.

He did not respond.

She stepped closer and tapped him on the shoulder. "Excuse me."

He turned toward her. "Shut the—"

She drove the heel of her hand into his nose. Cartilage snapped and he grabbed his face, screaming.

The armed kid spun toward her with the knife, but Charlie was already coming at him. Though Lisa appreciated the gesture, she didn't need it. With a single kick to the groin, she dropped the boy to the ground, where he was unable to move, barely able to breathe. She may no longer be FBI, but like Charlie, she still knew the moves.

✝

Forty-five minutes later—after disarming the boys and taking the one with the broken nose to ER—Charlie and Lisa stood outside her Santa Monica apartment on Fifth Street. A nearby magnolia filled the air with a sweet, heavy fragrance.

She shook her head. "I'll say this, you know how to show a girl a good time."

"I should have been paying more attention."

"You were a little preoccupied."

"Yeah." He paused. "I'll see you tomorrow then."

It was more statement than question, and she glanced away.

"Something wrong?" he asked.

"Maybe . . . maybe we'd better let things cool for a little while."

He looked at her.

"I just don't want—you know, I don't want you wasting your time, that's all."

"I can wait."

"You can't wait forever, Charlie."

He held her with those powerful steel-gray eyes. "If that's what it takes, I can wait."

Every part of her wanted to say yes—except the part that knew what was best for him. She looked down and shook her head. "I don't think so, Charlie. I don't. . . . " She shook it again.

He remained silent. She could feel his eyes searching, probing. Without warning, she rose onto her toes and gently kissed his cheek. Before he could respond, she turned to the apartment.

"Lisa."

She gave no answer, but unlocked the door and stepped inside.

"Lisa."

Without looking at him, she forced a smile and shut the door. Leaning against it, she closed her eyes and swallowed back the conflicting emotions.

"Lisa."

She wasn't sure how long he stayed there, calling her name, but eventually he stopped. Another moment followed before she heard his footsteps turn and fade into the night. She slowly slid to the floor and sat. Pulling her knees to her chest, she wanted to cry. But she didn't. She couldn't. And that made the ache all the more unbearable.

The phone down in the kitchen startled Thomas. He was sitting in the hallway outside Will's room, praying—something he'd been doing the past few months when he couldn't sleep (and when he was sure he wouldn't get caught). He struggled to his feet and quickly padded down the carpeted stairs to the kitchen, hoping to pick up before Sharon woke and answered on the bedroom extension.

He'd been tough on the boy, laid into him pretty hard. Too much was at stake not to. Still, he tried to be understanding. He knew from firsthand experience the trials and tribulations of being a preacher's kid. What he hadn't suffered personally, his younger sister, Lisa, had. That and more. Which was why he did his best to be lenient, cutting Will more slack than he himself ever got. But it was hard. Every day he bit his tongue, fighting to swallow back the voice of his father that kept wanting to escape from his throat.

And yet, the more he gave, the more Will took. The latest example was Thomas's visit to Vice Principal Muller. Originally, Will had been suspended for one week. Thomas had been able to negotiate it down to one day.

And Will's response? Nothing but attitude.

Thomas snapped on the kitchen light and winced. Crossing to the wall phone, he answered, "Hello?"

"Pastor? Sheriff Hutton here. Hope I didn't wake you."

"No, I, uh. . . ." He rubbed his forehead. "I'm up."

"Good. I figured the sooner you know, the better."

"Know?" He glanced out the window. Gray drizzle snaked down the glass—another spring morning in Washington State.

The sheriff continued. "We got another."

Thomas swallowed.

"Preston Anderson. Does the name ring a bell?"

He felt his stomach starting to knot.

"Pastor?"

"Yes." Thomas cleared his throat. "He's one of our members. An elder, actually. What happened?"

"Another accident. Least that's how it appears."

"Appears?"

"We found another Bible verse. In the car."

Thomas hesitated, then asked the question he dreaded to ask. "Was it . . . on our bulletin?"

"No, Pastor. Your church stationery."

✝

"Why are you always being so mean to me?" Jazmin mumbled from beneath her blankets.

"I'm not being—"

The kid was good. Even though she was deaf and unable to read Charlie's lips from under the covers, she instinctively knew his response. "Yes, you are! Mean, mean, mean!"

He reached down and shook her leg.

"Don't touch me."

"Jaz."

Another shake.

"I'm awake! Quit harassing me!"

Charlie took a breath, grateful for the self-control all those years in Delta Force had taught him. If she had been anyone else—a fellow soldier, a new recruit—her insubordination would be met with a bucket of ice water followed by orders shouted into her face to get down and give him fifty or one hundred. (The twenty-mile run would be optional.) But this creature, with so much emotion and so little logic, seemed unable to grasp even the basics of discipline and chain of command.

He shook his niece's leg again. "Let's go."

With a heavy sigh, she threw back the covers, sat up,

and glared at him. Well, as much as a single, half-opened eye can glare. "You have to be the rudest human being on the face of the planet."

"Tell that to your first-period teacher."

"She's a Nazi."

"One more tardy and you get Saturday detention."

The thirteen-year-old plopped back down on her pillow. "Right, like that's *my* fault." Before he could answer, she changed the playing field. "You blew it with Lisa, didn't you?"

He hesitated. Ever since Jazmin was exposed to the Voice of God the previous year, she had developed an uncanny ability to sense situations. "To hear deeper things," she said. "Sometimes I even know what people are thinking." Of course Charlie was skeptical, but there were those times. . . .

Pushing the strawberry blonde hair from her eyes, she continued. "How many times have I told you, women want what they *can't* have."

Charlie started to reply, but she cut him off. "You just can't go around throwing yourself at us."

"Nobody's throwing themselves at—"

"And telling us whatever's on your mind."

"People appreciate honesty."

"Excuse me? *Excuse me?* We're talking women here."

Charlie shifted topics to something he understood. "Do you want oatmeal or eggs?"

"I want you to leave me alone." She reached for the covers, but he'd learned a few tricks from their months together. He'd already gripped the blankets, making it impossible for her to pull them back.

"Oatmeal or eggs?"

"I'll eat at school."

"Oatmeal or eggs?"

"Eggs! All right?" Her heavy sigh made it clear she was dealing with a moron.

"Eggs it is." He dragged the blankets off her. Now she would either lie there and freeze or get up and storm toward the bathroom.

She did neither.

Pulling into a fetal position, she moaned pitifully. When he didn't respond (another trick he'd learned), she yelled, "I wouldn't have all those detentions if you'd drive me to school like all the other parents. You can be such a Nazi sometimes."

Charlie knew he should let it go. He could outthink and outmaneuver any enemy in the field, but win an argument with her? Never. Even when he won, he somehow lost. No, he should just drop it, walk away. But the comeback was so obvious, the life lesson to be imparted so clear. Against his better judgment, he waited until she was looking at him and said, "We live five blocks from the school."

"What's that got to do with anything?"

"Five blocks. You can walk."

"Walk? With these blisters?" She raised a foot a couple of sizes too big for her child body.

"You're the one who wanted to buy those silly thongs."

"Flip-flops. They're called flip-flops. Thongs are what

you *won't* let me buy. Even though everybody wears them."

"Thongs?"

"Flip-flops," she sighed. "The subject is flip-flops."

It was happening again. Like some prehistoric mammoth, Charlie's lumbering legs of reason were being wrapped around and around by the rope of her lightning-quick irrationality. Still, this time he could break the cords. The logic was so clear.

"The choice is yours, Jazmin, not mine."

"Right. I can choose to become some fashion geek, just 'cause you're too lazy to drive me to school."

The mammoth staggered. "You can buy whatever clothes you want, as long as you deal with the consequences."

"Except thongs."

"Young ladies don't wear thongs."

"My point exactly."

The mammoth dropped to his knees. But he was strong; he could rise. "We're talking about you being late for school."

"*You're* talking about me being late for school." The cord wrapped tighter. "And that's my whole point."

"No. The point we're discussing is you being late for—"

"The point is, we're always 'discussing' what you want to discuss. Never what I want to discuss. You, you, you. It's always about you."

"Jazmin, if you're late one more day, you'll have to make it up in Saturday detention." There. He couldn't have made it any clearer.

With sufficient melodrama, she rose to her feet, his army sweatshirt hanging around skinny arms and boney knees. Was it possible? Had he won? Before he could stop himself, he had to add a final word: "Right?"

She rolled her eyes and pushed past him with her own final word:

"Nazi."

Chapter Three

A men, forever glory."
Jason Ballard continued reciting as he dipped the stick with the knotted washcloth into the chalice.

"The and power the and kingdom the is."

He sprinkled it over the bowed heads standing before him and the altar, just as he'd seen Father Riordan do with holy water when he was a kid.

"Thine for evil from us deliver."

But the wine mixed with goat urine was not holy water. Nor was the naked, shivering woman spread out before him on a fallen log a sacrifice. Well, at least not a *holy* sacrifice.

He knew some of the guys were there just to sneak peeks at her from under their hooded robes. But that's how it always was. No matter how selective he tried to be, there were always a few just hanging around for the thrills . . . the booze, the drugs, the sex.

But the other acolytes, especially the girls like Heather, or even Ashley, were there for more serious reasons.

"But temptation into not us lead and."

The candles they held made their plumes of breath glow almost supernaturally, like a brooding presence waiting to answer their prayer with its unseen power . . . not unlike the power of the Stillaguamish River that silently flowed nearby.

He saw one of the younger girls sway. Another reached out to steady her. Little wonder. With the wine and acid they'd put down, he was surprised they could even stand. But that was the price of calling upon the power. The submission necessary for the Magick to work.

Kristof had made it clear. If power was to be released, the Black Mass had to be followed to the letter. These were not empty words he recited. Not some childish game. The power had already been unleashed and their faithfulness rewarded. Twice.

This would be the third.

"Debtors our forgive we as debts our us forgive and bread daily our day this us give."

Already they had drained the cat's blood and hung the body on a fir branch above the woman. Already, they had written the man's death decree in the animal's blood and burned the parchment to release its power.

"Heaven in is it as Earth on done be will thy, come kingdom thy."

Now it was just a matter of finishing the prayer. Then as before, Lucifer, the Prince of the Air, and Jesus Christ, the Savior of the World, would begin their work.

"Name thy be hallowed, heaven in art who Father our. . . ."

Jason paused, waiting as the glassy-eyed participants

looked up—some dazed, others with smiles of anticipation. When he had everyone's attention, he bowed his head and finished the prayer.

"Amen."

✝

Samuel Mugridge was holier than most.

Churchgoer. Part-time youth worker. A year before he'd helped the high school group with their drive to sponsor Ugandan orphans. The previous Thanksgiving he was down in Mexico helping them build a church. Amazing how many girls didn't even know how to swing a hammer. Good thing he was there to help and guide them. But that was Sam. Always willing to help and guide.

Of course, he wasn't perfect. His ex was the first to point that out. It's not that he didn't find her attractive, but who said getting married meant you couldn't look anymore? Nothing wrong with appreciating the beauty of the opposite sex. And if Sam couldn't get enough of that beauty in person, there were always the DVDs he rented.

Meg put up with it for a while, believing what he said about it spicing up their sex life . . . until she found the magazines.

Women. Go figure. How could she be jealous over some airbrushed, silicone-enhanced bimbo he'd never met and never would? Of course, the porn wasn't the only problem between them. Her counselor said it was merely a symptom. Well, symptom or not, the bimbos proved more faithful than Meg ever did. After two years, she left him. The airbrushed images remained. And, except for the cat who'd gone missing the last three or four days, they were all he had to come home to after a hard day at the office.

Of course, he never made their presence public knowledge. Some of his church pals still lived back in the twentieth—no, make that the nineteenth—century. Except for some tatted-out Goth who worked at the video store late on Fridays, he doubted anyone knew or cared.

Bottom line: if this was Sam's only vice, he was doing just fine.

That's why, as he sat on the sofa, stocking feet propped up on the coffee table, sound blasting through his Dolby 5.1, he was surprised to see the word ADULTERER begin flashing on the seventy-inch screen. At first he thought it was part of the flick. But after twenty or so seconds it became a drag, so he reached for the remote and hit Fast Forward, 2-X.

The word continued to flash.

He clicked to 4-X.

It continued, neither speeding up nor slowing down.

He went to 16-X.

The same.

Then 32-X.

128-X.

Scowling, he shuttled ahead to the next scene.

The word continued flashing.

He clicked to the next.

Same thing.

If this was supposed to be a joke, some director's commentary, it was pretty stupid. Finally, he pressed *Eject*.

The picture disappeared, but the flashing continued:
ADULTERER . . . ADULTERER . . . ADULTERER.

He hit the Off button. The flashing continued:

ADULTERER . . . ADULTERER . . . ADULTERER.

With an oath, he dragged his feet off the table and set them in water. Where it came from, he had no idea. Maybe the dishwasher was overflowing. They'd had problems with it when they first moved in. Or maybe a pipe had burst in the bathroom. Unfortunately, he had little time to wonder. His entire body jerked with such violence that he could not scream. He could not breathe. Except for the contractions that seized him, he could not even move—only fall, splashing face-first into the inch of water that was charged with 220 volts of electricity.

Though the radio alarm glowed 4:12 in the morning, Thomas fumbled with the nightstand phone and tried his best to sound awake. "Hello."

"Pastor?"

"Yes."

"Robert Hutton again. Snohomish County Sheriff."

His head immediately cleared. "Did you find something?"

"About the church reader board? No."

Thomas sighed. The previous evening, someone had accessed their electronic reader board, changing the title of the week's sermon to a Bible verse.

"We do, however, have another."

"Another?" Thomas asked.

"Samuel Mugridge? Name ring a bell?"

"I don't—I'd have to check our direc—"

"He's from your congregation, trust me."

Thomas closed his eyes.

"We need to talk."

"Yes, of course. When?"

"Why don't you meet me at his apartment—say, around one?"

"Tom?" Sharon's voice mumbled beside him.

He covered the phone. "It's okay, sweetheart. Everything's all right."

The sheriff continued. "By then the press will have cleared out."

Thomas nodded. "Yes . . . yes, that's a good idea. Thank you."

"You definitely got yourself a problem here, Pastor."

"Yes, I understand."

"Good. I'll see you then."

"Yes, I'll see you—"

The soft click cut him off.

Sharon turned to him. "Someone from church?"

"It's okay," he said, returning the phone to the nightstand. "Don't worry, go back to sleep."

She gave a smile and did just that.

But not Thomas. He lay on his back, staring up at the ceiling, thinking, debating. It was time. He'd put it off long enough. With a sigh of resignation, he slipped from the bed, put on his robe, and shuffled into the hallway. After checking on Will, he headed down the steps and into the kitchen. It still carried the faint scent of salmon from last night's dinner. He snapped on the light, squinting at its brightness, and headed to the phone. He opened the cupboard above it. On the inside of the door, Sharon had taped a list of important phone numbers—friends, family. Near the bottom he found a California number. One he called only when he had to.

Chapter Four

hree? Three murders and you don't—"

"Will you just—" Her brother glanced about, making sure no one overheard as they sidestepped the puddles in the apartment parking lot. "Keep it down, all right?"

But Lisa wasn't in the mood for keeping it down. "Three murders, and you just now get around to asking for my help?"

"I wasn't—"

"Tommy, L.A. is two hours away!"

"You *hate* flying."

No argument there. In fact, her first stop after landing at Sea-Tac was the ladies' room—not to empty her bladder, but to change into a blouse that didn't carry the faint aroma of a Big Mac that hadn't completely made it into her air-sickness bag.

They forged through the rain toward the old brick building, Thomas trying to keep an umbrella over them as she continued her lecture. "You should have called sooner. This is serious business."

"I didn't . . . I wasn't sure there was a connection."

"Yeah, right."

"What's that supposed to mean?"

She gave him a look before starting up the concrete steps.

He followed. "Lisa?"

She yanked open the door and was greeted by the blue-green flickering of a bad fluorescent and some deputy sheriff just out of puberty. "Sorry, ma'am." He moved to block her. "The place is—" He spotted her brother and changed gears. "Hello, Pastor."

"Hello, Martin." Thomas closed the umbrella. "Nasty out there."

The man-boy nodded.

Thomas introduced them. "This is my sister, Lisa Harmon. Lisa, Deputy Johnson."

The kid touched his hat. "Ma'am."

"She's retired FBI."

The deputy blinked, unsure what to do with the information.

"She used to do this for a living." Thomas waited, then continued. "Solve these types of cases."

"Oh . . . right." The kid stepped aside, somewhat clumsily.

But Thomas wasn't finished. Turning to Lisa, he said, "Martin's mother has been head of the school board"—he turned back to Johnson—"how long, almost ten years now?"

"Yes, sir."

Lisa gave a nod.

"How is she?" Thomas asked. "Feeling any better?"

"A little, yes."

"Good, good." He looked to Lisa and explained, "Cancer."

"I'm sorry to hear that," she said.

"Yes," Thomas agreed, "it's been hard for everyone." Then, brightening, he added, "But she's a fighter. Isn't that right, Marty?"

"Yes sir, she is."

"Yes, she is," Thomas repeated. "Well, if you'll excuse us." He motioned his sister forward. Lisa took her cue and started down the hallway of worn carpet, blistered paint, and the smell of mildew. Thomas followed, calling back to the deputy. "You be sure to tell her hi for me, all right?"

"I will."

"And let her know we're praying for her."

"I'll do that," the young man said. "Thanks, Pastor."

Thomas gave a wave as he joined Lisa's side and they headed toward the open door near the end of the hall.

Lisa shook her head. "You're good. Real good."

"I'm compassionate. You should try it some time."

"You should mean it sometime."

"Pastors show interest."

"So do politicians." Before he could answer, she brought them back on topic. "Three victims. All from the same church. And you're telling me you saw no connection?"

"I'm telling you, I couldn't be certain. I didn't want to create a panic."

"Or a mass exit."

"Meaning?"

"How big is your little fiefdom these days—four thousand, five thousand members?"

"You think I'm trying to cover this up?"

"I think you know bad publicity when you see it."

The threadbare carpet grew spongy under their feet.

"Listen, just because Dad occasionally abused the pulpit doesn't mean—"

"*Occasionally?*"

"Hello, Pastor."

Lisa looked up to see a good-looking sheriff in an olive-green, fitted uniform standing in the doorway. He was definitely cut, mid-forties, strong jaw, dark hair, darker eyes. A real player.

"Glad you could make it," he smiled, definitely giving off a vibe.

She returned it, then immediately rebuked herself. With the help of friends and counseling, she'd purposely dropped out of the game, for almost two years now. Then, of course, there was Charlie and whatever they had—or didn't. Either way, she wasn't about to step back onto the field . . . no matter how incredible the chin or the eyes.

"And you are?" he asked.

Thomas answered. "This is my sister, Lisa Harmon, FBI."

"Retired FBI," she corrected.

The dark eyes flickered. He was definitely sending out feelers. "A little young for retirement."

"Yes, well," she cleared her throat, "we retired each other."

He nodded with a faint smile indicating he caught the subtext. She doubted it, since the subtext had nearly included a prison term. He stretched out his hand. "Rob Hutton." They shook. His grip was firm and professional.

"What exactly happened here?" her brother asked.

Hutton turned back to the room. "Same as the other two. Late evening, early morning. Everything made to appear like an accident."

"Appear?" Lisa asked.

He motioned them inside the tiny apartment.

The carpet was sopping wet. On the floor next to the sofa and cluttered coffee table, complete with the remains of Chinese take-out, the crude outline of a body was marked in masking tape. Ten feet away, out of context in such cheap, cramped quarters, stood a big-screen TV. To the left was a hallway leading to a bathroom and bedroom. And to their immediate right was a kitchenette.

Hutton nodded toward the stove. "The electrical came undone. Wires were hanging less than an inch from the floor, so when the water reached them, they—"

"Water?" Lisa interrupted, looking down at the carpet.

"Stopper in the bathtub. Door closed. He had the DVD cranked up so loud, he couldn't hear it running."

"DVD?"

"These." Hutton held up a couple of disks. The cover of one contained lurid poses of underage girls on farm equipment, surrounded by dead, plucked chickens. If he expected to shock her, he was disappointed. "When he finally got up to take a leak or whatever, he stepped into the water and . . . Kentucky-fried pervert."

Lisa stepped past him and walked over to the stove. "Anything else? Any other clues?"

"Nothing yet. And if it's like the others, there won't be." He joined her, perhaps a little too close. "The guy's meticulous. And, as far as we can tell, none of the victims saw it coming. Well, except for the warnings."

"Warnings?"

Hutton looked back to her brother. "You didn't tell her?"

Thomas cleared his throat. "Not yet."

"What warnings?"

The sheriff answered. "For the first, there were the highlighted words in the church bulletin: 'Thou shall not kill.'"

"How did he die?" Lisa asked.

"Heart attack. But the good doctor departed under some strange circumstances."

"Doctor?"

Thomas replied. "He volunteered part-time at an abortion clinic."

Lisa swore softly.

The sheriff continued. "Second victim received his warning on your brother's church stationery."

"Thou shall not steal," Thomas said.

"And what was his job?"

"He worked for National Corp," her brother explained. "Newly appointed VP of their credit card division."

Lisa arched an eyebrow. "And this guy? What warning did he get?"

Thomas took a breath, then answered. "Our electronic reader board, the one advertising Sunday's sermon?"

She nodded.

"The title had been: 'How Can God Serve You?'"

"And?"

"Last night it was changed to Matthew 5:28."

"Which is?"

"Anyone who looks at a woman lustfully has already committed adultery."

Lisa slowly shook her head. No wonder he called. Her big brother was definitely in some deep water.

The sheriff's cell rang and he pulled it from his pocket. "Hutton here."

Lisa looked back at the oven, sorting through the facts.

"You sure?"

She turned to the sheriff, who was glancing at his watch.

"Right. I'll be there in forty." He snapped his phone shut and looked at her. "There's something else you're welcome to see, if you want. Up in the mountains."

"Another one?" Thomas sounded unsteady.

"Another death?" Lisa asked.

"Not exactly."

Chapter Five

"Who?"

"He calls himself Kristof. At least according to the kids."

Lisa and Sheriff Hutton continued, single file, through the wet undergrowth of ferns, salal, and wild huckleberries. She was soaked to her thighs. "Kids?" she asked.

Hutton nodded. "Mostly high schoolers. Of course, they claim they don't know anything—taken a blood oath so they won't say a word—but we're getting bits and pieces."

Thomas had returned to the church to begin damage control. Despite his efforts, the press had gotten wind of the connections. Even with his spin-doctoring, she knew he'd have his hands full.

Now it was just she and Hutton. Not that she minded. He seemed a decent enough man, and he definitely showed interest in her, which was always good for the ego. But there was no way she was getting involved, much less having a relapse. Those days were long gone, with or without Charlie Madison. Truth be told, Charlie was one of the reasons she could hold the line. Even in her weaker moments, when things got hot and heavy between them, he was the one to show the strength and cut it off. No surprise there. At one time the guy wanted to be a minister—though that wasn't exactly proof of moral character, at least from Lisa's experience.

Up ahead she heard voices and a barking dog. Hutton held a branch so it wouldn't fly back into her face.

She took it and asked, "By 'blood oath,' are we talking, like, a secret society?"

"A coven."

"Witches?"

"They play harder ball than that. Satanists, I suspect."

"I didn't know there was a difference."

"To them, it's huge. But to the shrinks, it's all the same: Loners. Outcasts. Kids searching for family, or just trying to get control of their lives."

Lisa mused. It almost sounded like her own childhood. In the distance she heard the squelch of a walkie-talkie. "And Kristof?" she asked.

"A leech exploiting the kids. His real name is Howard Campbell. Went AWOL after getting kicked out of SOCOM down in Fort Lewis."

"He was in Special Ops?"

"Yeah. Until he began shooting off his mouth and looking for Process recruits."

"'Process' . . . as in the old Charles Manson group?"

"And the Son of Sam, and a half dozen others."

"I thought they were history." She stepped in a rabbit hole, nearly twisting her ankle.

"They keep sprouting up in different forms. Latest batch insists that Jesus Christ and the devil are brothers.

And as their true disciples, their mission is to bring the two together in love and wrath."

"Love and wrath?"

"Or sex and violence, take your pick."

"Sounds like you've done your homework."

"We get our share of nutcases up here. Anyway, we're pretty sure Campbell or Kristof is living in these mountains somewhere, manipulating and using the kids."

"You think there's a connection? Between the murders and this group? You said they're just kids."

Hutton glanced back at her naiveté. It was a stupid comment, and she looked down, pretending to avoid another hole.

"Far as we can tell, they've had meetings at this location each night of the murders."

"That's it?" she asked.

He gave no answer.

"That's not a lot to go on."

"You're sounding like your brother."

"Yeah, well, we come from a long line of deniers."

"How's that?"

She let it go. Lisa never talked about her father and felt no inclination to do so now.

Hutton pushed back the final branch and they stepped into a clearing. The undergrowth had been trampled into a circle about thirty feet in diameter. Just beyond it lay the river. Three other officers were scouring the area, along with an agitated German shepherd, its nose to the ground, sweeping back and forth.

"Morning, gentlemen."

The men greeted him with various degrees of respect.

He turned to the closest, a middle-aged officer with thinning hair and flaccid, buttery jowls. He was squatting over something on the ground.

"What's up, Ed?"

He examined a small piece of paper, careful not to touch it. "Same ol' same ol'."

"What do you have?" Lisa asked.

Ed scowled up at her.

"FBI," Hutton explained. "Retired."

Ed stabbed the paper with a small twig and held it up for a closer look. He nodded his head toward a branch near the edge of the clearing. "Sacrifice is over there."

Lisa turned to see the remains of an animal—a rabbit, maybe a large squirrel—hard telling since it was skinned.

Ed called to the dog. "Jackie. Come here, girl." The dog looked up from her sniffing. "Over here, sweetheart."

She ran to him, all paws and excitement. She was barely out of puppyhood and showed plenty of affection with her wet, eager nose.

"Okay, girl," he said, turning from her, "easy, easy."

She settled down and he held out the paper. If she was animated before, she went ballistic now, barking non-stop.

"Good girl," Ed said. "Okay, okay." He shouted to a woman officer just beyond the clearing. "Hendricks, give me a hand here."

The officer called, "Come here, Jackie. Come on, girl."

The dog spun around and bounded in her direction.

Hutton motioned to the paper "Pot?"

"Big surprise," Ed said as he produced an evidence bag.

"And that animal on the tree?" Lisa asked. "You said it's a sacrifice?"

He dropped the paper into the bag. "A cat."

"Out here?" Hutton asked.

"Domestic." Ed nodded over his shoulder. "The pelt was tossed there. Had one of those electronic implant things in its shoulder. We just checked Animal Services."

"And?"

With a slight groan, he rose to his feet. "Her name was Lucky. Belonged to a real estate agent down at Smokey Point."

"Smokey Point?" Hutton asked.

"Yeah." Turning to the youngest officer, he called, "Keatch, what was his name?"

"What?"

"The owner, what was the owner's name?"

"Mugridge," the officer shouted back. "Samuel Mugridge."

Lisa exchanged looks with Hutton.

"We tried calling him at home," Ed said, "and at his office. Only got answering machines."

"Yeah." Hutton nodded. "I don't think he'll be returning many calls today."

From outside the clearing, Jackie gave a startled yap, followed by desperate yelpings.

Ed spun around. "What's going on? Hendricks?"

"It's Jackie!" the officer called from the woods. "She's hurt. She's—"

The two deputies dropped what they were doing and raced toward the noise. Lisa and Hutton followed.

"What is it?" Ed demanded. "What happened? Jackie!"

The dog continued yelping in obvious pain.

Keatch was the first to arrive and began swearing.

Ed was next. "Cut her down!" he shouted. "Get a knife and cut her down!"

Lisa arrived to see the officers surround the dog. The animal was suspended at eye level, twisting and squirming in some sort of homemade trap—two squares of alder poles laced together with vines.

"She smelled the dope," Hendricks shouted. "There's a big stash right here."

Ed grabbed the trap, stopping it from twisting. "Easy, girl."

But the dog continued to yelp pathetically, and for good reason. Her sides were bleeding.

"They used it as bait," Hendricks yelled, "to draw her in!"

The dog focused on Ed, her yelps turning to whimpering and whines, begging for help.

"It's okay, girl," he said, "it's okay."

But it wasn't. In the center of the two alder squares were a dozen wooden spikes, six to eight inches long. Most had pierced deep into the animal's body.

"Careful," Hutton warned. "Those points could be poisonous."

But Ed paid no attention. His voice was thick with emotion. "You're going to be okay, girl, you're going to be all right." Shouting, he demanded, "Would somebody get a knife?"

Keatch handed him one and Ed began cutting the rope above the trap. "Who would do this?" he yelled. "She's just a dog. An innocent dog. What kind of monster would do this?"

Mostly to himself, Hutton muttered, "A very experienced one."

It was then Lisa knew they needed help. If they really were dealing with a Special Ops, they'd have to know how he worked. They'd have to know his training, his capabilities, and how he thought. Then there was the whole religious angle. Although there were probably a dozen individuals who could offer their expertise, only one came to her mind.

"Hasn't it ever dawned on you that Hitler and Darwin have the same number of letters?"

"I'm sorry, what?"

Jason Ballard leaned forward and repeated. "I'm sorry, what?"

The class snickered, though Jason had spoken with just enough sincerity so Mr. Ramsey couldn't bust him.

The teacher pushed up his glasses. "I'm not sure I understand the connection."

"Between Hitler and Darwin?" Jason scorned. "You're kidding me, right?"

"No. Enlighten us, please."

Jason glanced around the biology classroom. Most of the kids were careful not to let their eyes meet his. And for good reason. All morning the rumors had been flying . . . another Mass last night, another murder. Their respect for him had skyrocketed. Or was it their fear? Either way, it felt good.

The only two he caught watching him were the geeky preacher's kid that Kristof ordered him to recruit, and of course, Heather. Faithful, obedient-as-any-dog Heather. Black miniskirt, translucent skin, a half dozen scars on each arm from cuttings. They'd even done a little blood-letting together before he got tired of her. Still, she'd do anything for him. Even bed the geek if he chose. That was the power he had. The power that grew stronger at every sacrifice.

With exaggerated patience, he sat back up in his seat and explained the obvious to his teacher. "This whole concept of natural selection. I mean, creating a superior species . . . give me a break."

"And your point is?" Ramsey said.

"My point?" Jason glanced around the room, wondering if he was the only one who noticed the teacher was an idiot. "My point is that Hitler was just practicing Darwinism. Let's face it, if the Jews, retards, and gays are genetically inferior, then the guy was right. Stoke up the ovens and get 'em out of the gene pool before it's too late."

More snickers.

Ramsey cleared his throat. "I fail to see the similarities of an anti-Semitic madman to—"

"No, you see," Jason interrupted. "You see perfectly."

Ramsey swallowed, unsure how to respond.

Jason saved him the trouble. "And that's what makes you a hypocrite."

You could hear a pin drop. Students literally stopped breathing.

"Mr. Ballard—"

"You're a church guy, right?" Jason asked. "Calvary Cathedral?"

"My religious affiliations have nothing to do with what I teach."

"Apparently not. Tell me, how can you sit in church, listening to all the God-talk about how He created the world and everything . . . and then turn right around and tell us we're the product of a couple amoebas getting the hots for each other?"

More snickers, louder.

"Mr. Bal—"

"Hypocrite!" Jason felt the power welling up inside. "You're a hypocrite and a liar."

Ramsey's ears grew pink. Though his voice was cool and even, you could hear it quivering underneath. "I'll have to ask you to leave."

"And with the hypocrites there shall be much weeping and gnashing of teeth." Kristof had ordered him to memorize the verse for this occasion. Now he understood why.

"Mr.—"

Jason rose to his feet, the power surging through his veins. He raised his arm, pointing a long black fingernail at Ramsey. "Thus saith the Lord."

"If you don't leave, I'm calling Security."

"I shall vomit you out of my mouth!"

Ramsey turned toward the telephone intercom underneath the blackboard. "All right, you had your warning."

But Jason Ballard would not give him the satisfaction. He spun around and stormed toward the door, his trench coat flowing behind, his combat boots kicking aside a chair, more for show than anger. It was an announcement. A decree.

He knew the cops would drag him in again. Let them. It was a free country. Freedom of speech. Freedom of religion. Of course they'd try to intimidate him, use him to find Kristof. Let them do what they could. There was no stopping it now. Even if they caught him, there was no stopping the power.

The end of the world was quickly approaching.

Chapter Six

Uncle Charlie." Jaz lowered her voice so she wouldn't make a scene. "What are you doing here?"

He leaned toward the open passenger window of the SUV. "You're always complaining about having to walk. I figured I'd give you one less thing to gripe about."

She glanced over her shoulder to the students swarming out of Jefferson Middle School. They seemed like they didn't notice, which of course was a major put-on. She could practically feel their eyes burning into the back of her skull.

He reached over and opened the door. "Hop in."

She climbed in and melted down into the seat. It wasn't until they pulled away that she looked over to see what he was saying.

". . . again, haven't you?"

"What?"

He tried signing. "You've been flipping people off again, haven't you?" At least that's what his hands said—though she doubted that's what he meant. The poor guy had been taking American Sign Language classes for a couple months now. She gave him an A for effort, but an F for success. Let's face it, watching those big meaty hands try to sign and spell out words was like watching a gorilla play the piccolo.

"What?" she repeated.

He tried again. This time she watched his lips. "You've been smoking again, haven't you?"

"Pleeease." She slunk lower, dragging her hair into her mouth to chew. In reality she was sniffing it for evidence. One puff. All right, maybe two. That's all she'd had behind the gym. But the guy had a nose like a bloodhound.

He tapped her arm once, then twice before she looked. "You're not answering me."

The way she figured, she had two choices: Lie to him, which always made her feel guilty. Or change topics. She chose the latter, since she was like the world's champ at topic avoidance. "Lisa called, didn't she?"

He stared at the road, poker-faced.

"Lisa called and needs your help. Right?" She saw his jaw tighten and waited.

Finally he answered. "Did you . . . *sense* that?"

She shrugged, seeing no need to tell him about the text message she got from Lisa during fourth period. "She needs you and wants us to fly up there tonight."

He turned to her.

She cocked her head innocently, waiting for an answer.

He marveled, "That's really something."

She looked out the window, letting him think what he wanted. "So am I right?" She turned back to see him nodding.

"Everything but the 'we' part," he said. "I'm going up there. You're staying home."

"No," she shook her head. "That's not right. I distinctly felt it should be 'we.' You *and* me."

"Jaz, I don't think this is—"

"So what are you going to do? Leave me here all by myself?"

"You're thirteen. It'll only be a couple days. I think you can—"

"*Hello*, this is Friday."

"Meaning?"

"A weekend."

He still didn't get it.

She sighed. "A teenager? No adult supervision? Friday *and* Saturday night?"

He gave her another look. She gave him another sigh.

He countered, "I may have to stay longer. You'd miss school."

"So write me an excuse."

He paused—a tactical mistake she took full advantage of.

"Uncle Charlie, I've never been to Washington State. It would be an educational experience."

"It's your education I'm worried about."

"Then fly me home. If you have to stay longer, put me on a plane Sunday and send me home."

"Jaz—"

"I've traveled around the world. I think I can manage a few hours by myself on a plane."

He paused.

More weakness. Time to go for the jugular. "Please, Uncle Charlie." She gave him her best puppy-dog look. In the old days the guy may have been a killing machine, but he was a pushover when it came to puppy-dog looks.

He frowned hard at the road. Good. He was showing emotion. Now they were on her turf. Home court advantage. The rest would simply be a matter of working him . . . all afternoon if she had to.

With luck they'd be on a plane by nightfall. At worst, early morning.

✝

Will headed home, angling his way through a series of vacant lots. If life was fair, he'd have been suspended for at least a week. But of course, life wasn't fair. Not when good ol' Dad was there pulling strings. One day, that's all Muller had given him, and now he was back. What a joke. It was like Dad was some sort of pope that no one wanted to offend. Like everybody had to kiss his ring or his butt or something. Well, let them kiss away. He'd only begun.

"Will! Will Harmon. Wait up!"

He looked over his shoulder to see one of Jason's Goths running toward him. Puzzled, he stopped and waited.

"Hey." She arrived, pulling a black shawl around some very bare shoulders.

"Hey," he answered, and then somewhat clumsily added, "Heather, right?"

"Yeah." She tossed back her hair and flashed a killer smile—purple lipstick showing off some dazzling white teeth. She was gorgeous. Thin like a model. The black miniskirt and fishnet stockings didn't hurt, either. You'd have to be a fool not to notice her.

And Will was no fool. He hadn't been one on several occasions. But what did she want with him?

"Everybody's talking 'bout what you did Wednesday in the boys' john," she said.

"Yeah," he said.

She started down the path. "Cool. Very, very cool."

He joined her, his heart pounding a little.

"And what you did to Muller's shoes." She raised her shoulders in part shrug, part ecstasy. "I would love to have seen that. It must have been beautiful."

Trying to hide his excitement and slow his pulse, Will gave a simple nod. "It was all right."

They walked in what felt like hours of silence.

"This how you always go home?" she asked.

"Sometimes, yeah."

"Cool." She lifted her face to the afternoon light, showing a perfect nose and a delicate chin. "I've never been here. I like it."

"Yeah."

"Nice and peaceful."

"Yeah." He was sure he had more words in his vocabulary. At the moment he just couldn't think of any.

They continued walking.

Will cleared his throat.

More walking.

He cleared it again. "Your friend Jason, he put on a pretty good show in Ramsey's class."

"Oh, that." She cut him a smile. "Sometimes he gets a little worked up."

Will returned the smile, or at least he tried. In the process he noticed how the sun made her hair glow like shiny black cherries.

More silence.

"I always thought you took the bus," she said.

He turned to her, surprised she'd even noticed. "Yeah. I, uh, go this way when I want to think. You know, work stuff out."

"That's so cool," she said. She tossed back her hair. "Most boys, they're so busy with sports and junk, they take, like, zero time to think."

"Yeah," Will said. Then, for a change-up, he added, "But with this body, sports aren't exactly an option."

"I don't know," she said, looking off toward the mountains. "If you ask me, brains are a lot more interesting than brawn." Turning directly to him, she added, "And a lot sexier."

Will tried to swallow, though at the moment there wasn't much to swallow. Before he could think of a response, much less hope it would be intelligible, she said, "Your dad's a preacher, right?"

He imagined screeching brakes, saw himself thrown through the windshield, DOA before they ever started. "Yeah . . ." he said. Then he finished nailing the coffin by adding another, "Yeah."

"I think that's so cool."

He blinked. "You do?"

"To have all that spiritual heritage, those deep conversations about God, are you kidding?"

It was true. Between his father and grandfather Will did have "spiritual heritage." Up to his eyeballs.

"I think it's so hot," she said, "for a guy to have brains and spirituality."

If Will's mouth had been dry before, it was the Sahara Desert now.

"If you ask me, that's, like, *the* winning combo."

He didn't respond. Couldn't if he tried.

"Listen. Jason and some of the kids, we're having a get-together tomorrow night."

"Get-together?"

"Kinda like a party. He thinks it would be so cool if you joined us." She pushed back her hair and smiled. "So do I."

"Well, uh. . . ." Desperately, he tried to remember what night tomorrow was. A school night? A weekend? And what was his name again? Despite the confusion, he heard himself answering, "Things are kinda jammed right now, but you know, I'll check my calendar."

"That would be so cool." She turned to him and smiled.

He tried another attempt at swallowing.

Suddenly she reached down and took his hand. He stared dumbly as she put something inside and closed it. "Gotta go." Then, just like that, she did a 180 and headed off. "Call me, okay?"

He turned and opened his mouth. Nothing came. He tried again, this time with minimal success. "A number . . . I don't have your . . . number."

She twirled around. "It's in your hand, silly." Then she turned back and floated off into the sun.

He looked down and opened his hand to see the slip of paper. It had a phone number with little hearts drawn all around it.

Chapter Seven

On their way to baggage claim, before they even met Lisa, Charlie put in a quick call to Robert Quinn. He lived in Seattle now and had access to equipment that might be needed. The two had quite a history, serving together on several missions—the last in Jordan, though Special Forces were never officially in Jordan. It had been years since they talked, but bonds like that never dissolve. In fact, when Charlie's family was destroyed, it was Rob who flew down to be at his side during those weeks of drinking . . . and to slap him out of his self-pity when it was time to dry out. Like Charlie, he'd retired from Special Ops, but as an adrenaline junkie, he still needed an occasional fix—dodge a bullet here, neutralize a terrorist there. But since the local SWAT team frowned on hiring "senior citizens" (he was almost fifty), he finessed himself into a "contract employee" position for the FBI . . . as well as a few other nondisclosed agencies.

"I've got just what the doctor ordered," Quinn told Charlie over the phone.

"New toys?" Charlie asked.

"It's a whole new world out there, cowboy."

"Any chance of having something by tomorrow?"

"Sure, but you'll owe me."

"Put it on my tab."

Ten minutes later Charlie and Jazmin were down in baggage claim. It had been only a few days since his crash-and-burn routine with Lisa in Santa Monica, but it seemed like weeks. How he missed the petite, strong-willed beauty. Sure, she had her issues. Who didn't? But deep down at her core, they didn't come any better. Of course she never believed that about herself, but she didn't have to. That was his job. And he did believe. Enough for both of them.

When they greeted each other her embrace was friendly, but a little stiff. It saddened him, though he wasn't surprised. Of course she hugged Jaz more easily and for that he was grateful. It always pleased him to see the two girls together. Granted, they spoke a language he never fully understood and often felt was conspiratorial, but he was glad for Jazmin's exposure to an adult woman. To a *quality* adult woman.

A half hour later he was behind the wheel, driving them north on Interstate 5. True, it was Lisa's rental, but some things were nonnegotiable. As he drove, she filled him in on the details.

"The church has between four and five thousand members."

He whistled softly.

"Biggest in the county, and he'll do anything to keep it that way."

The accusation made him turn to her. She wasn't a

mean-spirited person, but you wouldn't know it from her tone. Before he could ask any more, Jaz spoke up from the backseat.

"Uncle Charlie?"

He glanced at her in the mirror.

"Could we move into another lane?"

"Why?"

She pointed ahead to a flatbed carrying a load of two-inch copper pipes. They hung over the back about three feet, a red flag whipping at their end. "I'm not crazy about that truck."

"This lane's faster," he said.

"I know, but—"

"We're fine."

"Please, Uncle Charlie."

He glanced back at the mirror. She looked desperate. Well, as desperate as she was with anything when she wanted to have her way. And, since it didn't cost him anything, he hit the blinker and pulled over one lane.

He turned back to Lisa. "What else is bothering you?"

"Three murders. Isn't that enough?"

He held her look and she glanced away. "What?" he repeated.

Still avoiding him, she answered, "I just get weary of all the performances, that's all."

He waited for more.

"I know he's a good guy, trying to do good things, but every time I come up here, it's like he's running for Mr. Congeniality or something."

"Doesn't the Bible talk about being at peace with all men?"

She threw him a look. Charlie knew he was on thin ice, quoting verses to someone who'd probably forgotten more Scripture than he ever learned. Odd, of all the topics they discussed, religion was the one that remained off-limits. It's not that she didn't believe in God; she just didn't trust many who did. Having both a dad and a brother as pastors didn't help. Particularly when her father scored such high marks in the hypocrisy department, his sexual abuse leaving scars from which she would never recover.

She looked back out the window. "I guess . . . I guess I just wouldn't mind seeing as much emphasis on the truth as on church membership."

The silence grew. Sensing her difficulty, Charlie changed subjects. "So tell me about this Kristof."

"SOCOM reject. Actually, he got through the training just fine. Even did a few out-of-countrys. But somebody ruined him with a bunch of Satanist crap, which he bought. Not only bought, but now he's selling."

"To the kids?"

She nodded.

"And you think he's behind the murders."

"That's what Hutton thinks."

"Hutton?"

"The sheriff. Bright guy. But you're the one with the experience. You know how these fellows think."

Charlie nodded and took a silent breath. The point was he'd been trying *not* to think like those fellows for years. Not after that thinking killed his wife and daughter. And later, when they were pursuing the Voice, his sister.

The squeal of brakes drew him from his thoughts and

back to the road. The flatbed with the pipes was skidding, trying to avoid a sofa that had fallen onto the freeway. The VW Bug directly beside them had no time to brake. Jaz screamed as the pipes from the flatbed exploded through the VW's windshield . . . a windshield that would have been theirs if Charlie had not heeded Jaz's warning.

✝

"It's going to be dark soon." Lisa tried hiding her exhaustion. "Feel like calling it a day?"

"Only if you do," Charlie said.

She set her jaw and continued. The guy didn't know the first thing about quitting. It took twenty minutes to arrive at her brother's house, make the intros, and head out. For two hours they were in the mountains, combing the bluff overlooking yesterday's ceremonial site. Sure, he may pretend to be Mr. Casual, Type B Personality, but on the inside he was triple A all the way. He never forced his untiring pace and determination on anybody, but if you wanted to play, you had to keep up.

And Lisa? There was no way she was going to be outmached. She'd mixed it up with the best in the Bureau and she wasn't going to let a little thing like dead-dog exhaustion slow her down.

Earlier, Charlie explained why they weren't revisiting the victim's apartment. "Local authorities have messed it up by now," he said.

"Perps usually return to gloat. What about a stakeout?" she asked.

"Amateurs do that. Not pros. And you're right, this guy's a pro."

"But up here?" she argued. "Shouldn't we be down there, where the kids hold their meetings?"

He shook his head. "This is the highest ground. Gives him a full view with easy egress."

"Why not that other ridge on the north side of the river?"

"He'd want to keep the moon at his back—avoid any reflection off binocular lenses."

Charlie definitely knew his stuff. Still, after all this time on the ridge, they'd not found a sign of anyone's presence. No cigarette butts, no footprints . . . nothing except a single broken fir bow, which they'd discovered nearly forty-five minutes earlier.

"Could be part of a blind," he explained as he rose from inspecting it. "Keep your eyes open for one or two more."

"It's a broken branch, Charlie. We're in the middle of a forest!"

"Do you see any fir trees?"

She looked around. There were plenty of alder, a few birch. But no firs, at least where they stood.

"Let's keep looking," he said. "He probably scattered them."

She sighed wearily. "That's a pretty thin clue."

"We could look for others."

She turned to him and saw a smile. Against her will, she asked, "Such as?"

"Searching under rocks."

"For?"

"For any bowel movements he may have buried."

"All right," she muttered. "I'm looking, I'm looking."

She worked her way across an open patch of ferns and

grass until she reached the edge of the bluff overlooking the river and ceremonial site. Thirty feet below, on the side of the ridge, she spotted a second fir bow. "Here's another," she called.

"Want me to go down and check it out?"

"I've got it," she said—though she would have paid good money for someone else to retrieve it. Gripping the salal vines, she eased herself over the edge and started down. She traveled about ten feet when she caught the whiff of something like rotten eggs. Sulfur. But there were no hot springs in the area, no mineral baths. So how could—

A shriek echoed against the bluff and trees. Like a hawk or an eagle. But louder.

And longer.

She gave an involuntary shudder, felt the hair on her neck and arms rising. She tilted back her head and looked up to see a shimmering darkness fill the sky. Translucent, like smoke.

Another shriek. More wail than scream. The chill spread across her shoulders and into her chest. Now she saw movement in the darkness. Synchronized. Back and forth. Back and forth. No, it wasn't smoke. They were wings!

"Charl—" The cry stuck in her throat.

The wings folded back and the darkness dove at her.

She ducked, letting go of the vines, and tumbled backward, head over heels. She spread out her arms, her hands grasping for something to catch. A glimpse skyward showed the darkness nearly on top of her. She screamed, bouncing against the rocky bluff again and again, until she hit a tree and her vision exploded into whiteness.

And then she saw nothing at all.

Chapter Eight

Jāz hadn't heard God speaking like this since her exposure to the Voice back in Rome over a year before.

Well, not *speaking* speaking. It wasn't like words or anything. How could it be? She was deaf. It was more like a whisper. No, not that, either. More like wisps of warmth. And with them came a type of understanding. She'd been getting a lot of that, ever since her encounter back in the Italian lab. But nothing like this. Nothing like what she heard in the music at the Saturday night church service.

Lisa and her nephew, Will, both found excuses to stay home: Lisa because she had a huge headache (getting knocked out will do that to a person) and because she was pretty shook over whatever she had seen on the mountain a few hours earlier. And Will stayed home because, well, he was a jerk. Seriously, the guy moped around the house grunting like some Neanderthal. He'd said like a grand total of ten words to her since she'd arrived. Not that she was interested. Pleeease, he was so majorly unhot, he belonged in the Arctic. But there was something going on inside him. Not the deal where he seemed all mad at everyone and everything. But something deeper. She knew it. She sensed it.

The church was huge, like what you see on TV, with rich burgundy seats as plush as any movie theater. Jaz sat up front between Uncle Charlie and Sharon, the minister's wife. Of course, Sharon suggested she sit in the "hearing impaired" section, but bag that. Jaz wanted to sit as close as possible to the giant speakers built into the walls on either side of the stage. That was the only way to really feel their vibrations.

In the sermon, which was more like a pep rally, Lisa's brother told everyone God was their best buddy, and not to worry 'cause He loved them all. "Even those news and media folks waiting outside." he chuckled. "In fact, if they hassle you, just invite them to one of tomorrow's services."

Of course, that got plenty of yuks. And it should. He was pretty funny. The drama team was good, too. And the videos? As slick as anything Hollywood had to offer. Even the announcements were cool, the way different types of print flew around the big screens. It was like the whole service was this perfectly produced show—way more entertaining than the church Uncle Charlie dragged her to back home.

But nothing compared to the music—part orchestra, part rock, even some rap. She closed her eyes to the vibrations, feeling the throb of the bass and the drums with their killer backbeat. From what she could tell, the keyboard and guitars weren't bad, either.

Then there were the singers. . . .

There were only eight of them, but they were as powerful as any choir. If she concentrated she could literally feel their words brush against her face as she read the lyrics up on the giant screen:

> . . . *exalt You above all things.*
> *Holy King of glory,*
> *Holy God my King.*

People were on their feet, singing and clapping. But there was more than the music. There was something inside it. She'd felt this a few times before with other music but could never put her finger on it. She looked at the words, concentrated on them, even began to sing them. Not verbally, of course. She had no idea where the melody was. But she sang them in her head:

> *You are my life,*
> *The center of my being.*

And, as she "sang," the intensity of the Voice increased.

> *Your glory makes me sing.*

Jazmin felt its warmth wash over her. She looked back at the musicians and singers, expecting to see something, anything.

But there was nothing.

A soloist stepped into the spotlight. An impressive blonde with an impressive figure she wasn't afraid to show off. She leaned over, pouring her heart out into the microphone. When she looked up her eyes were filled with tears.

It was a terrific performance, but it wasn't where Jaz felt the warmth. It came from the music, yes, but not there. And not from the band. So if it wasn't coming from the singer or the band, then where was it—

And then she saw her, one of the backup singers. She was plain-looking, with thick, Coke-bottle glasses and about zero percent fashion sense. But she seemed to shine. Not *shine* shine, as in light. But shine as in—well, as in the power of the Voice. You could practically see it rippling from her. And the way she held her hands at her sides, opening and closing them into fists, you could really tell something was going on.

Unfortunately, Jaz didn't have time to investigate. Suddenly the musicians were looking at each other all startled-like. Some even made faces. They tried to keep playing, but something was definitely bothering them. The orchestra was the first to quit, followed by the guitarists and keyboard. A few of the singers tried to plow ahead along with the drums, but it was useless, and pretty soon they stopped, too.

But something was still coming through the speakers. Jaz could feel it. Not music. More like talking. Or yelling.

She glanced at Sharon, who looked pretty upset. Then at Charlie, who was already checking out the auditorium and the ceiling above them. Another blast roared from the speakers. She looked up to the video screen and saw only the lyrics. She rose on her tiptoes to see what the interpreter was signing.

It was the same thing over and over again: "2 Peter 2:1, 2 Peter 2:1, 2 Peter 2:1."

Jaz guessed she was repeating what the speakers were

blasting. She turned to Sharon. The woman was already flipping through her Bible to find the verse.

"What is it?" Jaz shouted.

Sharon found the place and began to read silently.

"What's it say?" Jaz repeated.

She held the Bible out to her and pointed to the verse:

There will be false teachers among you . . . bringing swift destruction upon themselves.

✝

"What are you doing?" Heather shouted over the truck's CD. "Why we slowing down?"

Will turned to her. She was already three beers to the wind and now she was sucking on a silver flask of something. "You said a party," he shouted back. "There are no houses up here."

"Who said anything about a house?"

"It's too cold for a bonfire."

"There'll be plenty of antifreeze to keep you warm." Laying a hand on his thigh, she gave a sloppy grin. "And if the antifreeze don't work, there's always me."

He gripped the wheel tighter and accelerated. He'd heard all about Jason's little get-togethers. Who hadn't? The booze, the drugs, the sex. And, of course, the spells. None of that really interested him—well, except, of course, the sex. I mean that was the whole point of this little excursion, right? She'd sure made her intentions clear . . . calling him Saturday morning, Saturday afternoon, asking him if he'd drive them up here.

Of course he agreed. He was sixteen years old, for crying out loud. And still a virgin. It was definitely time for the PK to taste the real world.

It took a grand total of one lie to convince Mom he wasn't feeling good enough for Saturday night's church service. If Dad had been there, it might have taken a little more. . . . like sodium pentothal and a lie-detector test. But because of all the killings and stuff, he'd left earlier for church and wasn't there. Then again, Dad was never there. For as long as he could remember it was as if he had to get an appointment just to talk to the guy. Not that Will wanted to. Nowadays, talks meant fights. And Will was through with both.

Once the annoying deaf girl, her uncle, and his mom left, Will had struggled to push his beater pickup out the garage and halfway down the block before starting it up. Aunt Lisa was upstairs resting, but she was ex-FBI and pretty sharp for an old person.

Now the bridge and river lay just ahead. He glanced back at Heather. Her eyes were closed as she swayed to the rhythm of some screamer band. Through the fog, his headlights caught a dozen cars parked along the edge of the gravel road. He slowed and pulled in behind a rusting Toyota.

Heather mumbled something he couldn't hear.

"What?"

She mumbled again.

He popped out the CD. "What did you say?"

"I don't feel so good."

She didn't look it, either. In fact she was leaning forward like she was going to hurl.

"Hold on!" he shouted.

He threw the pickup into park and bailed out. He ran to her side, barely getting the door open before she rolled her head toward him and spewed, missing the interior by inches.

But not the new Converses he'd bought for the occasion.

Swallowing back his irritation, he asked, "You okay?"

She answered by hurling again, this time catching the leg of his jeans.

When she finished, he wrapped an arm around her waist and helped her out of the truck. She felt cold and damp. Her hair hung over her face in strands that were wet with drool. Not exactly the sex goddess he remembered from the day before.

That's when he heard the screech—like an owl, only longer.

"D'you smell that?" she slurred.

He thought she meant the vomit, until he caught the stench of something like rotten eggs.

There was another screech. Louder. Closer.

They both looked up, searching the sky. Not that they'd see anything with the thick canopy of evergreens.

But they did see something. A black mist appearing through the branches.

Heather swore. "What is it?"

It gave another shriek that grew into a wail. As it grew, so did the blackness—thicker, darker. And it was waving, moving up and down. Wings! They were wings! They stretched nearly a dozen feet across. And they were diving at them!

Will pushed her back inside the truck. "Get in!"

She needed no second invitation.

He slammed her door and raced around to his side.

The wail grew louder. Part-animal, part-human.

He flung open his door and dove in. Stealing a quick peek above, he saw a darker shape in the center of the wings. Like a person. Eight to ten feet tall.

He shut the door and started the engine.

"What is it?" Heather shouted.

He dropped into Drive and hit the gas. Wheels spun, spitting gravel as they slid, barely missing the parked Toyota.

"What is it!?"

He cranked the wheel harder, throwing them into a 180. He straightened out and stomped on the gas. They fishtailed and for a moment he lost control. Finally regaining it, he looked into the mirror and saw nothing but their own dust.

"What is it?"

The shriek faded, but Will continued picking up speed. Whatever it was, the farther they got away from it, the better.

†

Mark Ramsey woke up shivering. His mind was thick as sludge. His temples pounded. Eyes still shut, he winced against the pain and reached for his blankets. But he couldn't find them. He felt a bristly dampness against his buttocks and shoulders. Forcing one eye open, he saw he wasn't in bed, but lying on grass. Wet grass, in a darkness that was not his bedroom.

Despite the throbbing in his skull, he managed to rise into a sitting position. Looking down, he saw he was naked. He tilted back his head, eyes fluttering from the pain. Up above, a tree with leaves he couldn't identify, stretched over him. Beyond it were low-hanging clouds, pewter gray with the reflection of city lights.

He heard a rustling behind him, the snort of a horse. He was in a pasture. Somehow he'd wound up in a pasture. He frowned, trying to remember.

There was O'Brien's Sports Grill, which he frequented on Saturday nights. The game on the screen. Mariners up by two. The bottle redhead three stools over. His obligatory move. Her obligatory shutdown.

He remembered climbing into his car, thinking how strange it was that he'd left it unlocked. He recalled the white cord coming around from behind, yanking so hard into his neck he could barely breathe, holding him in place as a tiny burn pricked his right arm.

Back in the pasture, he heard another snort, closer. And the smacking of lips.

He turned and saw a giant, leathery face staring back at him, huge pink and black nostrils flaring. He cried out and scrambled to his feet. The movement scared the creature, and a black, hairy arm the size of a tree knocked him back to the ground.

Ramsey looked up at it and screamed, which frightened the monster even more. It lunged at him, baring large, almost human teeth.

A gorilla! He was in a pasture with a gorilla! No, not a pasture. His eyes darted, catching glimpses of rock, a watering hole, a distant fence. He spun around and crawled away on his hands and knees until the animal grabbed his foot. He fought, kicking back, landing a blow in the creature's chest.

It roared in anger and rose to its full height.

Ramsey kept crawling until he felt hands wrapping around his waist. They picked him up. He screamed, arms flailing, fists pounding against fur and muscle. By luck he landed a blow to the creature's face.

The ape howled and threw him onto the ground.

Catching his breath, Ramsey scampered back to his hands and knees. Only then did he see the glowing eyes of another creature looming before him. He veered to its left, gasping, trying to crawl away, but the first animal would have none of it. Once again it caught Ramsey's foot. He kicked free but it caught him again.

"Help me! Somebody help!"

It snorted angrily as it pulled him across the grass.

"Help me!"

It scooped him up and raised him high off the ground. Then, eyes glaring with rage, it roared and flung him into the rock wall.

Ramsey hit hard and tumbled to the ground. He rolled onto his back and saw the animal lumbering toward him.

"Please," he whimpered, "please."

Only then did he see the white banner of butcher paper behind the creature's head. It was stretched between two trees, with words clearly printed in giant block letters:

That was the last thing he read as the gorilla picked him up and flung him into the wall again. And again. How many times, Mark Ramsey would never know.

Chapter Nine

Getting a CD of the evening's service wasn't hard. The sheet music with lyrics for the song was almost as easy. The worship leader, some forty-plus fossil who dressed like he thought he was twenty, must have thought it "cute" that a deaf kid wanted to learn the song, so he gave her a copy.

But learning it was the last thing on her mind.

Jazmin was an expert in acoustics—well, at least her parents had been, which meant she was. Sort of. The point was, there was something about the song that night that was connected to the Voice. Actually, it wasn't that big of a surprise. Asia, Africa, South America, even sixth-century Greece thought music was somehow connected to the power of the cosmos. And "power" was definitely what she'd experienced at the service . . . and what she hoped to experience again.

Minutes earlier, when Will had been showering, she stole into his room and borrowed his CD boom box. Now she had it in the guest room she shared with Lisa, who was still downstairs with the grown-ups.

First she played the CD, keeping her hand on the speaker

so she could feel its vibrations. She sat cross-legged on the quilted bedspread, eyes closed, straining for the slightest feel of energy, the slightest warmth that had been so present earlier that night.

The choir sang:

> *I exalt you above all things.*
> *Holy King of glory,*
> *Holy God my King.*

But Jazmin felt nothing. Whatever she'd experienced in person wasn't transferred through the CD player. No great revelation there. Even in Switzerland, and later, Rome, when they played the Voice, they hadn't been able to use regular speakers. The things had nasty habits of disintegrating. Not blowing up—that would have been too normal. Instead, the speakers, which like most speakers were made of paper, simply turned into wood and sawdust. That's what happened when things were exposed to the Voice, they turned back into their original elements. Which is why they had to use special speakers—long rods made of special crystals and stones.

Anyway, since playing the CD didn't work, Jaz decided to feel for recurring rhythms. They might act as a conduit for the power. South American shamans used rhythm lots of times in their practices. So did the Yirkalla Aborigines and the Tibetan monks. Even the metal and rap artists knew something was going on. And for good reason. Everything about human beings is made of rhythms . . . beating hearts, brain waves, even the contractions of their intestines. Not to mention the rest of the universe . . . from the vibration of starlight, to atoms, to subatomic super-strings. If the right music could vibrate with the right rhythm to affect people's bodies and surrounding world, who knew what could happen?

Yes, sir, there was lots going on in the land of vibrations. And, as her parents had proved, much of it was associated with a very specific set of vibrations . . . the words that spoke the universe into existence. The Voice of God.

When her search for special rhythms failed, she divided the lyrics into syllables, reciting them over and over again, stressing certain accents and beats.

> **I**-*ex-alt-You-a-bove-all-things.*
> *I-ex-alt-***You***-a-bove-all-things.*
> *I-ex-alt-You-a-bove-***all***-things.*
> **I**-*ex-alt-***You***-a-bove-all-things.*
> *I-***ex-alt***-You-***a-bove***-all-things.*
> **I**-*ex-alt-***You***-a-bove-***all***-things.*

Nothing. No pattern. No sensation of any kind.

Maybe it was a combination—some sort of harmonics between the words, the music, and the rhythms.

She placed her hands on the speakers and read the sheet music, reciting the words as best she could in time with the music:

> *I exalt You above all things.*
> *Holy King of glory,*
> *Holy God my King.*

Still nothing.

Keeping her hands on the speakers, her eyes glued to the music, she tried to sing, matching as best she could the pitch of the words to what she felt:

You are my life,
The center of my being.
Your glory makes me sing.

And the result?

More of nothing.

In frustration, she dropped her head and half-mumbled the words—not a mindless mutter, but a search for something deeper, anything that could be hidden or locked inside them.

And then she felt it. Ever so slightly. A tiny ripple.

She stopped.

The sensation stopped.

She started again, more slowly this time.

I exalt You above all things.

She continued the verse, slowly chewing on its meaning, making it as real as possible.

Holy King of glory . . .

The sensation grew, spreading its warmth through her body. She adjusted herself on the bed and concentrated harder, pressing in on the words, trying to unpack their meaning:

Holy God my King.

The warmth grew, not only inside, but also around her. Not as much as at church, but similar to it.

> *You are my life,*
> *the center of my being.*
> *Your glory makes me sing.*

Was this the key? Not the music. Not the lyrics, but the intensity in which she thought the lyrics? Sure, there was something about the melody. Sure, there was something about singing the words. But the energy seemed to be the most present when she concentrated on what she was saying, when she focused and meant it. And if that was the case . . . then it wasn't the music affecting the power of her mind, but her mind affecting the power of the music.

She hit *Replay.*

Again she spoke the words with the music, making them as real as possible. Again she felt an increase of power until suddenly there was . . . a coldness.

Something was pushing back the warmth. Before she could investigate, the air pressure in the room changed. Someone had opened the door. She turned to see Will standing there, hands on his hips, demanding, "—my CD player?"

Before she could answer, he stormed in and grabbed the boom box off her bed. "Nobody gave you permission to come into my room and—" He turned and headed back for the door.

She was off the bed in a flash. "Will!"

He crossed the hallway to his room.

"Will!"

He stopped so quickly, she ran into him. Flustered, she demanded, "Why do you always have to be such a jerk?"

"Why do you have to be such a pest?"

He turned away and entered his room, slamming the door. Well, at least he tried to slam it. But Jaz's foot was already there, and she followed him inside. The place smelled like dirty gym socks.

He spun around at her. "Do you mind?"

That's when she saw something over his shoulder. Something weird on his computer screen. The source of the coldness. "What's that?"

"What?"

"That." She pointed at the image of a giant bird. Or was it a butterfly? Either way, its wings were jet black. She tried moving around him, but he blocked her. She looked to his face and caught the last of a phrase:

"—junk on the Internet."

But she knew it was more than just junk. Not only by his expression, but by what she felt—from him *and* the monitor. The coldness was connected. It was hard to explain, but in some way, they were the same, or *would* be the same. Not only a coldness, but a sadness. Deep down inside.

She pushed back the feeling and raised on her tiptoes to see the monitor. Actually, it didn't have your typical butterfly body with head and antenna and all that stuff. Instead, it had the body and face of a man.

"That's gross." She faked to the left then twisted past him to the right. "No, really, what is it?"

He turned and crossed to the desk, reaching for the mouse.

"No, don't change it. Tell me what it is. Please?"

He hesitated and then, like he needed to tell somebody, he took a breath. "They call—" He turned his head and she missed the rest.

"I'm sorry, what?"

He turned to her. "Mothman. They call it Mothman."

"Like in the movie?"

He looked at her surprised. "You saw it?"

"Some of it, yeah. Pretty creepy."

He nodded. "Yeah. It was first spotted back in—" He turned and slipped behind the keyboard to start typing.

"Excuse me." She tapped his shoulder. "You have to face me when you talk."

He turned back to her and repeated himself so slowly and with such exaggeration that she could barely read him. "I . . . said . . . in . . . 1966!"

"I'm deaf, not blind."

"What?"

She shouted back with equal exaggeration. "I'm . . . deaf . . . not . . . blind!" She hoped the comedy would lighten things up.

It didn't.

He turned back to the computer and brought up three more drawings—two by okay artists, the third by an obvious amateur. In some ways, the thing looked like an angel, except for its black wings. But forget the feathers. These wings were all leather and rubbery. More like bat wings.

He turned to her. "In November 1966, two couples were

driving near Point Pleasant, West Virginia, when they got attacked by this."

Jaz leaned closer.

"It was about seven feet tall. They tried to get away, driving, like, a hundred miles an hour, but it kept on attacking and clawing at their roof."

She shrugged, disappointed that such a brainy guy could fall for an Internet hoax. Then again, maybe it was geeks like him who dreamed the stuff up in the first place . . . when they weren't attending *Star Wars* conventions.

"The thing was sighted off and on in the area for over a year."

"Ruining how many hookups?" she asked.

He ignored her and brought up another pencil sketch. It had a lot more detail than the others. "Lots of folks saw it. Townspeople, firemen, a doctor's wife, some airline pilot."

Hoax or not, the thing was definitely giving her the creeps. Besides the cold, there were those eyes—bulging, like the UFO thingies on the Sci Fi Channel. The fact that they were red didn't help.

She frowned, trying to remember the movie—at least the parts where she wasn't hiding under the pillow. "Didn't something really bad happen to the town, like a bridge blowing up or something?"

Will brought up another image. A grainy black-and-white photograph of a collapsed bridge. He turned back to her. "The Silver Bridge over the Ohio River. It was rush hour. Forty-six cars were lost."

"And everybody thought there was like some sort of connection or something?"

He entered some keystrokes and another photo came up. This time in color. It was a modern building with domes and stuff.

"What's that?"

"Chernobyl."

"What?"

He pointed to the caption under the picture: "Chernobyl."

"What's that?"

"A nuclear reactor that melted down in Russia."

"And?"

More keystrokes brought up another amateur drawing of a man with wings. Not exactly the same, but close. "This creature was seen in and around the area a few weeks before it happened."

He brought up another photo—the Twin Towers—and another sketch of a similar creature. "This was seen in New York during the first few days of September 2001."

Jaz could only stare.

He entered one last set of keystrokes, waited for a video to load, and hit Play.

It was a shaky home video. Some poor village—tiled roofs, water tanks—definitely not America. And hovering over the roofs was a Darth Vader–type guy, complete with black cape.

"What's this?" she asked.

"Santa Rosa, Ecuador. A week before it was destroyed by a massive earthquake." He hit Enlarge and zoomed in.

Now the cape didn't look like a cape at all. But wings.

"Can you get any closer?"

He hit Enlarge again.

The image got so grainy, it was impossible to see much of anything. Except for the eyes. There was no mistaking their red color.

Jaz shuddered. "Why . . . why are you so interested in this?" He hit Freeze Frame at a point where Jaz could clearly see the two glowing red dots.

"I was up in the mountains tonight."

"When we were in church?"

He nodded, continuing to stare at the screen.

"And?"

"And this is what I saw."

✟

"I'm just saying that since you're here, it would be nice to see him." Thomas took his seat across the kitchen table from Lisa and Charlie. The smell of eggs and bacon filled the air.

"Nice for who?" Lisa asked.

"He's our father. He asks about you all the time."

"He's got Alzheimer's. He barely knows his own name."

"But he talks about you," Sharon said. She turned from the stove with a platter of eggs.

"That's right," Thomas agreed. "He thinks about you a lot."

"I bet he does," Lisa muttered.

Thomas gave her a look, then tried again. "It's a twenty-minute drive. We could drop by after this morning's service. Grab a bite to eat with him in the cafeter—"

"This conversation is over."

"Lis—"

"I said, it's over!"

An uneasy silence filled the room. Uneasy, but not surprising, at least for Thomas. It had been this way every time she'd come up to visit. Why did he think it would be any different now? Particularly under these circumstances.

The past eight-and-a-half hours had been hard. Somehow, Thomas had finished the evening's service, patched things up with the congregation, and sent them home with what he hoped were words of comfort. Afterward, Sheriff Hutton grilled him and the staff, particularly the tech support people, for a good three, four hours with no clues . . . until one of the deputies discovered a receiver hidden in back of the video mixer. Then the grilling began all over again.

The best they figured the message had been transmitted from a passing vehicle.

The investigation was still going on when Thomas called it a night and headed for home around 1:45 AM. He had two more services coming up in the morning.

But of course neither he nor anybody else in the house had been able to sleep. That's why now, at—he glanced at his watch—4:20—Sharon was serving them an early breakfast of bacon, eggs, and hash browns. She'd do it all over again when the kids got up. And probably something lighter for him, just before he traipsed back to church. But that's how it was with Sharon. She was always there. All these years. What she put up with never ceased to amaze him. And what she saw in him was even more of a puzzle.

He liked Charlie the moment he met him. His soft-spoken candor was similar to the farmers who still remained in the area. Quiet, unassuming—as plain and true as the earth they relied upon. Imagine his surprise when he learned the man had retired early from Special Ops in hopes of entering the ministry. Of course, there was much Thomas wanted to say on the subject, but for now he simply hoped it wouldn't ruin him, that Charlie would be one of the lucky ones who refused to allow ministry to become business. With his quiet, straight-talking style, maybe he would.

After the group said grace and passed around the platters of food, their talk turned back to the killer.

"And when you do find him," Sharon asked, "what will you do?"

Lisa looked up from her plate. "What do you mean?"

"Will they let you capture him? Since you're not law enforcement officers, can you still arrest him?"

"Actually," Lisa said, "arresting is not what we have in mind. More like blowing the mother to kingdom come."

Without missing a beat, Sharon asked, "And they'll allow that?"

"They'll have a hard time stopping it."

As they spoke, Charlie dug something out of his pants pocket that looked like a large ballpoint pen.

"What do you have there?" Thomas asked.

Charlie set it on the table. "It's a transmitter."

"A tracking device?" Lisa said. "Where did you get that?"

"A friend had it delivered when we were in church."

"Along with a receiver?"

He shook his head. "It uses cell phone technology. We get close enough to plant it on him, my friend connects us to NSA, and—"

Lisa finished the thought, "We track him just like any other cell phone user."

Charlie nodded. "It's accurate to within a couple feet, at least in the populated areas."

"Except in places where there's no signal," Thomas said.

"You still have those?" Lisa asked.

"Here and there. Depends how deep you go into the mountains. Last winter some campers—"

Thomas's PDA vibrated, and the table froze. He pulled it from his pocket and looked at the screen. It was Sheriff Hutton.

"Hello?" he answered.

"I'm afraid we've got another one," the sheriff said.

"From the church?"

"Mark Ramsey. High school science teacher."

Thomas swallowed and looked around the table. All eyes were on him. "Where is he? Where did it happen?"

"Down in Seattle. The Woodland Park Zoo."

Chapter Ten

"But Sheriff Hutton is right there." Lisa pointed past the penguin pool to a small group of men standing in front of the gift shop. Beyond them was the outdoor gorilla exhibit, where there was even more activity. "We're assisting him in the investigation."

"I'm sorry," the roly-poly cop said. "This is a crime scene, and unauthorized personnel are not—"

"That's what I'm saying, we *are* authorized personnel."

"Who have no credentials."

"We're retired. I've explained to you that—"

"I'm sorry, ma'am, but you'll have to step back behind the yellow tape."

Lisa's ears grew hot. Not a good sign. She felt Charlie's hand on her arm. Another warning. She refused to heed either.

"Listen, pal, we didn't drive all the way down here for our health. We were specifically asked—"

"Ma'am, please. I've requested you to step behind the tape. If you fail to obey my orders, then I'm left with no recourse but to—"

"Your orders?"

"Ma'am."

"Your orders?"

She saw him glance at Charlie. An obvious plea, man-to-man, to help calm the hysterical female . . . which really set her off.

"Don't look at him! You're talking to me!"

The cop stiffened. "Yes, I am." With a touch of melodrama, he reached for the riot stick on his belt. "And I've clearly repeated my order for you to—"

But it was going to take more than some pumped-up doughnut-eater to deter her. "Listen, I don't care—"

Charlie's grip tightened. "Let's go."

She shook him off.

"There's nothing we can do."

"We were specifically called down here to—"

"We can wait over there." Charlie motioned to the picnic area beyond the tape.

"We were specifically—"

"Actually," the cop corrected, "I'll have to ask you to wait outside the park."

"Outside the park?"

"Given the inability to control your outbursts."

"Outbursts!?"

Again Charlie took her arm, his voice infuriatingly calm. "Let's go."

"But—"

He repeated more firmly, "Let's go."

His tone brought her to her senses. She shook him off and stormed up the lane on her own—angry at the ultimatum, even angrier at her reaction. What was wrong with her, anyway? She was always the calm and professional one. But this. . . .

A moment later Charlie arrived beside her, matching her stride.

"Whose side are you on, anyway?" she demanded.

"We're in Seattle. Out of Hutton's jurisdiction."

"He's the one who called. He's the one who—"

"Even if he wanted, he couldn't give clearance. You know that. Not if some big city detective wants to throw his weight around."

She knew he was right—though she didn't give him the satisfaction of admitting it. Instead, she picked up her pace, distancing herself from him. And he let her. That's one of the things she admired about the man. And hated. He gave her her space . . . whether she wanted it or not.

But this time, she wanted it. Because it wasn't just the murders or her experience on the mountain. It wasn't even about a brother whose concern for appearances always made her crazy. It was also about her dad. No secret there. Never had been. Not after it made the papers. But every time she came home, Tommy piled on the guilt. And this morning was no different. Granted, it was the abridged version—no doubt for Charlie's sake. But abridged or not, it always came down to something like:

"He barely remembers who he is, let alone what he did."

"I remember loud and clear."

"And you're still the victim—back then and today."

"I did the therapy."

"I'm not talking about your 'acting out.' I'm talking about Dad. I'm talking about God."

"Yeah, well, me and the Big Man still got a few things to work out."

"But it's got to start with Dad."

And so the argument continued, year after year, with no progress except for the increasing aggravation and, of course, the guilt.

Lisa approached the carousel near the north entrance and slowed her pace—Charlie's cue that it was safe to approach.

He arrived and asked. "Feel like stopping for coffee?"

She nodded, and they continued forward in silence. The parking area looked like a used police car lot. There were over a dozen empty cruisers as well as two or three vans. Apparently crime fighting was slow on Sunday mornings.

By the time they reached the first car she'd cooled down enough to admit she'd been a jerk. But when she turned to apologize to Charlie, she saw a red dot quivering on his chest.

"Look out!" With no time to explain, she threw herself at him. She was too slight to bring the big man down, but she managed to knock him off balance . . . just as the first shot *ker-plunked* into the side panel of the car in front of them.

Charlie understood. He dropped and pulled her down on top of him so he'd take the impact of the pavement. As they fell, a second shot shattered the car's safety glass inches above their heads. He released her and they scrambled to an adjacent van, flattening themselves against it as two more bullets sank into the cruiser immediately in front of them.

If they had guns, they'd be in their hands by now,

though Lisa doubted they would do any good. Looking at the holes before them, she knew it was a high-powered rifle with scope—the shooter no doubt in the zoo behind them, perched atop a roof or in a tree.

As soon as the shots ceased, Charlie moved to action. "Stay here."

"What?"

He rose, stooping. "I'll draw them away. When it's safe, go for your car and meet me in the street."

Before she could protest, he darted to the right and ran between more cruisers, keeping his head low, but raising it from time to time to draw fire—a shattered window, a ricochet, more punctures of sheet metal.

As he ran, Lisa strained, listening for the shooter's location. Of course he was using a silencer and she heard nothing. She waited until Charlie was thirty feet away before starting. She worked slowly and methodically, careful to keep out of sight. For now it was important Charlie be the one to take the risk. Her turn would come when she got to the car.

The rental was a cream-colored Camry parked beside one of the vans. She arrived and, staying low, dug into her pocket to pull out the key. It was an electronic lock. For the life of her she couldn't remember if she had to press the remote button to unlock it, or if she could simply insert the key. Pressing the remote would beep the horn and flash the lights. A dead giveaway of her location. But if she used the key, would that set off the alarm?

She decided on the remote and pressed the button. The car beeped, the lights flashed, and she waited for fire.

There was none.

Slowly, carefully, she opened the door and eased up into the seat. She didn't slam the door but closed it just enough so it wouldn't chime when she inserted the key. For the same reason, she buckled the seat belt. Now she looked through the windshield at the zoo directly in front of her.

She inserted the key and turned the ignition. The Camry started up and quietly idled. She dropped the gear into Reverse and gently pressed the accelerator.

The car did not move.

She pressed harder.

Still no movement, until she remembered the emergency brake. Cursing herself, she released the brake and slowly backed out of the space. Once she was clear, she shifted into Drive. She headed toward the street but, thanks to a three-foot retaining wall, she had to turn and run parallel with it.

Finally she arrived at the exit and spotted Charlie to the right, already forty yards down the road. She turned onto the street and picked up speed, confidence building. She slowed beside him and reached over to open the door.

He jumped in. "You okay?" he asked.

"Yeah." They accelerated and she pushed back her hair. "You?"

He nodded. On the dash in front of him, he spotted a business card. He picked it up and Lisa caught a glimpse of the wording. Something about a janitorial service.

"What's it say?" she asked.

He flipped it over and immediately shouted, "Stop the car!"

"What?"

"Stop the car! Get out!" Without explanation, he

reached over and shoved the transmission into Park, throwing them forward with a horrendous noise. Before they stopped, he threw open his door. "Get out, get out!"

"What are you—"

She barely had her seat belt unfastened before he'd crossed to her side and was pulling. "Come on!"

They stumbled into the street. Rush-hour horns honked and brakes squealed.

"Charlie?"

They crossed into the opposite lane.

"What are—"

Suddenly, the car exploded. The impact was so powerful they flew forward, tumbling onto the asphalt. Charlie instinctively threw his body over hers as pieces of automobile rained down around them. She heard cars screeching, slamming into one another.

Only when the pieces stopped falling did he roll off her. She raised her head and looked across the street. A smoking chassis was all that remained.

"That's my rental!"

Charlie remained silent.

She staggered to her feet, astonished, outraged. "My insurance won't cover that!"

He rose beside her. The business card was still in his hand.

She turned to him and saw it . "What is it? What's it say?"

He looked down and flipped it over. On the back three words were printed by hand:

BOOM!
YOU'RE DEAD

Chapter Eleven

Thank God for iPod.

Over the past six months, the little invention had become a permanent part of Will's wardrobe, his survival kit for sanity—at least when the folks were around. Popping in those little white ear buds was like wearing a Do Not Disturb sign around his neck. And the beauty was, if he wanted to know what they were saying, all he had to do was hit Pause and eavesdrop. Yes, sir, it was a wonderful thing. Dad could ramble on all he wanted about God's mercy, but iPods were proof that there really was a loving God in heaven. More so with this newest pain in the butt . . . the thirteen-year-old with diarrhea of the mouth. Honestly, did she have the slightest idea how to quit talking? And now that he had made the mistake of telling her about last night, there was no stopping her.

"Did it really look like that?"

"Can I meet Heather?"

"Can we go back up there?"

"Wouldn't it be cool to get it like on video or something?"

Of course, she was forbidden under penalty of death to mention anything about it to his parents. But it didn't stop her from mentioning it to him . . . again and again, and again some more. And yet, even as he sat with her in the back of the family's Volvo, heading for the required Sunday encore of last night's service, he was beginning to think she might have a point. Maybe it would be good to go back up there and investigate . . . in the daylight . . . with witnesses and a camera.

The techno band, Hypnoises, was pounding away through his earbuds when he noticed his dad pulling into the service entrance of their sprawling church. He was obviously hoping to avoid the press by going in the back way.

Not a bad idea, except it looked like the press had the same one.

As the car pulled to a stop Sharon and Jazmin reached for their doors, but Will had other ideas. "I'll stay with you."

Dad shook his head. "This is not up for discussion."

The others were stepping out, but Will stood his ground. "I can handle it."

"Son."

"What? You afraid I'm going to say something stupid?"

"No, of course not."

"That's it, isn't it? You're afraid I'm going to embarrass you."

"Will, this is not your battle. I'm simply trying to protect you from—"

"From what? Making a fool of myself? Making a fool of *you*?"

"Please, son, get out of the car."

"I'm a big boy. I can—"

"Now. Get out of the car now."

For the briefest second, Will thought of challenging him. What was he going to do, drag him out? The press would love that, wouldn't they?

Then again, so would the kids at school.

"Fine!" He opened the door. There would be other battles, other times. This was not the hill to die on. He climbed out, making sure he gave the door a good slam.

Of course, his mom was already there, trying to smooth things over. "Will. . . ."

She was always smoothing things over. But not this time. This time he turned and stormed toward the west entrance. But not before catching a final glimpse of his dad. The man wasn't even looking. He'd already started the car forward, off to make another grand appearance to his people.

So what else was new?

†

"And that doesn't seem odd to you?"

Jason Ballard looked up with feigned innocence. "What's that?"

"You threaten your biology teacher at school on Friday, and forty-eight hours later he shows up dead?"

"I thought you said he died this morning."

"That's right."

"So isn't that closer to thirty-six hours?"

Sheriff Hutton said nothing, but there was no missing his frustration. Jason helped out by throwing in a smirk.

The man ignored him and walked around the steel gray

Bill Myers

96

table. Jason didn't bother to watch. He knew what was going on. It was the same dance they'd been through twice before. Twice before they tried to stick something on him, and twice before they failed. Truth was, Jason was getting to like the dance. He liked playing with their heads.

"'I'm going to vomit you out of my mouth,'" Hutton quoted. "What do you call that?"

"I call it the Bible." Jason stretched, leaning back in his chair. "You should try reading it sometime. It's got some crazy stuff."

Hutton walked away. Too bad. Jason was hoping for a little more competition. Still, you couldn't blame the dude. He'd been up all night—already down to Seattle and back. He had a right to be a little off his game.

For the third time, Jason felt his cell phone vibrate. Heather, no doubt. She'd been calling like every twenty seconds. Freaked about what she claimed to have seen last night. Pretty lame excuse for not showing up, but she seemed convinced it was true. Maybe it was. Kristof always said something would eventually happen.

Hutton's assistant stepped forward. Some runt of a deputy with too few brain cells and too much caffeine. Jason knew his daughter from school.

"You accused him of being a hypocrite, teaching evolution," he said in his best *CSI* imitation. "And suddenly he winds up in a gorilla cage, torn to pieces?"

Jason yawned. "Sorry, Deputy. I'm not seeing the connection."

"With a banner reading 'Survival of the Fittest.' You don't see that as a coincidence?"

"A coincidence?"

"Yes, a *coincidence*."

Jason frowned. "No, I don't think so. Now *irony*, you might have something with *irony*. But *coincidence*, that's really not the correct term in this—"

"And where exactly were you when this *irony* was taking place?"

Jason sighed wearily. "I told you. I was at a party with some friends."

"In the middle of the woods."

"We like our privacy."

"Right."

Jason turned to him. "Actually, the privacy thing, that's more for the girls. They get a little loaded—not on booze or any *illegal* substances, just high on life—and then they like to have a little, how can I delicately put it . . . coeducational recreation."

The men said nothing and he continued. "Chicks nowadays, they're like sex addicts. You know what I'm talking about, right, Deputy? If not, just ask Sherry or Cherry or whatever your kid's name is. With her rep, she ought to be able to fill you in on *all* the details."

For a brief second, he thought the runt was going after him, until Jason threw a pointed look over to the one-way mirror. Maybe somebody was there, maybe there wasn't. Either way, they were probably getting it on tape.

Containing himself but giving his Adam's apple the workout of its life, the runt asked, "Have you or have you not been practicing a bunch of sick, occultist rituals?"

"If I'm not mistaken, the constitution calls that freedom of religion. And, yes, we have been."

The sheriff stood to the side, leaning against a beige

cinder-block wall. "So you admit your group stole and killed Samuel Mugridge's cat."

Jason looked up at the ceiling and sighed in exaggerated patience. "As I said before, we're not the only ones who use that site by the river. I don't know if you know it, but those woods, they can be full of all kinds of unsavory characters."

"Tell me more about your religion," Hutton said.

"You thinking of joining?"

Hutton waited.

Jason shrugged. "Nothing to say, really. 'Cept the end of the world is coming, and we've been chosen to help usher it in."

"And how is that?"

"Come on, guys." Jason stifled another yawn. "We've been through this a dozen times. Don't you have any new material?"

"How is that?" Hutton repeated.

Jason recited, "Through the Ultimate Unification."

"Of—"

"Jesus Christ and Satan."

"Complete love and complete wrath," Hutton quoted.

"Yin and yang. You got it. The two greatest powers of the universe, coming together for the grand finale."

Hutton pushed away from the wall and shoved his hands into his pockets. Oh, brother, now he was going for the aw-shucks, Jimmy Stewart routine. Do these guys ever learn?

"Doesn't it strike you as, oh, I don't know, just a little unusual that all of the victims are from the same church?"

"Calvary Cathedral?" Jason asked.

The sheriff nodded. "Why do you think that is?"

Jason shrugged. "Maybe 'cause it's the biggest in the area. Kinda like a symbol or something."

"Maybe."

Jason couldn't help adding, "Or maybe 'cause some people don't even consider it a church."

That did it. Jason almost smiled as Runt took the bait and pulled up a chair. "Why wouldn't they call it a church?"

Jason scoffed.

Even Hutton was falling for it. "No, please, why is that?"

"It's just . . . I mean, they claim to follow God and everything, right?"

Hutton nodded. "Right."

"But you never hear anything about sin. You never hear anything about having to get clean to meet God."

"Why's that important?" Runt asked.

"Read your Bible."

Hutton sat on the table beside him. "Why don't you educate us?"

"Please."

"No, I'm serious."

Jason looked from one to the other, then answered. "Holiness begins in the house of the Lord."

"Meaning?"

"In order for Jesus Christ to return, the first thing He's gotta clean up is His house and His people."

"And how is that accomplished?" Hutton asked.

"How is His house cleaned?"

"Yes."

By now both men were leaning toward him, practically drooling.

Jason looked up, paused for effect, then grinned, "Got me."

Realizing they'd been had, they pulled back.

Jason continued, all smiles. "We just pray that His will be done, that's all."

"While throwing in a few orgies on the side," Runt piped in.

"Love *and* wrath, gentlemen," Jason said with a grin. "Love and wrath."

"And Kristof?"

He turned back to Hutton. "Who?"

"Harold Campbell?"

"Sorry, no bells."

"You have a short memory," the deputy growled. "We bring this guy up every time you come in."

"Oh, *that* Harold Campbell." Jason hesitated. He scrunched his face into a thoughtful frown, letting the tension build. They waited, trading discreet looks. Then, when he was sure he had them, he shrugged. "Sorry, never heard of him."

Runt turned away. Hutton closed his eyes. And Jason smiled. He couldn't believe he got them twice in a row.

Regrouping, the sheriff reached for a pitcher of water on the table. He poured himself a glass and took a sip. "Why so many?"

"So many?" Jason asked.

"So many murders. Serial killers usually take months, years—savoring their deeds, enjoying the fear they're creating."

Jason nodded. "Unless, of course, this guy isn't a serial killer. Maybe he's planned it out months in advance."

"What do you mean?" Runt asked.

"Maybe he's not doing it for himself. Maybe he couldn't care less about the kill thrill."

"Why would he be doing it, then?" Hutton asked.

"Maybe he's on a mission."

"A mission?" Runt was pretending to be all casual again. "Like what? A religious mission?"

Jason shook his head. Did they really think he was that stupid?

The sheriff moved closer. "If he was on a 'mission,' like you say . . . when would you guess it to end?"

Jason chuckled.

The sheriff persisted. "I'm serious. When?"

"That's easy."

"When, Jason? When do you think the killings will stop?"

"When Jesus Christ returns."

"And that will be. . . ."

Jason took a breath and wearily quoted, "When the house of the Lord is cleansed and purged of all unrighteousness."

†

The good news was, neither of the two morning services had weird stuff happen as it did Saturday night. The bad news was, by the third go-round, Jaz was bored out of her skull. Seriously, how could Sharon sit there service after service, smiling and laughing at the same jokes she'd already heard? Talk about a cure for insomnia. And the music? Jaz was hoping for a repeat performance of the night before, but this time it was different. Oh, she still got a little "Voice buzz" and stuff when they sang, but nothing like Saturday. That's why, as the third service got up and running, she was more than happy to head back and check out the nursery. Even hanging with ankle-biters was better than sitting through the same routine all over again.

Of course she had second thoughts when she pushed open the door and was greeted by a herd of rug rats and the smell of baby wipes. Luckily there were plenty of moms around to do the work. One in particular caught her attention. She stood near the one-way window that looked out into the sanctuary. She was the singer from the night before—same Coke-bottle glasses, same lack of fashion sense. Only this time she held a baby in her arms.

Jaz gave her a nod, and the lady returned it with a smile, almost like they were pals. Grateful for a connection, Jaz waded through the babies to meet her.

"Hey," the lady said.

Jaz nodded back. "Hey."

They stood a moment. Jaz shifted to her other foot, not exactly sure where to take it from there.

Fortunately, the lady helped out. "You're the pastor's niece."

Jaz shrugged. "Sorta. I mean, not really, but, yeah." Trying not to sound like a total mental, she added, "Maybe . . . someday."

The lady gave her a look like she hadn't exactly proven her case, so Jaz jumped back in. "You're one of the singers."

She nodded.

"Why aren't you up there onstage?"

"We rotate. The church has lots of talented—" As she spoke she turned back to the window.

"I'm sorry." Jaz touched her arm and the woman turned back. "I'm deaf. But I can read lips, you just have to face me." She plowed ahead. "I'm Jazmin, like the flower, but people call me Jaz, like the music, but with only one z."

The lady pushed aside a clump of mousy brown hair. "I'm Cindy, like—well, like nothing, I guess."

Jaz liked her instantly and felt they should shake hands or something. But since Cindy was carrying an armload of kid, she settled for another nod—about what, she wasn't sure. Another awkward pause followed.

"Your baby?" Jaz asked.

"Yes."

"My mom's dead."

"I'm sorry to hear that."

"Yeah. My dad, too." She shrugged. "It happens."

"Yes." Cindy glanced down. "It happens."

Jaz sensed she was thinking about her husband or lover or something like that. And that it hadn't been too long ago. Refusing to allow another pause, Jaz continued. "I saw you up onstage last night."

"Yes, I saw you, too."

"You did?"

Cindy nodded.

"Were you. . . ." Jaz hesitated and started again. "When you were singing, was something going on with you?"

"What do you mean?"

"I mean, I don't know." She shoved her hands into her pockets. "It was like I felt this power or something. And it was coming . . . well, it was sorta coming from you. Mostly."

"Me?"

"Yeah. It's kinda complicated. And your hands. You kept opening and closing them. It looked like something was really going on."

The woman stared at her for a moment, then glanced out the window and spoke.

"Sorry." Jaz touched her arm reminding her to face her.

Cindy turned back, looking a little uneasy, almost embarrassed. "I was . . . I know this sounds strange, but when something like that happens, I'm . . . fighting."

Certain she got it wrong, Jaz asked, "I'm sorry, what?"

"I was fighting."

"You were singing."

She looked down at the baby. "Yes."

Jaz could feel her closing up so she talked faster. "I mean, you were doing more than that, right? I could see it. I could feel it. I mean, I could feel something."

Cindy kept looking at her kid. "Yeah, me, too. Feel it, I mean."

"But what? What were you feeling?"

"I was fighting against something."

"By singing?"

She looked up. "By worshiping, yes."

"You were fighting by worshiping? How does that work?"

"I don't know." She looked out the window, caught herself, and turned back to Jaz. "Ever since I was a little girl, I . . . sensed things. Especially when I sang."

Jaz knew all about sensing things. And she felt a wave of

relief to think there might actually be somebody out there who understood what that meant. But just to be safe, she played dumb. "What do you mean?"

Cindy looked around the nursery and spotted a Bible on one of the changing tables. "Would you grab that for me?"

"Sure." Jaz crossed over and scooped it up.

Cindy gave a quick glance around the room. She wasn't trying to be secretive, but you could tell she'd be just as happy if no one overheard. "People don't much talk about it, at least around here, but . . . turn to Second Chronicles."

Jaz looked at her, not understanding.

She nodded to the book. "It's in the Bible."

"Oh." Jaz flipped open the Bible and started searching.

Cindy touched her shoulder and she looked up. "It's right after Kings."

"Sure, right." She continued the hunt, working from the back.

Another touch. "It's more toward the front."

Grateful for the clue, Jaz looked until she finally found it. "Second Chronicles. Right. Got it." Then, looking up, she asked, "What about it?"

"Turn to the twentieth chapter, starting about verse twenty-one."

Jaz scanned the page, found it, and looked back to her.

Cindy gave a quick explanation. "Way back when Jehoshaphat was king of Judah and the people were—"

Jaz snickered and Cindy stopped.

"Sorry." Jaz grinned. "But there was really somebody named that?"

Cindy smiled and nodded.

"Poor dude."

She agreed and continued. "Anyway, his country was surrounded by three separate armies. And they were all coming to destroy him."

"That can't be good."

"It wasn't. But instead of fighting with swords and weapons—well, go ahead, read it."

"What, out loud?"

"If you don't mind."

It was Jaz's turn to glance around the room. Finally she looked down, found the place, and began:

> *After consulting the people, Jehoshaphat appointed men to sing to the LORD and to praise him for the splendor of his holiness as they went out at the head of the army, saying: "Give thanks to the LORD, for his love endures forever." As they began to sing and praise, the LORD set ambushes against the men of Ammon and Moab and Mount Seir who were invading Judah, and they were defeated. The men of Ammon and Moab rose up against the men from Mount Seir to destroy and annihilate them. After they finished slaughtering the men from Seir, they helped to destroy one another.*

Jaz looked up, surprised. "Did I read that right? The armies wiped each other out?"

Cindy nodded and pushed up her glasses. "All three of them."

Jaz looked back to the book. "And you think that's because this Jehoshaphat and his guys, because they sang?"

"And worshiped the Lord. That's right."

Jaz stared at the verses. "Crazy."

"And that's not the only place. There's Joshua, where the priests blew their horns and the people shouted until the walls of Jericho fell down. And in the New Testament, when Paul and Silas were in prison, singing. They were worshiping and an earthquake hit, causing their chains to fall away and the prison door to open."

"So that's what you were doing onstage? Fighting stuff by worshiping?"

Holding her gaze, Cindy gently nodded.

"But what kinda stuff?" Jaz asked. "What were you fighting?"

She hesitated. "I don't . . . know. There's something going on. I mean, more than the murders. There's something—"

Her head jerked up to the speaker above the window, then out to the service. The members of the congregation had frozen for a moment, then immediately started looking around and talking to each other.

Jaz stepped closer to the glass. "What happened, what's going on?"

Cindy pointed to the giant TV screens on either side of the stage. On them was another Bible verse:

GOSSIPS, SLANDERERS . . .
THOSE WHO DO SUCH THINGS DESERVE DEATH.
ROMANS 1:30 & 32

Chapter Twelve

And here we go." The busboy reached for Carla Brown's water glass.

"No, we're fine," the elderly lady protested. "The Diet Cokes are all we need."

But he'd already turned the glass over and started pouring. "Water is nature's elixir of youth. They say you should have eight glasses a day." He flashed her a dazzling smile.

She couldn't help returning it.

"Then again, with such wonderful complexions, I'm sure you two girls already know that, don't you?"

Across the table, her sister, Susan Brown, suppressed a giggle.

Of course he was just flirting. Everyone knew that. Land sakes, he was a third their age. And one of those gay, homosexual types, at that. He had to be, the way he filled out that black, skin-tight T-shirt of his. Why, Carla could practically see his abs, or whatever they were called. Still, the attention felt good . . . even at her age.

He reached for Susan's glass.

"No, really," Susan protested. "If I drink any more, I'll simply burst."

"Now you don't want me cross with you, do you?" His grin grew even brighter.

"Oh, no." Susan's face flushed slightly. "That would never do."

"Besides, such lovely ladies need to set an example for others." He lowered his voice, glancing around the room. "And, believe me, these folks need all the help they can get."

More giggles from Susan.

More smiles from Carla. She raised her glass. "Well, since you put it that way. . . ."

"Drink up, girls. If not for yourselves, at least for the others."

"All right." Susan laughed. "But just to keep you happy." She lifted her glass to Carla. "Cheers."

"Cheers," Carla replied, and they drank.

"Now, if I can get you anything else, be sure to let me know." He turned and sashayed back to the kitchen, his pants as tight as his T-shirt.

Catching each other's stares, both sisters broke into giggles. This was something they could talk about for days.

Charlie leaned against the pine paneling in Thomas and Sharon's family room. He was sipping from his third or fourth Seahawks mug of coffee. It had been a long morning. And by the look of things, the afternoon wasn't going much better. After answering a few hundred questions from the authorities and securing a ride from one of Hutton's deputies, they finally returned home. Charlie had given Jaz permission to hang out with Will. He seemed a good boy, from good stock . . . though the "boy" part was still reason for suspicion. Of course, Charlie had put the fear of God into him—actually the fear of an ex–Delta Force Ranger, which was far more immediate and far less understanding. Hopefully that would keep things in order.

He turned back to the conversation and asked Thomas, "These topics, are they ones you've addressed from the pulpit?"

The pastor leaned his head back on the sofa, staring up at the ceiling. Exhaustion had definitely set in. "Topics?"

"Adultery, stealing, gossip—"

"No. We seldom talk about those things."

"Or anything else of relevance," Lisa quipped from the hearth. Like her brother, she was also on edge, something about nearly getting killed and having her rental car blown up from under her.

Still staring at the ceiling, Thomas replied, "My sister thinks I'm not judgmental enough in my sermons."

"Sermons?" Lisa said. "I thought they were comedy routines."

"We're reaching out to a community with the love of God."

"You're building a fiefdom with watered-down pablum."

"Love is *not* pablum."

"Neither is truth."

Thomas closed his eyes, trying to drop the subject. "Please."

But if there was one thing Lisa was not good at, it was dropping subjects. "You tell me what's more loving: warning someone they're driving off a cliff, or wishing them a nice day and, oh, by the way, 'Be sure to stop by the offering box on your way down'?"

Charlie looked on silently. The two definitely knew how to press each other's buttons.

Thomas raised his head. "And love and mercy, where do they fit in your world? Oh, that's right, they don't exist, do they? No matter how sorry a person is for what he's done, or how long ago he did it, none of that matters."

Now Charlie knew what they were really talking about. Or whom. Truth is, he and Lisa had had the same conversation more than once, during those late-night hours as they got to know each other, as he fell head-over-heels in love with her. Despite her baggage, there was no denying his feelings. He just prayed someday they would be reciprocated. And if she couldn't love him, maybe she would learn to love somebody else. She was too good a person not to.

Drawing the group back to point, he quietly observed, "Well, whatever you're choosing for sermons, it's obvious someone is using your pulpit for their own topics."

Thomas agreed and started counting them off. "Porn, gossip, stealing. . . ." He frowned, trying to remember the others.

Sharon helped. "Abortion . . . evolution."

"All with real-life illustrations," Charlie said.

"Or dead ones," Lisa corrected.

The group nodded in silence.

"And this latest, this gossip verse. Any idea who that would apply to?" Charlie asked.

Thomas sighed. "More like, who *wouldn't* it apply to. When it comes to gossip, I'm sure we've all done our share."

"Except. . . ." Sharon hesitated.

Charlie turned to her.

"Except what?" Thomas asked.

"What about the Brown sisters? They're always complaining about someone, right? I mean, they're the sweetest persons you'd ever want to meet, but they love finding faults in people."

Thomas gave another sigh. "And sharing their 'concerns' with anyone who will listen."

"The Brown sisters?" Charlie asked.

Sharon nodded. "A couple of elderly spinsters."

Thomas almost smiled. "God's self-appointed hall monitors. Every church has them. Comes with the territory."

Charlie and Lisa traded looks.

"Where do they live?" Lisa asked.

"Sisco Heights—a few miles south of Arlington."

"You have an address?"

"Sure." Sharon started to rise, then stopped. "But you won't find them there. At least, not right now."

"Why not?" Charlie asked.

"It's Sunday afternoon."

"And that means. . . ."

"Bingo at Lawton's."

"And Lawton's is?"

"A family restaurant, over at Island Crossing, near I-5. The two always eat dinner there before they play. Just like clockwork."

Lisa was up and grabbing her jacket off the rocking chair. "Can we borrow your car?"

"Will has it," Sharon said.

"What about the pickup?" Charlie asked.

"Sure," Thomas said, "the keys are under the seat. You don't think—"

Charlie grabbed his own coat and followed Lisa toward the front door.

"Do you want me to come?" Thomas called.

"It's probably nothing," Charlie said as Lisa opened the door.

"Are you sure? Because—"

"It's nothing," Charlie repeated. "We'll be back in a few minutes."

They stepped outside, the storm door slamming behind them, as they headed down the porch steps, then broke into a run.

†

"Thanks so much, ladies." Terri was one of their favorite waitresses even though she'd just come out of a divorce. She set the check on the table and started to leave.

"Excuse me, Terri?" Carla opened her billfold as Terri turned back to her. "Seventeen dollars and eighty-nine cents, correct?"

"Yes," Terri answered, "something like that."

"Exactly like that," Carla said as she pulled out a twenty-dollar bill. "Two French dip sandwiches and two Diet Cokes. Seventeen dollars and eighty-nine cents. It's been that for the past two years, and it'll be that today."

The waitress smiled. "I'm sure you're right, Miss Brown."

Carla nodded, digging out two quarters from her change purse. "And here's a little something for the busboy." She cleared her throat. "Is he new?"

"Yes, ma'am, first day."

"Little old for a busboy."

"Yes, ma'am." Terri gave a knowing smile. "But none of us are complaining, if you know what I mean."

"Hmm." Carla's look made it clear she didn't approve of the comment. Then, setting the two quarters on top of the twenty, she motioned for Terri to step closer. Lowering her voice, she continued. "I don't know whether you noticed, but Susan and I have every reason to believe he is a homosexual."

"Really?"

Carla nodded. She coughed slightly and reached for her glass of water. "You be sure to tell your manager that."

"Yes, ma'am."

She took a swallow. "I mean, who knows what type of diseases they're carrying nowadays." She gave Terri a knowing nod then coughed again. Something had stuck in her throat.

"Are you all right?"

Carla nodded and took another drink. "Must be something in the French dip." But even as she talked her tongue seemed to be growing numb. "Too much salt."

"I'm sorry to hear that. Do you want me to—"

She shook her head. Coughing again, she took another drink. She noticed Susan reaching for her water as well.

Terri frowned. "Are you sure you're okay?"

Carla waved her off and started to stand. "Whoth calling the numberth tonigth?"

"Pardon me?"

Carla scowled. Her tongue had grown thicker. "For bingo, whoth callingth. . . ." She stopped. How embarrassing. Only then did she notice it was becoming difficult to breath.

"Miss Brown?"

She turned to the waitress and opened her mouth. It was hard to catch her breath. Across the table she saw Susan fanning her face and also coughing.

"Miss—"

The room shifted slightly. Carla reached down to the table and steadied herself. What was going on?

"Here," Terri said, grabbing a chair. "Maybe you'd better sit down."

She agreed. At least to catch her breath. She sat and reached for the water to take another drink, hoping the coolness would ease the swelling. It didn't. Instead, she gagged and began coughing, spraying water across the table and dribbling it down her chin.

People were turning, looking.

"Gaacious." She grabbed a napkin.

She tried another drink, but gagged and coughed even more. That's when she realized she could barely swallow. Her throat was swelling shut.

Across the table, Susan was coughing harder.

Terri's expression had gone from concern to fear. She was talking. Carla could see her lips moving, but she couldn't hear . . . not over her gagging and choking. It took

all of her concentration just to draw air into her lungs—
tiny, gasping gulps that came harder with every breath.

"Aay canth. . . ." She fought for another gulp of air then
forced out the word, "Brreee. . . ."

By now *everyone* was staring.

"Aaaaa. . . ."

She could no longer speak. Her throat too full, her
tongue too thick. Her tongue! That was the problem! It
had swollen up like a sponge, filling the back of her throat,
making it impossible to breathe. She stuck it out like a
two-year-old.

"Haap meee," she wheezed.

The edges of her vision grew pale. She opened her eyes,
trying to focus. Where was Susan? She could no longer see
Susan!

Suddenly some fool was shouting into her face. "Can
you breathe? Can you breathe?"

She glared, wide-eyed. *Did it look like she could
breathe?*

He dragged her to her feet and threw his arms around
her from behind, jamming his fist into her stomach. Again.
And again. But she was not choking. It was her tongue!
Her gigantic tongue! If she had a knife she'd cut it out.

Everything was white now. The restaurant noise fading,
coming from another world. There was only her tongue!
Her tongue, that was all she thought of. Her tongue! Her
tongue, her tongue . . . until she thought of nothing at all.

Chapter Thirteen

Lisa was out of the pickup and heading for the restaurant before Charlie even turned off the ignition. The parking lot's mercury vapors had already kicked on, replacing the day's dull glow with a harsher blue. The place was one of those down-home family restaurants—wraparound porch, rocking chairs, baskets with preserves for sale on tables covered in checkerboard cloth.

Lisa had barely started up the half dozen steps when the front doors opened. A good-looking man in his late twenties emerged—just over six feet, shortly cropped hair. Even in his jacket, she could tell he frequented the gym.

He spotted her and slowed to a stop on the second or third step. "You may not want to go in there just yet."

"Why's that?" she asked.

"It's a bit, how shall I put it? Macabre." He glanced over at the main road. "We called 911. They should be here any minute."

Charlie joined her and the man's face brightened, obviously liking what he saw. "Well, hi, there."

Charlie gave no response.

"You called 911?" Lisa asked. "What happened?"

"A couple of sweet old ladies. They must have had seizures or something."

Charlie moved into action, quickly taking the steps and passing him.

"I wouldn't bother."

He stopped at the door.

"They're already gone. Deader than doornails."

"What happened?" Lisa repeated.

"They certainly weren't heart attacks, I can tell you that much. Not with their eyes bulging like that, and those awful tongues sticking out." He gave a shudder.

Charlie exchanged looks with Lisa.

"Food allergies, if you ask me. I've seen it before. My cousin, Doris, she's allergic to peanuts. Just a teensy-weensy bit and she goes into, what is it, anaphy-something-or-other."

"Anaphylactic shock," Charlie said.

"Yes, that's it."

"Both of them?" Lisa asked.

"They were sisters. Maybe it's genetic. So sad." He gave a sigh, then continued down the steps past Lisa.

"Don't you want to stick around?" Charlie asked. "See the excitement?"

The man checked his watch. "Actually, I have an appointment . . . to create a little excitement of my own, if you know what I mean." Then, holding Charlie's look, he added. "Unless, of course, *you* had something in mind— you know, to convince me to stay a little longer?"

Lisa saw Charlie tense and thought it best to change subjects. "Were you a customer?"

"Actually, no. I work here."

"Mind if we ask you a few questions?"

He threw another glance up at Charlie. "Are you law enforcement officers?"

"Undercover," Lisa lied. "Special division."

"I see. Well, listen, dear." He produced a small, burgundy pouch that he unzipped. "It's not like I'm being difficult or anything, but as I said, I do have a previous engagement." He pulled out a pen and business card. "Nevertheless, I certainly want to cooperate." He jotted something down then turned and trotted back up the steps to Charlie. "So here's my cell." It was a bold move. Bolder still when he arrived and dropped the card into Charlie's shirt pocket. "If you should ever want to call me for anything." He gave it a gentle pat. "And I do mean any—"

Charlie had enough. He grabbed the man's hand.

"Ow, you're hurting me."

Still clutching it, he looked at the man's thumb, then into his face.

Unimpressed with Charlie's homophobia, Lisa was about to call him out when the young man flung Charlie's hand aside and spun around. Having obviously taken a few self-defense classes, he made a roundhouse kick and caught Charlie in the chest, sending him staggering into the door. The event was over before it started.

The man raced down the steps past Lisa. But Charlie was already on his feet. He leaped from the top of the stairs and caught him by the waist, bringing them both crashing down onto the gravel parking lot.

"Charlie!"

The man jabbed at his larynx, but Charlie deflected the blow and head-butted him in the face.

"Charlie! Stop it!"

They scrambled to their feet. The young man attempted another roundhouse kick. Charlie dodged it and moved in from behind. He threw his arm around the man's neck and delivered a kidney punch into his back, and then another.

"Charlie!" Lisa stepped in and grabbed his arm, leaving him open to receive a powerful elbow into the gut. With an "Oaf!" Charlie released him, and the kid raced toward his car.

Shaking off the pain, Charlie started to follow until Lisa threw herself in front of him.

"Charlie!" She hoped her presence would bring him back to his senses.

"Get out of the way!" he shouted.

She heard a car door open and turned to see the man climbing into a gray Honda Accord.

Charlie broke past her and sprinted after him.

"Charlie!"

The car lurched forward, heading directly at him. Charlie leaped out of the way, managing to spin around and kick out the left taillight. Mud and gravel sprayed over him as the car fishtailed and headed for the road.

Without missing a beat, Charlie was up and racing for the pickup.

"Charlie!"

"Come on!"

"He didn't mean anything! He was just—"

"That's him!"

"What?"

"That's Kristof!"

"Sorry," Heather said with a shrug. "I was pretty wasted."

"But you remember it screaming," Will insisted, "and the giant wings."

She gave a shudder. "That I remember."

"And it came from up there." He pointed to a bunch of branches above them. "Right there."

She looked up to the branches, frowned, then shrugged again. "Sorry."

He sighed and stepped away from the car, brushing past Jaz and crossing the ditch that ran along the side of the road. Jaz did her best to read his lips while wrapping her arms around herself to keep warm. It was weird—the farther up the road they drove, the colder she got. Not because it was in the mountains or anything; it wasn't that type of cold. It was the other. She knew part of it was nerves—the power of suggestion and all that. She just wasn't sure how much.

"This is the place, though." Will stopped and turned to Heather. "I mean, you can see everyone's tire tracks." He motioned toward the woods. "This is where you guys meet, right?"

"Marker's right there." Heather pointed to a black ribbon tied around a fir tree behind him. Below it, all the ferns and undergrowth were trampled. She crossed the ditch to join him, leaving Jaz alone at the car. And then, for good measure, she took Will's hand, making it clear she'd staked out her territory.

As if Jaz cared. Honestly.

Still, what Will saw in the pile of bones was beyond her. Besides overdoing it in the makeup department, the Goth-wannabe was emotionally stunted. Like it was a crime to crack a joke or smile or something. But there was more. Underneath Heather's jaded exterior, Jaz felt that she was very, very tired. Like she was worn-out.

The couple started toward the woods. Before she could catch herself, Jaz called, "Will!"

He turned to her.

She shrugged, trying to be all casual. "You sure you want to go in there?"

Heather snickered or sneered, or both. "You chicken?"

Jaz could only stare. Talk about mature. But before she could think of a witty comeback, Will pushed aside a branch and stepped into the shadows. Of course, Heather followed. And, not wanting to be left alone in the cold, or whatever it was, Jaz crossed the ditch and joined them.

She hated bringing up the rear. It was impossible to see their lips moving. Not that she had time. Not with dodging all the branches Heather let fly back at her. After about the hundredth one, you could tell they weren't exactly accidents. Yes, sir, real mature.

They'd traveled around fifty yards into the woods when Will spotted something and slowed.

"What's up?" Jaz asked.

Of course, he didn't bother answering.

To see, Jaz had to stretch her neck and jump a little. Thirty feet away, off the trail and mostly hidden by ferns, a large black object hovered. She could feel the coldness wrapping around her. Instinctively, she moved closer to

Will and Heather. The object slowly rose, then turned to face them. Only then did she realize it was a guy. An older teen wearing one of those long black trench coats like in *The Matrix*.

Heather broke from Will and ran to him. Will followed a little more slowly. Everybody seemed to know everybody . . . well, except for Jaz. When she arrived, she interrupted whatever they were saying and stuck out her hand to introduce herself. "Hi, I'm Jaz. Like the music, but only one *z*."

The boy gave her a cooler-than-cool nod. "Jason," was all he said before he knelt back down. He was definitely hot. And definitely troubled, which made him all the more interesting. At his feet lay a big animal, like a reindeer or something. It had huge brown eyes that would have been cute if it weren't for the flies crawling all over them.

"Ew, what is it?" she asked.

No one bothered answering, so of course she tried again. "Is that like a moose or something?"

Only Will looked up. "It's a buck."

"Like a deer?"

"Like a deer." He stooped down to join Jason and Heather. So did Jaz—as much to read their lips as to look at the animal.

"So it *wasn't* part of the ceremony?" Heather was asking.

Jason motioned down the path. "We were at the river doing our thing. Didn't hear it screaming 'til we were all done."

"Screaming?" Will said. "Deer don't scream."

Jason looked back to the animal. "You tell him that."

Will swallowed. "Was it a screeching sound—real high and kinda long?"

Jason glanced up at him, then slowly nodded.

Jaz felt the cold getting colder.

Heather wrinkled her nose. "What's that smell?"

"Rotting flesh," Will explained.

"Rotting flesh don't smell like that," she said.

"You think somebody shot it?" Jaz asked. She was out of sync with the conversation, but what else was new? "Like hunters or somebody?"

Jason picked up a stick and slipped it under the animal's back leg. It took both of his hands to raise it up. Where the sex organs were supposed to be, everything was gone. Cut out. Lots of dried blood, but the actual cuts looked as neat as any surgery on TV.

The cold grew deeper. Heavier.

"Cattle mutilations," Will said.

Jason turned to him. "What?"

"Like in Texas. Where they have UFO sightings, sometimes they find perfectly healthy cattle killed. Not for meat or anything, just for their sex org—"

All three heads jerked up and spun around.

Jaz turned but saw only trees and shadows. She looked back at the group. Apparently they didn't see anything, either. But that didn't stop them from rising to their feet and trading looks of major panic.

"What's going on?" she asked.

No answer.

"Guys, what's—"

"Shut up," Heather said.

Everyone kept staring into the forest, straining to hear. Then suddenly they jumped.

Jason was the first to take off. He practically knocked Jaz over as he scrambled past them and up to the path.

Heather was right behind him.

Will motioned to Jaz. "Go!"

"What?"

He grabbed her hand and yanked her forward. "Run!"

"Why?"

They stumbled up onto the path and started for the car. Heather and Jason were in the lead, throwing scared looks over their shoulders. Will and Jaz were right behind.

And behind them?

Jaz didn't look until they were practically at the road. And when she did, she wished she hadn't.

Chapter Fourteen

hy do you think it's him?"

Charlie gave no answer as he focused on the road heading for the freeway. Kristof had distanced himself by forcing oncoming traffic to swerve wildly to the side. Charlie refused to follow his lead but hoped through dogged persistence to wear him down and not lose him in the process.

Lisa repeated her question. "Why him?"

"It's doubtful both sisters suffered anaphylaxis."

"Doubtful, but not impossible. There are special drugs that can bring it on. And the thumb on his right hand, you only get a callous like that from the firing range."

A gap appeared in the opposing traffic. Charlie sped up, passing an older couple who insisted on traveling a safe five miles per hour below the speed limit. He was directly beside them when a van pulled out from an approaching intersection and turned toward them. Charlie cut back in front of the couple, barely making it in time. They flashed their high beams at him in protest, and when he glanced into the mirror, he saw the old duffer offering him the universal hand gesture of ill will.

They reached the freeway and slowed at the north entrance ramp. "See anything?" he asked.

She looked down the ramp. "Nothing."

They moved across the overpass, Lisa still checking to the north, Charlie looking out his window toward the south. He spotted the broken taillight 150 yards away, moving into the fast lane. He hit the gas, bringing them to the southbound ramp where he took a hard left, throwing Lisa against her door.

"Seat belts" was his only apology.

They raced down the ramp, picking up speed as Lisa resumed her line of questioning. "Being a gun nut isn't enough to make a person—"

"He doesn't fit the profile." Charlie merged onto the freeway. Traffic was heavy and the Honda momentarily disappeared from his sight as he made his way toward the fast lane. "A gay who spends hours on the firing range?"

"You wouldn't be stereotyping, would you?"

He threw her a look. "Who purposely drives one of the most common vehicles on the road."

"He's a waiter, Charlie."

"Who leaves the scene of the crime wearing a government-issue waterproof chronograph wristwatch?" When he finally spotted the car, it was too late. It had slipped back into the slow lane and started up the next exit ramp.

"Over there." He pointed to the ramp. For the briefest moment they ran parallel with it before the overpass blocked their view. He slowed and hit the emergency flashers, watching the mirror as he angled across traffic toward the emergency strip. Lisa rolled down the window and stuck out her head, motioning to the other drivers they were going over. They were fifty feet beyond the overpass by the time Charlie reached the strip and came to a sliding stop.

"Watch the entrance up ahead," he ordered. He threw the truck into reverse. "Make sure he's not coming back on."

"Got it."

He hit the gas and they shot under the overpass, backtracking toward the exit ramp. Lisa leaned farther out. She looked over the roof in case the Honda was crossing the overpass and entering the opposite northbound lane.

Charlie nearly arrived at their exit when she banged on the roof. "He's over there!" She dropped back into the cab. "He's heading north. Traffic's jammed. He's using the emergency lane."

Charlie glanced at the overpass. It was clogged and would take forever to get across.

"Hang on!" He accelerated, the reverse gear whining in protest, as they continued backward down their emergency lane.

Lisa climbed back outside. "He's still there!" she shouted.

In the mirror Charlie saw they were quickly approaching a disabled RV. Traffic was too heavy to return to the slow lane, so he grabbed Lisa's back pocket and pulled her inside. She dropped down and he cranked the truck hard to the right. They shot up a steep embankment, hitting several low-growing junipers. The ride was rough and for a moment he nearly lost control, until they passed the RV and dropped back down onto the emergency strip.

Lisa said nothing. Neither did Charlie.

They were coming up to the first overpass, the one they'd originally taken. It would be faster to go against the traffic and continue right up the entrance ramp.

Faster, but not safer.

Reading his mind, Lisa shouted, "Go for it!"

He veered onto the entrance ramp, fighting a stream of oncoming traffic. Most vehicles had the sense to avoid him. Only a guy in a BMW felt his rights were more important than his life. In a dangerous game of chicken, he forced Charlie off the road, where he took out a reflector post or two . . . or three.

They reached the overpass and Charlie hit the brakes, turning the pickup as they slid to a stop. He dropped into first gear and they lurched forward, racing across the overpass to the northbound entrance . . . only to pass the Honda heading the opposite direction for the southbound.

Charlie's eyes locked onto the driver's for a brief moment. Just long enough to see the man was cool and completely professional.

Charlie spun the truck around, tires smoking, bumper trading paint with the guardrail, while drawing a symphony of irate horns and more hand gestures.

The Honda was thirty feet ahead.

Will fumbled with the car keys, cursing himself for locking it.

"Hurry!" Jason banged on the hood.

Will nodded and dropped the keys to the ground. "Oh, man!"

He stooped to grab them as Heather shouted to Jason. "Where's your Harley?"

"I'm not riding it with that thing on my—"

The shriek brought him to a stop.

Will rose with the keys and for the first time clearly saw it. Black wings stretching eight, maybe ten feet across. Between them was the body of a human. Translucent, like thick vapor, though he clearly saw the leathery texture of its face. But it was the eyes that held him. Red, like the drawings on the Internet. What the drawings did not show was their power, the way they bore into his mind and seemed to paralyze him.

Once clear of the trees, it flared open its wings and dropped toward them.

Heather panicked and broke away from the car. The movement caught the thing's attention and it veered for her. Spindly arms reached out from under the wings and grabbed her shoulders. She screamed, her own arms flailing. The misty hands wrapped about her waist and started to rise. But she was too heavy to completely lift from the ground. With wings beating the air, it pulled her backwards, her feet dragging in the gravel.

Jason sprinted after them and managed to grab her arm. The creature delivered a powerful kick to his chest and the boy fell to the road, stunned. Heather kept screaming as they crossed the ditch and headed toward the woods.

Will finally came to, shaking off the power of the eyes, and spotted Heather. He ran after her. He heard Jaz shouting at him but paid no attention.

The creature arrived at the forest's edge and folded back its wings to avoid the branches. Heather was not so lucky. A broken snag from a fir tree sank deep into her side. The screaming stopped instantly, but the pain in her eyes said she was all too conscious.

The thing flapped and pulled, hissing in frustration, but the branch had wedged firmly between her ribs.

Will spotted a broken limb on the ground. Operating on everything but logic, he scooped it up and ran at the creature, screaming.

"Will!" Jaz yelled.

He arrived, swinging the branch like a baseball bat. The limb passed through the vaporous body, but the thing gave a startled cry and turned on him, snarling.

This time avoiding its eyes, Will again raised the branch. But before he could swing, the creature's talonlike toes slashed through his shirt and into his stomach. Though only mist, they tore into his flesh. He gasped, nearly falling, until he used the branch for support.

The thing released Heather and flew up. It rose into the sky and began to circle.

Will turned back to Jason. Jaz was kneeling at his side, helping the dazed boy to his feet.

"Grab Heather!" Will shouted. "Get her into the car!"

"What about you?" Jaz yelled.

"Do it!" He looked up to see the thing continuing to circle. "Do it now!"

The couple ran over to Heather as the creature gave an eerie scream. Will watched it pull back its wings and begin diving . . . straight at him. He regripped the branch, staring at the chest, the wings, anywhere but the eyes.

It continued its approach. Fifty feet away and picking up speed.

He hefted the limb onto his shoulder.

Twenty feet.

He leaned back, preparing to swing. Suddenly it changed course, rising and veering to the left, just as Will swung and missed.

He spun around and watched it circle, obviously preparing for another attack. Stealing a look at Heather, he saw Jaz and Jason pulling her off the tree. Suddenly he wondered what he was doing. This was insanity! But he had little time to think as the creature tucked back its wings and began another dive.

Will lifted the branch and waited.

It was sixty feet away.

He took a breath.

Forty.

And then, knowing it was wrong even as he did it, Will looked into the creature's . . .

Suddenly he remembered the cat he shot when he was nine years old. It was just a BB gun. The cat wasn't supposed to die. But it did. And with the memory came the guilt. He hadn't thought about it in years, but now he was stooping over it, seeing the blood fill the gaping eye socket, draining onto the lawn.

Twenty feet. The mist appeared more solid.

Moved with guilt, Will watched himself reach down and touch the cat's blood-soaked fur, his throat tightening with emotion—

Until the creature struck.

It knocked Will onto the road, rolling him head over

heels into the ditch. When he finally came to a stop, he was staring up into the glowering eyes. His body ached and his mind reeled—but not from the blow. From the shame. And the guilt.

Until the misty talons sank into his head and he lost all consciousness.

Chapter Fifteen

I don't care where he is. Tell him Lisa Harmon—"

The dispatcher's voice interrupted. "Is this business or personal?"

"Business or personal?"

Charlie threw her a cautionary look from behind the wheel. It did no good.

"Did I mention we're in pursuit of a serial killer?"

"Ma'am, there's no need to take that tone with me."

"Tone? What tone?"

"Once again I must ask, are you an official agency?"

"Call the state patrol, tell them we're just north of Marysville and need some serious backup—"

"If you're not an official agency, there's nothing I can do except warn you that interfering with police business is both dangerous and illegal. I would encourage you to—"

Lisa slapped shut her phone and glanced at Charlie. She expected another look of admonishment. Instead, he was reexamining the business card Kristof, or whoever it was, had dropped into his pocket.

"What's it say?" she asked.

He handed it to her. "It's the same card he left for us at the zoo."

She took it and read:

God's Cleaning Service

She flipped it over to read the note he had scrawled on the back. It was another Bible verse:

*JUDGMENT WITHOUT MERCY . . .
TO ANYONE WHO HAS NOT BEEN MERCIFUL.*

Charlie swerved to the right, and she looked up as he cut across traffic. Just ahead, the Honda was darting toward another exit.

She stuck her arm out the window, signaling the cars behind while glancing up at the approaching sign. It was the Tulalip exit. These were her old stomping grounds. She knew the area like the back of her hand and had the memories (many she wished to forget) to prove it. Off to the right had been the old Thunderbird Drive-In where she'd garnered the well-earned reputation as the all-school sleep-around, doing any guy who showed any interest. Names were optional.

She closed her eyes and took a deep, cleansing breath. When she opened them, the Honda was approaching the top of the ramp. To the left, across the freeway and two miles away—"No," she muttered, "no, don't turn left"— was Cascade Valley Care Center, her father's home for the past three-and-a-half years.

The Honda arrived at the top of the ramp and turned left. Lisa's plea turned to a curse.

They followed, turning left on the overpass and crossing it. Up ahead, the Honda swerved in and out of traffic, its white taillight acting better than any tracking system. Five blocks later they crossed State Street, the main drag. Only then did Lisa notice the knot in her gut, and the coldness. She took another deep breath. This time it didn't go away.

Charlie glanced to her. "You okay?"

She stared straight ahead, giving only the slightest nod.

They eventually passed a gas station and a strip mall before they hit the residential area. The Honda was two blocks ahead, the nursing home another three after that.

"Try calling again," Charlie said.

She flipped open her phone. As she reached for *Send* she noticed how violently her finger trembled.

"He's slowing."

She looked up. They'd cut their distance from him by half.

The dispatcher picked up on the second ring. "Good evening. Snohomish County Sheriff's Department."

"Hi, it's—" Lisa's throat clogged. "It's me."

"I've put a call into Sheriff Hutton. He will return it when he—"

"We just passed through Marysville, heading east on 528. All I'm asking is that you send a car before he disa—" Lisa stopped.

"Hello? Hello, ma'am?" The dispatcher continued speaking, but Lisa did not answer. She barely heard. All she could do was stare at the gray Honda Accord with the broken taillight as it turned into the parking lot of Cascade Valley Care.

✝

Will woke up to singing. It was pretty bad. Actually, it was barely a song. But he recognized the words:

"Praise Him, all creatures here below."

He rolled his head to the right and saw Jaz. She stood three feet away, her back to him. Directly in front of her was the creature. It seemed a lot mistier than the last time he saw it.

"Praise him something-or-other la, la, la. . . ."

The thing tilted its head quizzically but came no closer.

"Praise Father, Son, and Holy Ghost!"

"Will! Get in here!"

He rolled his head to the left and saw his family's Volvo with the passenger door open. Jason sat behind the wheel motioning to him and shouting, "Get in!" as Jaz continued to sing:

"Praise God from whom all blessings flow."

"Will!"

He struggled to sit up, his head feeling full of cotton. He turned back to Jaz.

"Praise Him, all creatures here below."

"Will!"

With effort, he struggled to rise, fighting through a wave of dizziness.

"In the back with Heather!"

He obeyed, stumbling toward the car.

"Hurry! She can't do that forever!"

He opened the back door and fell inside. Only then did he see Heather leaning against the opposite door, unconscious, her shirt ripped and soaked in blood.

"Praise something, something, 'cause God is cool."

He turned back to Jaz, saw her stealing a look over her shoulder at them.

"Come on!" Jason shouted to her.

She backed away from the creature, inching toward the Volvo.

"Praise Father, Son, and Holy—" She spun around and dashed for the car. *"Ghost!"*

The creature screamed as Jaz leaped into the front seat. It dove at her and she slammed the door just before the car rocked under its impact.

"Go!" she screamed. "Go, go, go!"

Jason hit the gas and they spun out. He glanced at her and shouted, "What were you doing back there?"

"I don't know!" She turned to her window, then twirled around and looked out the back.

"You don't know?!"

The car rocked again, so violently that Jason almost lost control.

"It's a song!"

"No kidding!"

"I used to sing it in church—as a little girl!"

Above her shouting and the roaring engine, Will heard the thing give another long, loud shriek.

"Whatever it was," Jason yelled, "it did the trick!"

Another slam. This time the roof briefly buckled.

"Go!" Jaz yelled. "Faster!"

Jason pushed the accelerator to the floor. Heather

moaned and he glanced into the rearview mirror. "Put your hand on her wound!" he shouted at Will. "Stop the bleeding!"

Will gave a dubious look at the girl's wet shirt.

"Do it!"

He leaned toward her, searching for the exact source of blood, when the thing crashed into the back window so hard that the glass spiderwebbed. He ducked, hearing Jaz scream and Jason swear.

Another crash followed.

Will spun around and looked through the crinkled glass to see the thing kneeling on the trunk. It was raising the very branch he had used earlier. Once again, it crashed it into the window. This time the glass shattered, raining hundreds of pellets over them. Will threw himself across Heather, protecting her as the thing reached in, groping at his back. He hunkered lower, but a vaporous, clawlike hand found his neck and wrapped around it. The other hand appeared from the other side. Then it began to pull.

Will reached up, slipping his fingers underneath the claws, pushing at the vapors. Though mist, they had a substance that gripped so tightly he could barely breathe. He fought like a madman, kicking and thrashing as it yanked him upright. A moment later it dragged him through the opening. Glass broke away, scraping his shoulders and arms, his hips and legs.

Once he was out the window, the arms wrapped around his chest, pulled him off the car and down onto the road. He twisted and squirmed, digging his heels into the gravel, but it did no good. The creature raced forty feet down the road before cutting to the right, crossing the ditch, and dragging him into the forest.

✝

Charlie scrambled out of the pickup and ran toward the Honda. Of course it was already empty. He yanked open the door and tossed the tracking device under the seat. Turning back to Lisa, he shouted, "Take the front! I'll circle around back!"

She nodded.

"And be careful, he's probably armed."

Before she could respond, he turned and headed for the building. A three-quarter moon rose over the mountains behind it.

She stepped out of the truck. The early evening had grown cold, and she gave a shiver. So strange. She'd taken every precaution never to go near this place. It was one of the reasons she didn't come home. That, and the memories. Four years of confusion and guilt and terror. And, at sixteen, when she finally did blow the whistle on him, *she* was the bad guy. Even when the press had its field day exposing his hypocrisy, she was the accessory. After all, by then she was sleeping all over town. Maybe she *had* seduced him. And sometimes, to this day, when the booze and counseling didn't work, she lay in bed wondering that very thing. Maybe, in the beginning, her twelve-year-old body somehow sent the wrong message to the man she had so deeply worshiped and adored.

"You alright?"

She gave a start to see Charlie had returned to the parking lot.

"What are you waiting for?" she shouted. "Go!"

He paused to make sure she was okay.

"I'm all right, go, go!"

He nodded and disappeared back around the building.

With a breath to steady herself, she started forward. It was a beige, cinder-block structure, two stories tall. The double glass doors showed a brightly lit lobby and a receptionist counter/nurses' station inside. She arrived at the doors, took another breath, and stepped inside.

There was a trace of ozone in the air from the dehumidifier, and of course, the ever-present smell of disinfectant. She looked down the hall and saw no one. The receptionist counter was also deserted. The place was decked out in bright Easter decorations—cut-out bunnies on the wall, plastic Easter lilies, a basket with candy eggs on the counter. The holiday was nearly upon them. Or maybe it had come and gone. She couldn't remember.

She called out, "Hello?"

Two office chairs sat empty, their computer screens glowing. Quiet music played in the background, but no one was in sight. She leaned over the counter, making sure no one was hiding behind it. That's when she saw the blonde receptionist—late teens, powder blue shirt and white pants. Her eyes stared unblinking. Blood ran to the linoleum floor from a perfectly centered hole in her forehead.

Lisa raced around the counter. She dropped to her knees and confirmed what she already knew. There was no breath and no pulse. Leaning against the counter, she fumbled for her cell phone and opened it. Deciding against another bout with the sheriff's office, she dialed 911. The first time, it was busy. The second time, a young man picked up and asked, "What is the nature of your emergency?"

"We have a shooting." She was surprised at how breathless she sounded. "Cascade Valley Care Center. There's a man inside, with a gun. He's already shot—"

She heard the elevator across the lobby *ding* and froze.

The voice on the other end asked, "Ma'am?"

She gave no answer.

"Ma'am, are you there now?"

She closed the phone and held her breath, listening intently as the elevator door rattled open. She heard no footsteps, discerned no movement.

Slowly, she rose and peered over the counter . . . just as the elevator doors closed. She jumped to her feet and ran around the counter, checking the still-empty hallway. She arrived at the elevator, hit the button once, twice, a half dozen times, but was too late. It had already left. She stepped back, spotted the stairway to her right, and headed for it. She flung open the door and raced up the steps.

Reaching the second floor, she kicked open the door and immediately pressed against the wall. But there was nothing. No gunshots, no footsteps. She peeked around the corner and saw another empty nurses' station. Still ahead of the elevator, she darted across the deserted hall to check behind the counter.

There were no bodies.

The elevator dinged and she spun around to face it. Remembering she was unarmed, she spotted a fire extinguisher recessed in the wall to her right and ran to it. She yanked open the clear plastic door and grabbed the canister. She ducked around the corner just as the elevator doors opened. She hefted the extinguisher, feeling its weight in her hands. It wasn't as effective as her old Glock, but if she got close enough, it would do the job.

She held her breath. There was no sound.

She eased forward until the elevator came into view and she saw . . . nothing.

Cautiously, she stepped out. Was the elevator a ruse? If so, why? To pull her away from the first floor? To draw her up here, to the second? It made no sense. What was the purpose of—

Suddenly, music blasted from down the hall—two pairs of powerful chords, followed by hammering tympanis and two more chords. The opening of Beethoven's Ninth, the *allegro* movement. Lisa recognized it as quickly as she had the answer to her question.

This was no accident. That was her father's favorite piece of music.

"Do you hear the passion?" he would ask. "His desperation? That hunger for the Eternal?"

Whether she heard it or not made little difference. He had played it so often during her childhood that she knew every movement, every phrase. And she hated it almost as much as she hated him.

Unnerved, she looked down the hallway. The music came from one of the rooms. With another breath, she ordered herself forward. As she walked, she noticed how heavy her legs were becoming, how her feet seemed to drag. She pulled the fire extinguisher closer.

A nurse appeared at the far end of the hall, running toward her. Before Lisa could call out, the woman darted into what could only be the offending room.

Lisa continued, her legs growing more and more wooden. It was the strangest sensation, as if they had minds of their own. She stumbled slightly, moved closer to the wall in case she'd need its support. She took another step, and another, until her legs stopped altogether.

The room was less than twenty feet ahead.

Suddenly, the music ended. She listened intently, then called into the silence. "Hello?"

No answer.

"Hello?"

The nurse emerged. Late thirties, dishwater hair pulled back. "His DVD alarm," she explained. She shook her head. "Why anybody would set it for this time of day is beyond me. Is there something I can help you with?"

Lisa's first attempt to answer caught in her throat. She tried again. "Is Richard Harmon in there?"

"This is his room, yes. But he's downstairs."

"Downstairs?"

"In the cafeteria. It's dinnertime." She motioned to the fire extinguisher. "What are you doing with that?"

Once again the elevator dinged and Lisa spun around.

"Excuse me?" The nurse started toward her, shoes squeaking on linoleum.

Lisa answered without looking. "Go back."

"Pardon me?"

"The man on the elevator has a gun."

"He what?"

"He's already shot your receptionist."

The elevator doors began to open.

"Hide," Lisa ordered.

"But—"

"Hide. Now."

The squeaking shoes disappeared into a room.

Lisa followed suit, ducking into another. But once again, she heard no one step out of the elevator, detected no movement. And, after an eternity, the doors closed.

She eased her head back into the hallway. When she saw it was safe, she raced out and ran toward the stairs. Dumping the extinguisher onto the floor, she threw open the door and flew down the steps, turning at the landing, and practically running into a .45 pointed at her face.

"Will!" Jaz shouted. "Will!"

"Get back in the car!" Jason demanded.

"We can't leave him here!" Jaz turned away, refusing to see Jason's answer until he grabbed her arm and spun her around.

"Where do you suggest we start?" he shouted.

She shook herself free and ran down the road, following the drag marks of Will's shoes until they veered sharply and disappeared into the forest. She came to a stop, catching her breath, staring into the dark woods. She hated herself for not having the courage to go in, was unsure what to do if she did. "Will!"

Jason arrived beside her. "We have no idea where he is!"

"He's in there!"

"But where?"

Of course she had no answer. Fact was, the coldness or vibration or whatever it was she'd felt was completely gone. So was the smell.

"We'll come back," Jason said. "With the cops. We can't find him in there on our own."

"But, he's—"

"We've got to get Heather to a hospital."

Jaz faltered.

"We'll come back. I swear. But we gotta go. Now." He grabbed her arm. "Now!"

"Will!"

"We'll come back! I swear to God. With the cops, we'll come back!"

Finally, reluctantly, she allowed him to turn her toward the car . . . though she kept looking over her shoulder, just in case.

"I'm impressed." The voice had none of the effeminate quality Lisa had heard at the restaurant. "To be honest, I didn't think you'd make it this far."

She pulled away from the gun to get some breathing room and to confirm who was talking. It was Kristof, all right. She swallowed, then tried going on the offense. "What do you want? Why did you come here?"

"Didn't you read my card?"

"Card?"

"Seems you have a little problem with forgiveness."

Lisa's mind raced. The car chase, the Bible verse, this place—was it possible? She stalled. "What are you talking about?"

He motioned toward the second floor. "You've already figured that out."

Pieces were falling into place, though she still didn't believe it.

He continued, "Imagine my surprise when I did a little research on you and Daddy. That's some history you two have."

"You're right, it's history. A long time ago."

"Giving you even less of an excuse."

"So, this is all about me?"

"For now, yes."

She tried to answer but had momentarily run out of words.

He hadn't. "Refusing to offer forgiveness is a serious sin. 'But if you do not forgive men their sins, your Father will not forgive your sins.'"

"Surely you have bigger fish to fry than me with my little problems."

He nodded, suddenly sounding weary. "The harvest is plentiful but the workers are few." He took another breath. "Still, you must admit, your sin is very public."

As he spoke, Lisa felt a slight *whoosh*. Someone had entered the stairwell.

"It's a badge you've worn proudly these many years for all the world to see. A badge of clear and overt unrepentance."

She forced the man to keep talking, rule number one in any negotiation. "And your mission in all of this is. . . ."

" 'To prepare the way of the Lord.' So he may come 'in clouds with great power and glory,' with angels, ten thousand times ten—"

He jerked up his head, raised his gun, and shot . . . just as the fire extinguisher hit him. He staggered backward until his head slammed into the wall. He slumped, collapsing to the floor, gun clattering to the ground.

Lisa lunged to scoop it up, but there was no hurry. He was out cold. Ears still ringing from the shot, she looked up and spotted Charlie on the landing.

"You okay?" he asked.

"Yeah, you?"

He nodded, but the way he pressed his hand against his shoulder said otherwise.

She moved up to him. "Let me see." Pulling his hand aside, she saw blood spreading around a hole in his shirt. She gave him a look. He tried shrugging but winced at the pain. She undid his buttons and they both examined the wound. It was high enough to miss the lung but may have chipped the clavicle. Nothing life-threatening, as long as they kept pressure on it until they got him to the hospital.

Suddenly Charlie stiffened and shouted, "Kristof!"

Lisa spun around. The spot where the man had been was vacant, the first-floor door below them just shutting.

"Go!" He waved her on. "Go!"

She raced down the steps, gripping the .45. She threw open the door and saw Kristof staggering up the hall, ten yards ahead.

"Stop!" she shouted.

But he didn't.

She raised the gun, relaxed her elbows, and fired. The wall to the left of his head splintered with a cloud of paint and wood. Angry at herself, she re-aimed. "I said stop!"

He darted to the right, through a doorway with a sign reading *Cafeteria* above it.

Lisa broke into a run, but within a dozen steps, noticed

her legs once again growing weak. And for good reason. She knew full well what was inside that room. *Who* was inside it. Even now she could hear the clinking of dishes and the sound of elderly voices.

The unsteadiness grew. But she forced herself forward, each step becoming more difficult than the last. Finally, the entrance of the room came into view. Inside she saw old people. Everywhere, old people. She ordered herself to enter, but her legs betrayed her. Her heart pounded in her ears. It was growing difficult to catch her breath. Cursing herself for her weakness, she tried again, but nothing would cooperate.

Inside she heard the smashing of glass. She turned to see someone had thrown a chair through a back window. She caught a glimpse of Kristof hurling himself into the remaining glass and crashing through to the outside.

"Lisa!"

She turned to see Charlie calling from the stairwell door.

She looked back into the cafeteria. Her head was growing light. She knew her body was shutting down. She forced one leg into the room. Breathing was nearly impossible now, the pounding of her heart, relentless. Suddenly her knees became rubber. She stumbled back to the door frame as they gave out altogether, and she slowly slid to the floor.

Chapter Sixteen

They skidded to a stop in front of the emergency entrance.

As he crawled from the car, Jason turned to Jaz and shouted, "Help me get her out!"

Jaz waited in the back until he opened Heather's door. "Put your hand here!" She motioned where her own bloody hand was pressed against Heather's chest. He obeyed. She scampered out of her side and crossed around to help the semiconscious Heather from the back seat. Little pebbles of glass fell from the girl's shawl and matted hair.

Jason yelled over the roof of the car to no one in particular, "Can we get some help here?"

They half-walked, half-carried Heather toward the hospital doors. Pausing a moment, they leaned her against a pillar.

"Stay here," Jason ordered Jaz. "I'll get somebody."

She nodded and he took off—but not toward the hospital. Instead, he dashed for the car.

"Hey!" she shouted.

He climbed inside and slammed the door.

"HEY!?"

She turned back to the hospital to see a white-haired lady running out the doors toward them. "What happened?" she asked.

"She needs help!" Jaz shouted. "She's hurt real bad." She turned back to the car to see a tiny puff of smoke rise from the tires as it sped away.

A big bruiser of a man came out of the hospital. Some skinny guy with a gurney followed. Suddenly there was a ton of commotion, like on those hospital TV shows, as they loaded Heather onto the cart and raced her toward the sliding doors.

"She's got this big hole in her side," Jaz explained. "We were in the woods and—" Thinking better of it, she said, "She's got this really big hole."

They rolled into the lobby, then through more doors and toward a beige-curtained room. Someone grabbed Jaz's arm. She turned and saw the white-haired lady pulling her.

"—get you washed up," she was saying.

Before Jaz could answer, the woman led her to another curtained room and a big sink where she turned on the water. Suddenly Jaz felt so tired, she had to lean against the basin just to stand up. The old lady peeled off her sweatshirt, then rinsed her arms and hands. She was saying stuff, but Jaz didn't bother to look. Not that she could see, with the way tears kept filling her eyes. Talk about stupid. She wasn't the one who was hurt. She wasn't the one who got kidnapped by some, some. . . .

The tears came faster. So did the exhaustion. She could

barely stand and was grateful when the lady suddenly stopped and eased her into a nearby chair.

†

Lisa stood outside, sipping the nursing home's lukewarm coffee, wearily answering every boneheaded question the young officer could dream up: What was she doing in a high-speed chase? What was her prior relationship with the shooter? Where had her boyfriend run off to? Did they know—

"Ms. Harmon?"

She looked up to see a balding black man in his fifties approach. "Excuse us, son," he said to the officer.

"Who are you?" the boy asked.

He flashed a quick ID that Lisa didn't see. "I'll have her back in a second." Without waiting for a response, he gently took her arm and escorted her away. She knew he was a Fed by his polite insistence and the cheap suit.

"FBI?" she asked, raking her hands through her hair.

He nodded. "Robert Quinn. Rumor has it you need help finding a man."

She looked at him in surprise. "You're the one who scored us the tracking device?"

He said nothing.

"That was pretty fast," she said.

"Yes, well, I'm sure the paperwork will catch up someday."

She liked him immediately. "You know Charlie, then."

"We served in the military. Go back a long ways."

"You knew him when he—" She hesitated, unsure how to finish the sentence. *Back when he was a trained killer, back when he served the government in operations they de-nied existed, back when he was so valuable that the Assistant Joint Chiefs of Staff had asked him to reconsider resigna-tion?*

Quinn saved her the effort. "Yeah."

"I guess he had quite a reputation."

"So do you, Ms. Harmon."

"I was drummed out of the Bureau."

"That's one story. Another says you sacrificed a career to keep us clean." Before she could respond, he continued. "A task force is being assembled."

"Does Sheriff Hutton know about this?"

"He will. We're using his office as central command."

Lisa mused, imagining what turf wars were being fought over that one. No wonder the sheriff hadn't responded. He was probably battling even as they spoke.

"First Special Forces Group at Fort Lewis is also weigh-ing in."

Lisa arched an eyebrow. "People are getting serious."

"Special Forces likes to do its own housekeeping."

"So it's for sure. He's Special Forces?"

"One of their best."

"Same as Charlie."

"Same as Charlie used to be."

Lisa nodded, completing the thought: "Before he walked away and the bad guys killed his family."

Quinn looked at her, then changed subjects. "Where is he now?"

"In pursuit, I imagine. Our pickup and the Honda are both gone."

"Then we'd better get moving."

They started toward his car, a nondescript brown Saber.

"Excuse me," the young officer called after them. "Excuse me. I'm not done questioning the witness."

Quinn gave a pleasant wave and opened Lisa's door.

"Excuse—"

She stepped inside and he closed it behind her.

✝

Jaz paced back and forth in the ICU waiting room, trying her best not to explode. "You saw the hole in her side! Does that look like someone's playing games?"

She turned to the sheriff, who simply stared back at her.

"I can't believe this!" With dramatic flair, she threw herself onto the nearest sofa.

"Jazmin, sweetheart." Sharon rose from her husband's side and joined her. "In order to find Will, we have to know what really happened."

"I told you what really happened. How many times do I have to tell you what really—"

"Okay, I understand, that's what you *thought* you saw. But it was getting dark and there were plenty of shadows and—"

"Right, a shadow did that to Heather. A shadow smashed in your car window."

Thomas got her attention across the room. He looked pretty drained. "About the car," he said. "Where do you think it is now?"

"I don't know. Ask him."

"Will?"

"Will's still out there! The guy, ask the guy!"

The sheriff replied, "The guy who . . . ?"

"The guy who found the deer. The guy who drove us here. The guy who left with the car!"

The sheriff nodded. "What was his name again?"

"I told you, I don't know!"

"He didn't tell you?"

"I don't know, maybe, I can't remember."

The sheriff gave a disapproving frown.

"I had a few other things on my mind, alright?"

"Can you describe what he looked like, what he was wearing?"

"He was all Goth-like. Wore these really cool leather boots. I saw them in something like an Urban Outfitters catalogue. I was going to get me a pair, but they're way too expensive—least that's what Uncle Charlie says. Probably 'cause they're high quality, like suede, maybe calfskin—something you have to keep oiled all the time."

She looked to their faces. Blank expressions all around.

"Any idea of his age?" the sheriff asked. "His height?"

She erupted. "We've got to go back out there! If we're going to find Will, we've got to—"

Thomas broke in. "You're not even sure what road you were on."

"I told you! It was gravel! Up in the mountains!" Remembering another detail, she added, "Where they have their meetings."

"Meetings?" the sheriff asked.

"Yeah, Heather and that guy, they have like these ceremonies where they call on the devil and stuff."

"Heather's part of that group?"

Jaz nodded. "And the guy, he's their leader."

"Jason?" the sheriff asked. "Is his name Jason?"

"Yeah, sure, why not. Tats on his arms—a snake on one, a cross on the other."

"He had tattoos?"

"Yes."

"On both arms?"

"Yes."

"A snake and a cross?"

"Yes! Yes!" She was back on her feet. What's with these people? She's the one who's supposed to be deaf!

"Did he ever talk about a fellow named Kristof?" the sheriff asked.

Jaz blew the hair out of her eyes. "I'm talking about the creepy monster thing, not your serial killer."

"Maybe he was dressed up like one," Thomas offered.

"Who?"

"Kristof."

"Like what?"

"Your creepy monster thing."

She was really ready to blow.

"No, I'm serious." He was trying to be nice, but it made her feel like some stupid kid. "A big black suit, a scary mask. Who wouldn't mistake him for—"

"Bovine feces!"

"What?

She didn't bother repeating herself. Everyone looked at each other.

"Where's Uncle Charlie?" she asked. "Where's Lisa?"

"Why?"

"Why? 'Cause they'll do something. They'll go up there

and start—" She came to a stop, suddenly remembering. "What about that singer lady? From church?" She turned to Sharon and Thomas. "You know, with the real thick glasses? And the baby?"

"Do you mean Cindy Carlson?" Sharon asked.

Jaz nodded. "I bet she could help."

"How, dear?"

"Help to find him. It. The thing."

"How could she do that?"

"She feels stuff, too. Like me. And she fights against it. I bet if she went up there—"

"Fights?" Thomas asked.

"Like me with that monster."

"When you sang at it?" the sheriff said. Even through her deafness, Jaz could hear the attitude.

"That's right, when I sang at it. Just like she does in church. Just like she did when—" She stopped. They'd gone from trading looks to examining the carpet on the floor.

"I'm not making this up! Call the lady, she'll tell you. I bet she could help!"

"Jazmin." It was Thomas again. "Cindy Carlson is a talented singer. And I'm glad you two hit it off. But every church has, well, I'm not certain how to put this. . . ."

She shifted her weight. Of course he knew how to put it, if he'd just cut to the chase.

"Every church has its fringe element. Folks who get their emotions mixed up with what they think is supernatural."

"Like Jehoshaphat?"

"Who?"

"He's in the Bible. Sang a bunch of songs and beat those bad boys."

More traded looks.

Jaz threw herself back into the sofa. She may have scored a point, but it would mean another twenty minutes of lecture, which meant another twenty minutes of Will being out there all by himself.

Chapter Seventeen

Charlie followed the Honda north on I-5 and off at the 209 exit where the sky was lit up from a spring carnival. Kristof was several cars ahead when he veered off the road and into the adjacent pasture/parking lot. He turned off his headlights and quickly blended into the hundreds of other parked cars. Charlie followed but it was obvious he'd lost him. Eventually he slid the pickup to a stop, hopped out, and ran toward the carnival grounds, keeping an eye on the road should Kristof try to double back and escape.

His cell phone vibrated and he pulled it from his pocket.

"Hello, cowboy." It was good to hear Rob Quinn's voice again. "We're all set and ready to roll."

"That must be some kind of record."

"Like I said, you owe me."

Charlie nodded as he approached the ticket booth and dished out a wad of bills.

Quinn continued, "According to my GPS and little laptop here, you're standing in the middle of a vacant field."

"Not so vacant." He scooped up a ticket and headed

for the entrance gate, scanning the crowd as he walked. "They've got a carnival going. Must be spring break or something. Place is packed. You have a fix on his car?"

"Forty meters ahead at one o'clock."

Charlie frowned, looking over his shoulder. "Negative that. The parking lot is behind me."

"Big Brother don't lie, son. He's forty-three meters ahead of you and moving off to your right."

Charlie turned back to the grounds. He saw nothing but people, concession stands, games, and rides. Unless . . . had Kristof found the tracking device? A possibility, especially if he had a debugger. But why take it in with him?

Charlie's frown deepened. He gave the attendant his ticket and passed through the gate toward the thoroughfare. Games and concession stands stood on either side. The rides were at the far end. He worked his way through the crowd as briskly as possible without drawing attention.

"He's thirty-five meters now," Quinn said. "I'm putting you on speakerphone."

Charlie dug out his Bluetooth and attached it.

"Charlie?" It was Lisa.

"You okay?" he asked.

"Me?" She sounded irritated. "What about you? Last I saw, you had a hole in your shoulder."

"I found some duct tape in the back of the pickup. See if you can round me up a pile of antibiotics. Keflex is my current drug of choice."

"Will do."

Quinn came back on. "He's holding at thirty meters. Two o'clock. I've put a call in for backup."

"Negative," Charlie said.

"What?"

"Too many people here. We don't want him to panic."

"You don't have a gun, cowboy."

"He found the tracker. He's purposely brought me into a public place. Maybe he wants to talk."

"Or play you," Lisa answered. "Like his other victims."

Charlie entered the thoroughfare with its bright lights, laughter, and smells—everything from BBQ to battered corn dogs to deep-fried *churros*—the stench of rancid grease practically left a film in his mouth.

"He's stopped," Quinn said. "Twenty meters, three o'clock."

"Roger." As Charlie passed a gap separating the game booths, he spotted a fun house over on the north perimeter. It was the right distance and location. The fact that it stood two stories above the grounds only increased his suspicion.

He slowed as he passed the next booth, a basketball shoot, its barker calling out challenges.

"Still holding. Seventeen meters."

"Remember," Lisa warned, "he likes disguises."

Charlie turned to his left and saw a shooting gallery, the sound of its air rifles reminiscent of a handgun silencer. He closed his eyes a moment, shaking off the memories, then moved to the next game, a ring toss. Between the booths, he again checked the fun house. He was almost parallel with it now.

The next game was the fishbowl toss. Other memories rushed in. These he couldn't shake. His wife and little daughter insisting he try, and keep trying, until he finally landed a ping-pong ball in the bowl to win a goldfish, which lasted seventy-two hours before they held a tearful funeral service over the toilet. A harbinger of the double service less than a year later, where he buried something far more valuable—his only two reasons for living.

Suddenly, over the noise, he heard a little girl crying. Like his daughter. At first he feared he was losing it, that his mind was playing tricks. But as he searched the crowd, he spotted a four-year-old. She stood less than three meters ahead of him, in the space between the fishbowl toss and the next booth. In her hands she held an empty paper cone. At her feet lay a pile of cherry ice. Despite her father's attempts, she would not be consoled.

Charlie gathered his thoughts and refocused. He slowed as he approached the gap between the booths. The fun house came into full view to his right. Careful not to stare at it, he looked at the girl who continued to sob. Before he could stop himself, he was bending down to speak to her, to offer comfort — just as a bullet splintered the post where his head had been a second before.

He dropped to the ground, grabbing the girl and rolling her out of harm's way.

"Get down!" he shouted. "Everybody get down!"

The crowd pulled back. But not because of the gunman. They'd heard no shot, seen no bullet. They were moving away from Charlie.

"Get down!" he repeated.

"What's going on?"

He turned to see the father coming at him.

"Down!" Charlie shouted.

"What are you doing?"

Charlie looked over his shoulder. They were clear of the fun house. Safe for the moment.

The father grabbed his arm, yanking him. "Get away from her!"

"A sniper!" Charlie rose to his knees. "There's a sniper over at the—"

"Get away from her!" The man scooped his daughter into his arms. She began crying harder. "Get out of here!"

Quinn's voice rang in his earpiece. "He's moving. Sixteen meters, closing in."

"You think this is funny?" the father shouted.

Charlie rose to his feet.

"This how you get your jollies?"

Charlie turned toward the next booth.

"Twelve meters."

"I'm calling the cops!" The father reached into his jacket.

"Nine meters, three o'clock."

"You hear me? The cops!"

Charlie turned back to see nothing but angry and frightened faces glaring at him.

"Seven."

"Get out of there!" Lisa cried.

"Five meters."

Charlie turned, then quickly bolted between the booths.

"Yeah," the father shouted, "you better run!"

He cut to the left behind the booths and headed toward the rides.

"He's in pursuit," Quinn said.

Charlie continued running, passing two, three booths.

At the fourth, he turned left and doubled back toward the thoroughfare, between a cotton candy stand and a booth with greasy pizza under heat lamps.

"Thirteen meters, four o'clock."

A balloon vendor moved up the thoroughfare. Charlie darted behind him, then to the other side, to the last booth before the rides.

"He's at six o'clock, cowboy. Nine meters and still closing."

Charlie looked back up the thoroughfare. Where was he? How could he defend himself if he didn't know how the man was disguised?

"Six meters."

Time for a little recon. He stepped to the end of the booth, pushed aside the tattered drapes, and entered. It was a dart-throw game. The barker, a James Dean wannabe, complete with dangling cigarette, looked up.

"Who are you?" he asked.

"Boss wants to see you."

"Murphy? He's here?"

Charlie nodded and started pulling darts out of the board between the balloons. "Doesn't sound happy."

The kid swore and butted out his smoke in the dirt. A decrepit old-timer with a trophy-date twenty years his junior approached the counter.

"I'll cover 'til you get back," Charlie told the boy.

The kid gave a nod and headed for the drapes. He fumbled for breath spray to kill the smell of beer as Charlie glanced down the thoroughfare.

The old-timer held out a plastic Baggie of loose change and shouted, "We'll take three, please."

"Four meters, coming up to three o'clock," Quinn said through the earpiece. "He's dead ahead, Charlie."

Charlie continued searching until—there, he spotted him! Navy blue stocking cap, black-rimmed glasses, hands stuffed in a dark overcoat. Charlie pulled out of sight behind one of the stuffed bulldogs hanging from the ceiling.

"Three meters. He's passing. Four. Five."

"I said, we'll take three," the old-timer repeated.

Charlie continued to watch and wait. He would go on the offense, but not yet. Not until there was sufficient distance between them.

"Hey!" the old man shook his bag of money. "I'm talking to you!"

"He's at eleven o'clock now. Ten meters. Eleven—"

"Do you want my business or not?"

"Thirteen. . . ."

"Hey!"

Charlie turned to the old duffer.

"I want three darts!"

Charlie stepped forward and dumped his handful of darts onto the counter. "Here."

"I just want three."

"They're on the house."

"I said three."

"Senior discount."

"Oh. Well, all right then." He tilted the bag and dumped the change into Charlie's hand.

"We're at twenty meters now."

That was enough. Charlie headed for the exit.

"Aren't you going to count it?"

He pushed back the drapes and stepped into the flow of people. "Where is he?"

"Twenty-one and holding."

"He's stopped?"

"Probably searching."

Charlie started forward. He moved into the ride area, all the time keeping watch for the navy blue cap. "I don't see anything."

"Twelve o'clock. Still holding. You're at sixteen meters now."

Had he taken his cap off? Had he changed clothes?

"You're heading straight for him."

Charlie continued to search. "Double-check your readings. Make sure—"

"Everything's fine, cowboy. You're at twelve meters and closing in."

Charlie slowed, scanning the backs of people, their heads.

"Hold it. He's moving toward you now. Eight meters."

Charlie froze, glanced around for a quick cover.

"Five meters . . . three."

Spotting a group of tall, gangly boys, he moved behind them and slouched. He was no longer looking for stocking caps or dark coats—now it was anybody matching the right body size.

But he saw no one.

"Moving away again."

Charlie started forward, searching every person, every form. He spotted a trash bin. He quickly peeled off his coat and dumped it. Two could play the game.

"How far am I now?" he asked.

"Ten."

"Still in front of me?"

"Twelve o'clock. Dead ahead."

He continued to search.

"Hold it. He's moving toward you again."

Charlie slowed.

"Eight meters . . . seven. . . ."

It made no sense. The man was less than ten meters ahead, moving back and forth, yet totally invisible.

"Six meters. . . ."

"Charlie," Lisa warned, "he's walking straight toward you."

"Four meters and closing."

He saw everyone now. *Everyone.* And no one came close to the description.

"Dead ahead—two meters."

Pushing back the panic, Charlie forced his mind to slow and study every approaching face—male, female, young, old.

"He's directly beside you!"

He spun around. There were only kids. Nobody even close to the right size.

"He's there! He's right on top of you! He's—"

"Nobody's here! Nobody's—"

And then he looked up and saw the Ferris wheel directly above him. Of course. How could he be so stupid? The GPS was only two-dimensional, not three. There was no way to indicate how far apart they would be in height, not at this close range.

But he wasn't out of the woods yet. From the added elevation, Kristof could easily spot him. And drop him.

Except . . . as Charlie searched the cars above him he saw no one close to the description. They were all too young—kids, teens, a young couple with a toddler.

But Kristof *was* there. Somewhere.

Charlie stepped further under the ride. "Okay," he said. "I need to hear the slightest variation, the slightest change."

"What's going on?" Quinn asked.

"Later. I need you to be as exact as possible."

"Roger."

The cars were stopping now, loading and unloading.

"He's drifted away again. Five meters and holding."

Charlie looked to the farthest car going up. A mother and young daughter.

"Which way? Six o'clock or twelve. Six or twelve?"

"Twelve. Sorry."

He turned to the opposite car, the one coming down. It was a teenager in sweats and a Mariners hat . . . at least that's how he was disguised. The Ferris wheel started again.

"Moving," Quinn said.

That was him. It had to be. Charlie inched his way into the shadows, keeping his head down.

The wheel stopped.

"Holding at four."

It started again.

"Moving. Coming up to three."

Charlie darted under the car and behind it as the ride stopped and the car before it unloaded.

"You just ran through him, cowboy."

The ride started up again and the car dropped. Before it

came to a stop, Charlie leaped forward, wrapping his arms around the young man's throat from the back in a choke hold. The man twisted and kicked, but Charlie held tight. The attendant stood nearby, mouth open in surprise, as Charlie pulled Kristof over the back of the car. He felt the duct tape on his shoulder give way, his wound opening up as he threw him to the ground, using his free hand to search for a weapon.

The man squirmed like an amateur, putting up little resistance.

Unable to find a weapon, Charlie flipped him onto his back to deliver a blow to his face . . . when he saw the terrified eyes and the raw acne.

"Don't hurt me!" the boy screamed. "Don't hurt me!"

Startled, Charlie demanded, "Where is he?"

"Who? What are you talking about?"

Charlie glanced to the growing crowd, trying to understand . . . until a possibility surfaced. "The pen! Where's the pen?"

"The what?"

"Did someone give you a pen?"

"No, I mean, yeah, well—" The kid dug into his pocket. "This? Is this what you're talking about?"

Charlie yanked the tracker from him.

"I found it on the ground! I didn't know it was yours. You can have it, man! I'm sorry. It's just a pen, all right?"

Charlie looked up, surveying the crowd, realizing that by now Kristof was long gone.

Chapter Eighteen

It was as if he were asleep, but he wasn't.

Every one of Will's senses was alive and alert. It's hard *not* being alive and alert when you've just been drug through a rip in the fabric of the space-time continuum. At least, that's what the Mothman article on the Internet had said. It wasn't supposed to be an extraterrestrial from another planet, or anything like that. It was supposed to be an extra*dimensional*. Something that lived beside human beings but in another dimension . . . until a "portal" opened up, allowing it to slip into the human world.

Freaky theory, he knew. Though at the moment Will wasn't exactly living a theory.

He remembered the race down the road and through the woods. He remembered his face held tightly against the misty scales of the thing's chest. And he remembered the sudden blast of icy wind.

Followed by darkness. This darkness.

It was as if he was floating. Not in water, but in air—so thick he could actually feel its currents wash back and forth over him. Of course, it would have helped if he could have seen something. Anything. But it was pitch-black. He could feel, he could touch, he could even smell (particularly the stench of rotten eggs). But he could not see.

At least with his eyes.

And he couldn't hear.

At least with his ears.

But he could *feel* the sounds. Their voices. More like their emotions. And there were dozens of them, all around. Examining him. Not his body, but his mind. He could feel them pulling at his thoughts and memories. Holding them up to examine.

He could feel their thoughts as well. Confusion over what to do with him. And jealousy. A hatred so powerful, he knew they would destroy him if they could. But they couldn't. They were too afraid. It made no sense. He was *their* prisoner, not the other way around. Yet, as much as they hated him, they feared him even more.

The attack came without warning. A little explosion. A tiny burst of memory he didn't even know he had. It was so real, he actually smelled the roast his mom had been cooking, saw the dust motes in the final shafts of the afternoon sunlight.

He is eight years old, looking out the living-room window, waiting for his dad to pull into the driveway. Thomas has called around noon, promising him an X-Box marathon when he gets home. Will has dutifully pulled out the controls, arranged them on the carpet, and now he is waiting. And waiting. And waiting.

He and Mom eat alone that night. His mom is all chatty, even letting him make chocolate milk with some Hershey syrup. But nothing distracts him. When they are done and have cleared the table, he is back on the sofa, watching. And waiting.

Until bedtime.

Now he lies alone, smelling the freshness of his Star Wars pajamas just out of the dryer . . . the pillowcase that grows damp with his tears.

Such a little thing. It wasn't like Dad missed a birthday or broke some great promise. But it was so vivid, so painful, that even as the memory faded, Will felt the ache in his throat and the moisture filling his eyes.

No sooner did that memory fade before another began. . . .

†

"I never caught your name."

Charlie froze. He'd just opened the pickup door and saw a young man scooted down in the shadows, pointing a Sig 228 at him. He thought of taking his chances and leaping out of the way, but with the skills he'd already witnessed, he doubted he would succeed. Then there were the past opportunities. Charlie had made enough mistakes for the kid to have killed him several times over, if that's what he really wanted.

He decided simply to answer. "Madison. Charles Madison."

"They call me Kristof." He motioned Charlie inside. "You've had some training."

Charlie climbed into the pickup. "Retired army."

"More than that. Special Forces?"

"First Ranger Battalion."

Kristof completed his own introduction. "First SFG, Fort Lewis. You're a little out of practice."

"It's been a while." He waited, using the silence to read Kristof, knowing Kristof was doing the same with him. Finally he turned to him. "Now what?"

"I'd say a drive would be in order, wouldn't you?" He nodded toward the ignition.

Charlie closed the door and fired up the truck. "Where to?"

"So many possibilities."

"I don't suppose you'd be interested in swinging by the sheriff's station?"

"Sheriff Hutton is not on my list."

The kid knew his enemy by name. More importantly, he seemed to have an agenda. Charlie dropped the truck into gear just as his cell vibrated. The buzz in his pocket was faint but loud enough for Kristof to hear.

"Go ahead, answer it."

Charlie pulled out the phone.

"Make sure I can hear."

He flipped it open and held it slightly from his ear. "Hello?"

"Charlie?" It was Lisa. They'd already covered his failure at the fairgrounds. This was something else. "Meet me here at the sheriff's office as soon as you can."

"Tell her you're still in pursuit," Kristof softly ordered.

Charlie answered Lisa. "I think I see him up ahead."

"Char—"

"I'm continuing pursuit."

Kristof motioned him forward, and they started across the field toward the main road.

"There have been other developments," Lisa said.

"Tell her your battery's running low."

"With Jaz."

The concern hit Charlie hard. "Is she okay?"

"Tell her your battery—"

"She's been involved in something. Some sort of accident."

"Accident?" Charlie demanded. "What happened?"

"Tell her your battery is—"

He gave the kid a scowl to shut up.

"No, she's fine," Lisa said. "But that thing I saw up on the mountain—"

"But she's fine?" Charlie repeated. "Everything's okay?"

"Yes."

Kristof repeated, "Your battery is dead and you'll call when there's something to report."

"Are you sure?" Charlie asked Lisa.

To emphasize his point, Kristof chambered a round. Charlie ignored him.

"Yes," Lisa answered, "she's perfectly fine."

He relaxed slightly. "Listen, my battery is low. I'm going to have to sign off."

"We need you here, Charlie."

"I'll get there as soon as I can."

"Do you want backup? They're sending a special unit up from Fort Lewis. A chopper, too."

He threw a look at the kid, who was unable to suppress a smile.

"No, I'm okay. I'll call if I need help."

"You sure?"

"I'll talk soon." He closed the phone, and Kristof held out his hand. Charlie gave it to him.

"Jaz is?"

"A friend."

"You and your friend must be very close."

Charlie saw no need to answer.

The kid disengaged the phone's battery and slipped it into his pocket. He reached out again. "And the tracking device."

Charlie produced the pen and handed it to him. A moment later they arrived at the main road. "Now what?"

"Now you'll help me return to my somewhat demanding schedule."

After agreeing with Quinn that they'd contact each other as soon as they heard from Charlie, Lisa joined her brother. She knew he would need her support, and she agreed to ride back up to the site with Sharon, Jaz, the sheriff, and some mousy-haired singer from the church by the name of Cindy.

Apparently Jazmin had been more than a little persistent. From what little Lisa knew about deaf kids, that was a skill many had to cultivate to survive in the hearing world. And Jaz had that skill in spades, which was another reason the two of them hit it off so well.

She could appreciate that no one bought her wild story about a flying monster snatching Will away. But she also knew the girl seldom lied—well, not about big things. Of course, at thirteen she was a schizophrenic bundle of bravado and insecurity, but she never told whoppers like that. Then, of course, there was Lisa's own experience on the bluff directly above that same site just thirty-six hours ago. There was no missing the similarities.

They'd just left the gravel road. Jaz insisted the marks on it were left by Will's dragging feet. Now they were deep in the woods, following that same trail across broken branches and trampled undergrowth. With Sharon's prompting, Cindy was trying to explain what it felt like when she "did battle."

"It's like these ripples of darkness. Sometimes they're real small, sometimes they come in giant waves. And for Jazmin it's. . . ." She turned to Jaz, shining the flashlight into her own face so the girl could read her lips. "How do you describe what it feels like to you?"

"Cold," Jaz said, as she craned her neck around Sheriff Hutton to look up the trail. "Cold vibrations."

Thomas turned to her. He was still trying to be pleasant, but Lisa could see the strain and worry were definitely taking their toll. "When you say 'vibrations,' what exactly does that mean?"

Jaz looked at him, puzzled.

Trying to help, Lisa touched her arm and she turned. "Like in Rome?" she asked. "When all that stuff happened by playing back the Voice?"

Jaz shrugged. "Kinda. Only it's more like a *negative* voice."

"A negative voice," Thomas softly muttered. "Heard by a deaf child. Why am I not surprised?"

Lisa cut him a look and he glanced away. Both were grateful Jaz didn't hear.

Sheriff Hutton raised his hand and they came to a stop. He held out his lantern to reveal the same clearing he and Lisa had explored the first day she arrived. "I want everyone to stay put," he ordered. "If there's evidence, I don't want it disturbed."

They agreed, and he moved into the clearing, watching his every step. In the glow of the lantern and their darting flashlights, Lisa saw trash, cigarette butts, beer cans. Fortunately, there were no skinned animals. The man's search was meticulous, checking every piece of disturbed garbage and vegetation, trying to follow the faint trace of Will's trail.

As they watched and waited, Sharon turned back to Jaz. "I'm still not exactly sure what you mean when you say 'vibrations.'"

Jaz was only too happy to explain. "Everything around us is made of vibrations, right? I mean, that's what the current superstring theory is all about."

Sharon looked at her blankly.

"You do know about superstrings?"

Sharon glanced at Thomas.

Trying to hide her impatience, Jaz continued. "The latest studies in physics hint that the building blocks of matter are *not* subatomic particles."

More silence.

"You know, atoms and stuff."

"What are they?" Thomas asked.

"Vibrations."

Sharon frowned. "So this"—she plucked a nearby fern—"this isn't made of atoms?"

"Of course it is."

"Then. . . ."

"But the tinier particles that make those atoms are vibrating strings. And the frequencies that those strings vibrate at tell us what type of matter it is—kinda like different notes."

Thomas motioned to the woods around them. "So this is all . . . music?"

Jaz nodded. "Or words."

"Words?" he repeated. "Whose words?"

Jaz gave him a look.

Starting to understand, Sharon quietly quoted. "In the beginning was the Word. . . . Through him all things were made."

Thomas frowned. "So this vibration, that's what you felt from this thing?"

Jaz shook her head. "No. The *anti*vibration. That's why it was so cold for me and"—she motioned to Cindy—"so dark for you."

Thomas turned to Cindy. "And that's what you were fighting in my church? This anti-whatever?"

"Yes."

His frown deepened.

Cindy tried softening the blow. "There are other times, though—when God's presence is so thick that I just sit back and bask in His light."

"And what makes the difference?" he asked. "How loud we sing? How well?"

She shook her head. "It's not the loudness or quality. It's the intensity." She tapped her chest. "In here." A little more gently, she added, "It's also the sincerity of our prayers. And. . . ." She hesitated.

"Please," he encouraged, "go on."

"How serious the congregation is about pursuing His holiness."

Thomas looked at her a moment, then glanced away.

"Jazmin? Cindy?" Hutton called from the other side of the clearing. "Can you two come here a minute?"

Cindy motioned to Jaz and they stepped into the opening. Without being asked, the others followed.

"What did you find?" Thomas asked.

The sheriff shook his head. "Nothing. The trail ends here." He raised his lantern over a log that appeared to have been used for an altar. There were hardened puddles of black wax on either end. He looked to Cindy. "Do you feel anything now?"

The woman closed her eyes, waited a moment, then shook her head.

He turned to Jaz.

"Nada," she answered.

"Are you sure?"

They both tried again with the same results.

The sheriff scowled.

"Maybe you missed something," Thomas said.

"I don't think so, Pastor."

"He couldn't just disappear," Thomas argued. "I mean, if he was here, he didn't just vanish."

The sheriff gave a weary sigh. "I don't know what he did." With a look at Jaz, he added, "Or if he was even here. But I promise you this: we will get to the bottom of it. First thing in the morning we'll bring up a search party and comb every inch of the area."

"And until then?" There was no missing the concern in Thomas's voice.

"Until then, I would pray, Pastor." He turned and held Thomas's gaze. "I would pray very hard."

Chapter Nineteen

So you're saying Satan and Jesus are pals?"

"Christ commanded us to love our enemies," Kristof replied. "And since He had no greater enemy than Satan, He really has no choice in the matter."

Charlie pretended to chew on the statement, giving the impression he actually cared—one of the social engineering skills he'd learned from Special Forces. "So now they're working together: Jesus the Savior, and Satan is—what, His cosmic hit man?"

"Preparing for the Lord's return. That's correct. Perfect love combined with perfect wrath."

There was a moment of silence as the pickup bounced along the overgrown logging road, its headlights catching thick groves of alder and evergreens.

"And your part in all of this is. . . ."

"As God's priest, I'm to lead His children in hastening the day of the coming of the Lord."

"By . . ."

"Separating the sheep from the goats, the tares from the wheat."

"Seems the world might have more goats and tares than the ones you've selected."

"The world is not my concern."

"What is?"

"The church. To make her perfect. To present the bride to the Bridegroom without 'spot, blemish, or wrinkle.'"

"I always thought the church was supposed to be more of a hospital."

"How is that?" Kristof asked.

"A place people go to when they know they're sick."

"Ah, but if they refuse to get well. . . ."

"You'll help by destroying them."

"If they have sufficient time to repent and don't, they will be judged accordingly."

"Like Dr. Gibson, or that teacher, Mark Ramsey."

"Or Lisa Harmon." If he wanted a rise from Charlie, he didn't get it. "Her father's sin has always been public knowledge. So has her refusal to forgive him. Of course, she wasn't on my original list, but how could her appearance at this exact moment be anything but the Lord's timing?"

"So you'll be judging her, too."

"I have no choice." He pointed to a small trailer nearly hidden behind a stand of cedars. "There."

Charlie pulled in as close as possible and brought the pickup to a stop. What few sections of white that remained on the rusting trailer glowed in the moonlight. The rest appeared in dull grays and faded blacks.

Kristof motioned with his gun. "Get out."

Charlie turned off the ignition and did as he was told. Kristof crossed around the front of the truck to join him. "And bring the duct tape."

Charlie reached into the cab and grabbed the tape. He spotted a pencil on the floor and quickly slipped it into his pocket. It could easily serve as a shank.

"And I'll take that pencil, if you don't mind."

He nodded and handed it to him. The kid was good.

Plumes of white breath hovered over their heads as they threaded around the saplings and ferns, then between the trees to reach the trailer. "Nice digs," Charlie noted.

"I spared every expense."

They arrived at the front door and Kristof unlocked it. He stepped back and motioned Charlie inside. It was dark, except for the faint moonlight filtering through dirt-caked windows. Near the front, a red dot of an answering machine flashed.

"So," Charlie said as he continued to work the relationship, "tell me more about this group of yours."

Kristof headed to a nearby counter and removed the glass chimney from a kerosene lamp. It set on a small, crocheted doily. "Don't play me. We have too much to do." He produced a box of wooden matches, lit the lamp, and replaced the glass. The trailer filled with warm, yellow-orange light.

"*We?*" Charlie asked. "How do you figure *we?*"

"If I told you, it would ruin all the fun." He motioned to a camper's stool. "Take a seat."

On the table beside it lay a standard battle-dress uniform with a woodland camouflage pattern, an ECWCS jacket, a helmet, and a MOLLE backpack—gear he had not seen since his military days.

"Planning a little hike?"

"Sit down, tape your legs to the stool. Keep them high enough so your feet don't touch the floor."

"You really think that's necessary?"

"Don't you?"

He had a point. Charlie sat down and began peeling off the tape. Drawing his knees up slightly, he wrapped the tape around his legs and the stool once, twice, three times as Kristof rummaged in the cupboards above the lamp.

"When you're done, unbutton your shirt."

Charlie finished taping his legs and looked up to see Kristof turning with a bottle of bleach and a roll of paper towels. "That wound needs cleaning," he explained as he set the gun on the counter, easily within his reach.

Charlie shook his head. "Don't worry about it, I'll be fine."

"I'm serious."

"So am I. Just—"

With lightning speed, Kristof struck the side of Charlie's face. It was a painful blow, but Charlie gave him no satisfaction of response.

"Sorry," Kristof said as he straddled a chair before him. "I'm not used to giving orders twice."

Without a word, Charlie unbuttoned his shirt. The muscles had grown stiff and the tape stuck to the dried blood and matted chest hair. "I guess I should thank you for poor marksmanship."

"If I'd wanted you dead, you'd be dead."

So much for repartee. Charlie watched as the kid folded a paper towel and poured the bleach on it. The phone on the front counter rang, but he gave no indication of answering it.

It rang again.

Charlie continued gathering info. "I'm surprised you have phone service up here."

"I'm a communications sergeant."

"You tapped into a line?"

"Hard wire is more reliable up here, and harder to trace."

On the fourth ring, the answering machine kicked in with the single command, "Speak."

The voice on the other end was breathless. "This is Jason again." He sounded late adolescent, early twenties. "I don't know what happened, but we did it, man! Last night we had an honest-to-God manifestation. I'm talkin' the real deal!"

The two men exchanged looks.

"It attacked a couple kids. I think we'd better cancel tonight, 'cause it might get kinda—"

Kristof moved and scooped up the phone. "Hello, Jason."

Charlie strained to hear the other end but for the most part could only make out agitation.

In contrast, Kristof's voice was calm and controlled. "No, everything is good." He listened, almost smiling.

Charlie took advantage of the distraction and carefully surveyed the camper. There was no food out, no dirty dishes, no clothes that needed to be put away. Just the nearby lamp on the doily and a single towel neatly folded on the counter beside the sink. The guy was meticulous, a neat freak. This was good and bad. It meant he had everything carefully planned. A formidable opponent. But it also indicated he might have trouble improvising. If new or unforeseen situations arose, it might take him a moment longer to evaluate them and respond—and that moment may be all Charlie had.

Kristof continued on the phone. "No, that's a negative. Even if it does return, it won't attack you. Why? Because you're one of its priests."

The Sig was still out of reach on the counter but, spotting a glass saltshaker on the table, Charlie silently slipped it into his pants pocket. It was angular, with just enough weight to do damage.

"No, listen to me. The ceremony is still on. Something very important may happen tonight and we will need everyone there."

He listened patiently.

"Negative. It's on *our* side. You said it yourself, an honest-to-*GOD* manifestation." He listened. "That's correct. Yes. Later, then." The conversation was over and he slowly hung up.

"One of your disciples?" Charlie asked.

Kristof nodded. "Convinced himself he saw something last night."

"Something?"

Taking the tape, Kristof ordered, "Hold out your hands."

Charlie obeyed and watched as the man wrapped the tape around his wrists twice.

"So, do you believe him?" Charlie continued to probe. "That he saw something, I mean?"

Kristof hesitated. Finally he answered, "I have . . . dreams."

"Dreams?"

He rose and crossed to a drawer. "Sometimes it speaks to me."

"I'm sorry, 'it'? You mean the dreams speak to you?"

Kristof shook his head. "I wouldn't worry about it." He pulled open the drawer and produced a sterile syringe packet and a small vial.

Charlie stiffened. "What's that?"

He nodded to Charlie's wound. "For the pain." He sounded so nonchalant, he was nearly believable.

Charlie tried to sound equally relaxed. "That's okay."

Kristof tore open the packet and inserted the needle into the vial. Charlie watched as he drew out a small portion of the clear liquid.

"Really," Charlie said, "I'm good."

"This will make you better."

Every nerve was alive. Charlie waited until Kristof crossed back to him and reached for his arm before making his move—what little move he could make. He threw himself backwards, falling to the floor. Using his inertia, he rolled onto his back, face up, preparing to ward off the kid's attack. He was met by a boot to the temple—once, twice, so powerful his vision immediately blurred. He brought up his feet, stool and all, and drove the legs of the stool into Kristof's gut. The kid staggered backward and Charlie twisted around, lunging up, grabbing his pants leg, forcing him to fall. But the camper was too small and Kristof caught himself against the stove. Seeing the lantern on the counter, Charlie threw himself at it, managing to grab the doily and drag both to the floor. The glass shattered, splattering its kerosene across the cheap carpet. Flames dashed over the liquid in a quiet *whoosh*. Unfortunately, they also danced across the kerosene he'd spilled on his shirt.

Kristof swore as he turned and reached for the helmet on the table. Still on fire, Charlie again grabbed his leg. Despite the pain in his shoulder and the double vision, he hung on, flames licking his neck and face.

The kid kicked and twisted, but he was no match for Charlie's determination. Unfortunately, the helmet was. It took two blows into Charlie's face before he began losing consciousness. And still he hung on. If he could just bring Kristof down, pull out the saltshaker and smash it into his eye or temple or—

The third blow came.

There might have been a fourth. Charlie lost track as he slipped back to the floor, shirt in flames, receiving a final kick to the head.

The images of his father's failures came faster and stronger. But they were more than images. They were emotions. As deep and powerful as the first time Will felt them.

He is ten years old. Standing with his parents, looking at Holly on the examination table. The golden retriever has been struck by a hit-and-run.

"I'll take care of her!" he pleads. He looks to his dad, to his mom, then to the vet, then back to his dad. "She'll be okay, honest."

Dad glances at Mom, and Will knows the decision. Before they can stop him, he throws his arms around the dog's neck. If he could, he would pick her up and run away. He hears Holly's pathetic groan, sees her liquid brown eyes briefly focus on him.

"See! She's alive! She'll be fine! Won't you, girl, you'll be fine!"

"I'm sorry, son."

"Pleeease. I'll take care of—"

He feels his father's hand on his shoulder.

"No!" He buries his head into Holly's chest, smells her fur. She softly whines.

Dad's grip tightens.

"No!"

Now he is being pulled away, out of the room, into the hall.

"No! Holly!" How he hates the man. He won't even try to save her!

But it's more than what his dad does or doesn't do. It's how he lies. Hasn't he told Will to pray? And hasn't Will pleaded and begged and cried for God to heal her? Hasn't Jesus promised to answer his prayers, if he just believes hard enough?

Isn't that what Dad says?

And he had *believed*. With all of his heart.

And what did God do?

Nothing.

His father had lied. More important, God had lied.

The transition was subtle—his feelings of resentment toward his dad shifting toward God. It happened so gradually, Will barely noticed it.

And it continued. . . .

Now he stands in the middle-school band room. Class has just let out, and he anxiously waits by himself for the election results, trying to read Mr. Randall's face as he steps from his brightly lit office. All week Will has been praying to become the band president. Not that it's a big deal, at least to anybody else. *It's not as if people are standing in line for the position. It's just he and Brandon Collier, the all-school stoner. But he wants it. Just this little thing. Surely God will help him with a little thing like this.*

But surely God doesn't.

"Sorry, son." Mr. Randall shakes his head. "It was close. Maybe you could try out for drum major. That would be fun, wouldn't it?"

As with so many things in life, God let him down, God broke his promise. Again. And it is the memories of those broken promises, those little betrayals, that slowly moved Will from disappointment to resentment to rage. No longer rage at his father, but rage at his God.

✝

The ride back in the sheriff's van was silent even by Jaz's standards. Thomas and Sharon were pretty upset. Not that Jaz blamed them. Who wouldn't be? But at least they were starting to believe her.

Starting to.

Still, they weren't exactly thrilled when she suggested they bring the choir up to the location to start singing. "That would really shake things loose," she said. "Talk about kicking butt. If we all went up there and, you know—"

Seeing Lisa's look of warning, she should have stopped, but it's hard to stop in the midst of a major brainstorm.

"Seriously, we'd be just like that Jehoshaphat guy and his army." She turned to Cindy, who sat in the back of the van. "Or like you were talking about Jericho, where they shouted and blew horns and stuff? Talk about acoustical warfare."

Cindy gave a half smile and pushed up her glasses. No one else responded. But Jaz had never let a little thing like that stop her.

"And it's not just in the Bible. I mean, world-class scientists like Oliver Sacks have also been fooling around with that stuff. He had patients who went into seizures when they heard certain music. Others couldn't even walk 'til he played music, and then they not only walked, they started dancing! Others couldn't even speak until they heard certain music, and then they could sing."

She could have gone on forever and probably would have if Sharon hadn't rested a hand on her knee and given a sad sort of smile. Not sad like Jaz was a mental or anything, but sad like *you-really-are-just-a-stupid-kid-but-we-love-you-anyway* sad.

Eventually, they pulled up to the sheriff station, a tiny one-story brick building, and saw a military truck with a bunch of soldier-boys running around.

"What's going on?" Thomas asked.

Sheriff Hutton didn't look happy and muttered something under his breath that Jazmin couldn't read.

"Who are they?" Lisa asked.

"Idiots from Fort Lewis." The sheriff climbed out and started shouting. "Off the lawn! Taxpayers paid good money for that grass." He spread out his hands, waving them toward the sidewalk. "Get off my lawn!"

As the group climbed out of the van, the sheriff yelled at one of his deputies who had stepped outside. "No!" he was shouting. "We're going to find the killer and we're going to find him tonight!"

Thomas was immediately at his side, demanding, "What about our son?"

There was more talking, but Jaz didn't pay any attention. Because at that exact instant, she knew. She wasn't sure how she knew, she just sensed it. Like the other stuff. As clearly as two audio waves coming into phase, she was absolutely certain. "They're the same!" she blurted.

The group turned to her.

"There's a connection!"

Everyone traded looks.

"With what?" Thomas asked.

"I don't know. I mean, I do know, but I can't—"

"You think Kristof took Will?" the sheriff asked.

Jaz shook her head. "No. But he's still . . . connected. It's like his creepiness opened something up. Or maybe it's the other way around. Maybe the creepiness opened something in him. It's all mixed together, but there's a connection. They're definitely related."

The sheriff did his usual staring at her. Come to think of it, so did everybody else. Just like old times. She blew the hair out of her eyes and turned to see an older black guy in a suit step out of the sheriff's office. He started across the grass until Hutton yelled at him. "We put that sidewalk in for a reason!"

The man ignored him and kept right on coming. "I just received a text message from Charlie Madison."

Everyone stopped. Well, everyone but Jaz. She was too busy scoffing. Uncle Charlie didn't know the first thing

about text messages. He barely knew how to retrieve the
voice mails she sent.

"What's he say?" the sheriff asked.

"He replanted the tracking device on Kristof."

"You have a fix?"

"He's up in the mountains. No roads, as far as I can tell.
He's going cross-country."

No one said anything, and the black guy continued.
"A chopper's on its way. Between it and these soldiers, he
hasn't got a chance."

Chapter Twenty

Charlie woke up shivering. He opened his eyes to moonlight filtering through the fir branches above him. Despite the cold, he remained on the forest floor until he could assess the situation. He had little idea of his location or the time. The only fact he could verify was the relentless pounding in his head.

He sat up slowly, felt the strain of tape against his wound. He glanced down to see he was wearing the battle-dress shirt and jacket Kristof had laid out on the trailer's table, though his pants and boots remained the same. His arms were stiff as he reached up and unbuttoned the top of his shirt. The wound had been redressed with paper towel and duct tape.

Off to the left, he heard the snap of a twig. He froze and peered into the mottled shadows and blackness. There were no other sounds except frogs and the whine of mosquitoes. One of the insects landed on his cheek, just below his left eye. He felt the pinprick as it inserted its beak. But he would not move. Not until he was certain the snap had been caused by an animal and not a human. He lowered his eyes and searched the ground beside him. To his right he spotted the MOLLE backpack. Beside it, an M4 complete with a glowing green tritium sight.

The mosquito had its fill and flew away. Charlie waited another full minute before moving. First he searched for a long twig. When he could find none, he settled for the stem of a fern. He picked it, stripped away the fronds and, suppressing a groan, rose to his knees. Holding one end of the stem in each hand, he slipped it under the barrel of the rifle and slowly ran it underneath the weapon, careful to feel any resistance that would indicate a booby trap or mine.

The process took another full minute, delayed somewhat by his shivering. When he was sure it was clear, he lifted the weapon from the ground. It did not feel loaded. He checked the magazine. Only two rounds filled the thirty-round magazine. There may have been a third inside the chamber. He couldn't be certain.

Another twig snapped, fifteen yards away. He spun around and caught the form of a man decked out in similar battle dress. It was impossible to tell if he was approaching or retreating. It made no difference. For that brief moment, the old Charlie, the trained killer, took charge. He'd felt him stirring, wanting to rise when they were in the trailer—the creature whose past he tried so hard to forget, the one he pretended he could walk away from when he became a card-carrying Christian, back when he had the gall to think he could actually go into the ministry. It had been months, a year since he'd felt any trace of that person, but old habits died hard. Still, in that split second of indecision, Kristof had all the time he needed. As Charlie pulled back the bolt and fired, he was already leaping for cover.

Charlie's first shot was high. The second struck its mark but was not a kill.

"I've been hit!" a young voice screamed. "I've been hit!"

Another voice shouted through a field headset. "Stephens, is that you? Stephens?"

Rifle shots were quickly returned, splintering the tree high above Charlie's head. So wild and so panicked, he realized the obvious. He had not shot Kristof.

"I'm down!" the young soldier cried. "I'm down! I'm down!"

"Stephens!"

Charlie started forward to help until more shots were fired—just as wild, but no less dangerous. That's when he understood. The setup was complete. The die had been cast. Left with no alternative, Charlie Madison grabbed the backpack and bolted into the woods.

†

Thomas sat in the sheriff's cramped office, keeping a careful eye on Sharon. His wife was tough. She had to be to put up with him. Being a pastor's wife was not for the weak or fainthearted. Neither was being Will's mom.

The first dozen years had been a piece of cake. As a child, Will was a joy to raise. Pure delight. Then the testosterone kicked in. Within months he became moody and aloof. Once bubbling with lively thoughts and ideas, his conversations degenerated into monosyllabic grunts or silences seething with attitude. He loved solitude (or at least his solitude away from them) and sometimes would go missing for two, three, or four hours without checking in. But never this long. And not with a serial killer on the loose, whose victims were members of their own church or—Thomas stole a look at Lisa—his own family.

Without a word, he reached over and took Sharon's hand. It felt cold and damp. She was tough, but not this tough.

Across the office, all of ten feet away, two desks were slid together. At them sat Charlie's FBI friend along with a lieutenant who was commander of the in-training Special Forces squad they'd sent up. Beside them worked a communication sergeant just out of puberty whose equipment sprouted more cables than the back of Thomas's computer. A handful of deputies milled about, trying not to bump into each other.

"We have engagement," a voice called through the small black speaker atop the desk.

"Stephens!" another voice shouted through it. "Stephens!"

Sheriff Hutton stood looking over the sergeant's shoulder at the high-definition GPS screen.

"One man down." The first voice was doing his best to sound calm and professional. "Confirm, one man down. Company in pursuit."

"No," the lieutenant said into his headset. "Negative that. The risk is too great. I want a five-hundred-meter distance, no closer."

"But, sir—"

"We've got the tracker. We know where he is. Air support is on the way."

"Sir, he's only one man."

"Wait for the chopper."

"Affirmative."

The lieutenant ripped off his headset in frustration.

Hutton growled with equal displeasure, "Next time, don't send me trainees."

"He's one man," the lieutenant repeated.

"Who's already got your unit screaming like little girls." Hutton turned back to the family and spotted Lisa working on a cup of coffee. "How is that?" he asked.

"Might be better with steak knives."

"It gets that way after a day or two."

Thomas could tell his sister was feeling the pressure. Of course, it was hard to see under all that armor. But you didn't go through the childhood they went through without being able to read one another. Besides her concern for Will, she was obviously worried about her man. *Her* man. Oh, she could say they were just friends 'til the cows came home, but Thomas knew better. Charlie Madison had gotten inside her head, and there was nothing she could do about it.

"Pastor?"

He looked over at Cindy. She and Jazmin had been sitting together, comparing notes.

"What do you—" She stopped and tried again. "What would you think if I contacted a few of the choir members and we got together?"

"For prayer?" he asked.

"No, uh—"

"For singing," Jaz interrupted.

Thomas took a moment, waiting for his patience to arrive. Cindy had been through some tough times, losing her husband just last year. But there was still her reputation, coming from one of those signs-and-wonders churches.

"I could call them up," she said. "The ones who wanted could meet us over at the church."

"To sing," he repeated.

"To . . . worship, yes. And we could pray, too."

He held her gaze. "At the church."

She nodded.

He weighed the decision. To call it a singing session was out of the question. If Aaron Buchanan, or the rest of the board heard that, there'd be no end to his headaches. But if it was a "prayer vigil" that just happened to have a few singers, well, that was certainly appropriate. After all, Christians still believed in prayer. And yet, for somebody like Cindy to take the lead. . . .

"Pastor?"

He looked over at one of the deputies on the phone. "Yes."

"It's Cascade Valley Care. It's about your father."

Thomas traded quick looks with his sister.

"What about him?" Lisa asked.

"He's missing."

✟

The door to Jason's mobile home creaked loudly no matter how careful he was to open it. But if he pulled slowly, he could keep the noise down so his mom wouldn't hear it over the TV. She always fell asleep in front of the TV. Drunk, sober, it made no difference—she never remembered to turn the thing off.

But tonight he heard nothing. That was good news. It meant she was out partying. With any luck, she wouldn't be home for a day. Or two.

He stepped inside and was immediately hit by the smell of cat boxes. Trixie or Pixie or Dixie just had another litter, which brought them to a grand total of—well, he didn't know how many cats they had in the place. Not that it made any difference. As far as he was concerned, one was too many. Before he even turned on the light, they began rubbing against his legs, demanding to be fed.

He headed for the fridge.

He'd parked the preacher kid's car half a dozen blocks away. Figured he didn't need Sheriff Hutton stopping by again. He was pumped. Big-time. Not only about what had happened, but about what would happen. They'd done it! They'd actually called something up. And by the looks of things, it wasn't exactly one of the good guys. Kristof always said it was possible. The books, the urban legends were filled with these types of stories. But to actually see it . . . that was a whole other matter.

He opened the fridge, the old seal cracking and popping. Inside was the usual fare—beer, a box of Domino's pizza from two nights before, an open bag of bread, a jar of dill pickles, cottage cheese growing some cure for cancer, a bunch of Burger King ketchup packets. He grabbed a brew and checked out a package of bologna. It hadn't been closed, so the edges of the meat were dried and curled, but it would still work for a sandwich.

He pulled out the stuff and shoved aside the dirty plates on the counter, along with one of the cats who had jumped up to join him. Was he scared about tonight? You bet. But he also trusted what Kristof said about him being the priest and all, and that nothing would happen to him. It hadn't this afternoon, at least until he got in its way. And it hadn't the night before. Truth be told, Jason didn't even know when the thing had manifested.

Of course, the buck hadn't been so lucky. Neither had Heather or the preacher kid. But, as Kristof always said, "There's no stopping karma. 'As you sow, you shall reap.'"

The cat jumped back on the counter and Jason shoved her off. He finished making the sandwich and started chowing down. Grabbing his cell phone, he hit Speed Dial. With Heather out of the picture, someone else would have to bring the candles and junk. And right now, that some-one was probably Ashley. He couldn't remember the last time they'd had sex—she'd only partied with him once or twice, and that was with half a dozen kids—but she was looking pretty good, and it wouldn't hurt to get her more involved.

She picked up on the second ring. "Yeah."

"You wouldn't believe what came down today."

"More cops?"

"Better."

"You ever figure out what that smell was?"

"Long story." He reached into his wallet to double-check on the photo of tonight's victim. It had been cut out of some old yearbook. She had been definitely hot in her day, and you could tell she advertised it. Why she was next, he didn't know or care.

He leaned against the sink. "Heather won't make it to-night, so I'll need you to bring the candles and stuff."

"No prob, I have some."

"And a cloth for the altar."

"Fancy."

"Yeah, well, we might have a special guest."

"We're finally going to meet Kristof?"

"More special than that."

"What's more special than Kristof?"

Jason hesitated.

"Let me guess. Long story."

"Pick me up on the way."

"Where's your bike?"

"I'll tell you later."

"What about a sacrifice?"

Trixie or Pixie or Dixie was back on the counter, nosing her way into the bologna package and pulling out the final piece of meat. He smiled. "Bring a pillowcase. We're going to have more than one."

"More than one sacrifice?"

"I told you, it's special."

"Cool."

"Later."

Jason snapped the phone shut. He took another bite and chewed, watching the momma cat enjoy her last meal. In a moment, he'd find her babies. Might as well make it a family affair.

†

It had taken little effort to remove the old man from Cascade Valley Care. With all the earlier commotion, it was simply a matter of returning to his room, wheeling him into the closet, and hitting the fire alarm. When everyone had cleared out, Kristof wheeled him through the back door, loaded him into the pickup, and they were gone.

The old codger barely noticed or cared. And when he asked Kristof who he was, Kristof simply explained he was his son who had come to take his father for a ride.

The explanation was as good as any. And it wasn't entirely a lie. In many ways, he could have been Kristof's father. Strict disciplinarian. Religious. Hypocrite. Not that his father was in the clergy. He was second-generation military. But the man had strong views on the rules in the Bible. And even stronger views of God's wrath when those rules were broken. The scars on Kristof's back, and his broken arm at age seven, had proven that.

But, like all hypocrites, his father's sins were eventually exposed. For him, it was Jim Beam and women. Heavy on the women. Of course, the truth shattered the boy's world. Still, it wasn't the divorce or never seeing his father again that pushed him into the deeper, more secret truths. It was the lie. The hypocrisy of the man he feared and once adored as a god.

But the god had fallen without showing the slightest repentance. Unfortunately, cancer got him before Kristof could. But there were others. So many others. . . .

"Say, Dad?"

The old man was looking out the passenger window and gave no response.

"Did you know Lisa is up visiting?"

He turned slightly.

"Yeah. She wanted to say hi. That would be okay, wouldn't it? If she stopped by to say hi?"

His lips gave the slightest tremble. Finally they formed a word, at least part of one. "Li . . . ?"

"That's right. Lisa."

He turned toward Kristof. "Here?"

"Well, not here. But we're going to see her. Would you like that?"

He stared a long moment, then looked back out the windshield.

"You remember your daughter, don't you? What you did to her?"

He continued staring, but Kristof could see something going on inside. And that was good. There would be little satisfaction in calling down judgment if the guilty was unaware of his crime. Hopefully, the connection would grow stronger when he saw her and they were reunited.

Not only there, but in hell.

Chapter Twenty-One

Despite the cold and the mosquitoes, Charlie began to strip.

Earlier, when he'd escaped the shooting, he searched the sky for the Big Dipper. Once he found it, he located the two stars at the front of the cup, then counted their distance by four until he found the North Star. He had no idea how many men were pursuing him, or if they were attempting to drive him into a trap. So, using the stars to find north, he circled around. It should have been an easy maneuver, especially with their hushed radio chatter and the snapping of branches under inexperienced feet.

But as he circled, they circled.

How was that possible? Infrared scopes? He doubted it, or they would have attacked by now. So how did they know his location without seeing him?

Of course, he knew he'd been set up, what with his new wardrobe, the M4, and the government-designed MOLLE backpack. Everything was arranged to make them think he was Kristof. Now Charlie understood how he was to help. Kristof was about to kill again, and this little bait and switch with Charlie would give him all the time he needed. Clever.

But how had the soldiers found him in the first place?

It didn't take Charlie long to realize the answer to both of his questions was the same: the tracker. Kristof had planted it on him. And it was probably Charlie's old friend Quinn himself who was back at the sheriff's office, feeding the soldiers his location.

Very clever indeed.

The first thing Charlie jettisoned was the MOLLE. It was the most likely candidate for storing the device—though he knew that when they found the pack, it would only provide further evidence he was Kristof.

But after several minutes of traveling without it and still being followed, he realized the tracker had not been in the pack.

Next, he checked the rifle. But he found nothing.

That left him with no alternative but to strip. First to come off was the jacket. He'd already checked the pockets. Now he checked the lining and collar.

Nothing.

Next he unbuttoned his shirt, carefully slipping it off so not to tear open the wound. His hands shook from the cold as he felt along the seams. The result was the same.

Then came the pants. He'd already checked the pockets and hadn't found anything except the saltshaker he'd hoped to use as a weapon and the loose change the old man from the arcade had dumped on him.

Again, nothing . . . but the numbing cold and growing swarm of mosquitoes.

He did a rectum check and again found nothing. He

knew the device could not be ingested. Even taken apart, it was too large for him to have been forced to swallow it without gagging, particularly if he was unconscious.

So where was it?

His core temperature was dropping and he quickly re-dressed. It wasn't until he slipped back into his shirt, look-ing down at his meticulously taped shoulder, that he had the answer. With trembling hands, he took one end of the tape and carefully peeled it back. He paused to warm his fingers, then pulled off the other end. Next he tried to re-move the neatly folded pad of paper towel. But the blood had soaked into it and dried, thoroughly sticking to it. To avoid crying out, he inhaled sharply at the same time he ripped it away.

The edges of the wound had dried. The inside was still red and moist. He turned, bringing it more fully into the moonlight. And there, in the very center, he caught a glint, a reflection of metal. Kristof had removed the casing of the pen and inserted the guts of the tracking device into the hole of his flesh.

Charlie cupped his hands and blew into them to warm them again. He flexed his fingers, increasing the circula-tion and mobility. And, though he was shaking, he dug his thumb and index finger into the wound.

The pain shot through his body like electricity, and for a moment he thought he would pass out. But he continued digging until he got a firm grip on the metal, hard pieces that were not flesh, and pulled. In his haste, and because of the shaking, the delicate wires broke off and he held only part of the unit. Enough to prevent it from working? He didn't know. He couldn't take the chance. He closed his eyes, said a quiet prayer, and dug back into the wound, feeling for the nonhuman pieces, then gently, wiggling them back and forth, one by one, he pulled them out.

Jazmin's plan made more and more sense . . . well, at least to Jaz, which, as far as she was concerned, made it a majority. That's why she kept working on Sharon. Of all the people in the sheriff's station, Sharon had the softest heart, which made her the easiest target. Technically, of course, Jaz didn't have to ask permission for anything. With Uncle Charlie gone and Lisa heading back to the old folks' home, she was a free agent. Still, there was the minor problem of getting the singers together, let alone doing it at the church. And for that bit of permission, there was no better person than Sharon . . . particularly when her husband was preoccupied on his cell phone, wearing out the carpet with his pacing.

"So, what do you think?" Jaz asked.

Sharon hesitated, then turned to Cindy, who sat beside her. "Do you really believe you could raise folks at this hour?"

Cindy, who was not the world's greatest salesman, simply looked down and nodded, then shrugged, then nodded again. Not exactly a sign of confidence. Fortunately the tactile blunder was interrupted by Sheriff Hutton shouting at the younger army guy. Jaz didn't hear what he said, but by the way everyone jumped, and how the sheriff's face turned the color of a Christmas poinsettia, she guessed it wasn't good.

"We've lost him," the army guy repeated. "He's off the screen."

Charlie's pal from the FBI looked up from his own laptop. "Signal's gone for me, too. Must be at his end."

"How's that possible?" the sheriff yelled.

Neither man had an answer, which only made him madder. Not that Jaz blamed him. He had a lot on his mind—catching a serial killer, finding a kid dragged off by a flying monster, Lisa's dad suddenly disappearing. It had not been a good day. Or night.

He turned to the older army dude. "Where's that chopper?"

"En route."

"You said that thirty minutes ago."

Jaz didn't know much about heart attacks, but it looked like the guy was about to blow a gasket.

"There was some red tape," the older dude explained.

Jaz couldn't tell if he was being truthful or just protecting his butt. Either way, it didn't make the sheriff any happier. "And while they're filling out requisition forms, our killer gets away."

Jaz waited until things settled back down before she returned to Sharon. "So, what do you think?" she said. "It would only be for a little while."

The woman stole another look at her husband. You could tell she didn't want to go around him, but you could also tell she was getting desperate. Real desperate.

"We're just going to pray," Jaz assured her.

The woman gave her a look.

"Well, all right, and maybe sing, but just a little."

After chewing up her bottom lip, Sharon turned to Cindy. "You'll watch over her? Be in charge?"

Cindy nodded—this time without the shrug.

Finally, keeping her eyes on Thomas, Sharon reached into her bag and pulled out a massive set of keys. "All right." She handed them to Cindy. "Do you know the code for the alarm?"

She shook her head.

"Nine, nine, ninety-three—Will's birth date."

Cindy nodded.

"You'll let me know who shows up?"

"Yes."

"And call when you're done?"

Cindy pushed up her glasses and nodded.

Before Sharon could dream up any more rules, Jaz got up and headed for the door. Sharon was still telling Cindy stuff, but it didn't matter. They had permission and that's all that counted. Any rules broken after this would simply be a "misunderstanding." That was the beauty of being a teenager. People still thought you were stupid. And that meant you could always fall back to the first and most important law for any teen . . .

It's easier to get forgiveness than permission.

✝

The plump orderly turned to Lisa from her father's unmade bed. "You know the police were already here."

"Right," Lisa said, "I just missed them."

"They said it was cool. I could go ahead and make up the bed."

Lisa nodded. She stood in the doorway of the room, searching for any missed clues. Not that they'd be so easy to find from out in the hall. "Did they say anything else?"

"Who?"

"The police. Did they mention any leads? Take any evidence with them?"

The woman shook her head. "They seemed kinda irritated. Two calls the same night." She gave a phlegm-filled cough, confirming the smell of cigarette smoke on her clothing. "Not that I blame them. It's the most excitement we ever had. You can come in, if you want."

Lisa nodded but remained at the door. "And you don't see anything in here out of the ordinary."

"No, ma'am."

Lisa kneeled down, checking the floor and under the bed. Everything was immaculate—beige linoleum tiles ran to beige plastic kickboards, up to beige wallpaper, displaying faint patterns of darker beige oak leaves.

The orderly crossed to the other side of the bed. "Good man. Never gives me no trouble. Always following the rules."

Lisa rose stiffly. "Yes, well, he's big on rules."

"His son, your brother, he's pastor of that big church at Getchel Heights, right? Hear real good things about it. My sister and her new husband, her *newest* husband, they go there."

"Lots of people do." Lisa continued scanning the room, letting the woman chatter on.

"Me, though, I ain't got time for religion, least for now. Figure I'll have plenty once I'm dead. Time, I mean. Well, probably religion, too." She broke into a hearty laugh that broke into more coughing.

When she caught her breath, Lisa asked, "Did you check his dresser?"

"For what?"

"See if any clothes are missing?"

"Honey, the man can barely button his shirt, I don't think he'd be packing clothes."

"Unless someone took him . . . like on a trip or something."

The orderly hesitated, then shuffled toward the dresser. Lisa almost stopped her when she reached for the drawer handles. There'd been no sign of dusting for fingerprints—she doubted the crime scene boys had even bothered. Then again, whoever took her father (and the sick feeling in her gut told her who) would be smart enough not to leave such obvious clues.

The woman opened the top drawer and quickly rifled through it. When she was finished, she went to the next. "Really, not that much here, you know. Not like he ever goes out. Though from time to time, they take him for a drive. Not your brother—don't see him much, too busy. But his wife, Sharon or Cheryl or whatever, she's here most every Saturday. And, of course, the grandson."

Lisa patiently waited as the woman rambled on and checked the last two drawers.

"Yes, sir, he loves that grandson. Least when he knows it's him. I remember once, back when he was talking, asking me if I had extra change so he could tip him. 'Tip him?' I says. 'Why do you want to tip him?' ''Cause,' he says, 'pizza delivery boys only get paid in tips.'" More chuckling, more coughing. She closed the last drawer and looked up. "Everything's here, far as I can tell."

Lisa nodded.

"Well, it's been good talking with you." The woman headed past her and out into the hallway. "If you got any more questions, don't hesitate to ask. But I wouldn't worry none. I'm sure he'll show up. They always do."

"Thanks."

The woman gave a wave and continued down the hall.

Lisa turned back to the room, taking one last look. Only then did she notice something strange on the nightstand: a half-empty picture frame. The other six or seven frames, of every shape and size, were filled with photos of her brother and family—except for the five-by-seven frame. Half of its photo had been torn away and was missing.

She turned to the orderly, who had already disappeared, then back to the room and the nightstand. It was a pewter frame with an engraving she couldn't quite make out. She swore quietly and raked her hand through her hair. She could hear blood pulsing in her ears, feel tension spreading across her shoulders and into her neck. She hesitated, then took a breath and ordered her legs to move.

They obeyed, but stiffly, begrudgingly.

As she entered the room, memories from her childhood flooded in. The ugly ones she pretended weren't there. They came with such force and power that her head started to grow light.

But she could do this. She had to do this.

To her right, the bed approached. His bed. She shied away from it as best she could and finally arrived at the nightstand. She was so unsteady, she had to reach down to it for support. She focused on the closest photo: seven-year-old Will proudly holding a string of trout. Beside it was the wedding photo of her parents. She took another breath to steady herself. Beside her parents was a picture just of her mother, the Christmas before she passed away.

More than ever, Lisa saw her resemblance to the woman—strong chin, aquiline nose, dark, probing eyes. Behind that frame was a photo of her father wearing a cockeyed party hat that read *Happy 80th*. For a moment, she couldn't continue. He looked so old, so frail. So lost. Beside it was another photo of Will and his parents. And, looming behind all of them, perfectly centered, the only eight-by-ten in the bunch . . . Lisa's graduation photo from the FBI Academy at Quantico.

She blinked. She had no idea how he got it. Or why it was displayed so prominently. The image blurred. She brushed the tears from her eyes and returned her attention back to the half-empty pewter frame. The remaining portion of the photo was of her brother, grinning, his arm around somebody whose image had been completely ripped away. She gave her eyes another swipe and glanced at the inscription on the frame: *Like father, like son.*

She frowned, started to reach out and touch it, then had second thoughts. Suddenly her cell rang. She pulled it from her pocket, fumbled, and nearly dropped it before answering. "Hello?"

There was no response.

"Hello?"

But somebody was there. She could hear the breathing.

"Hello, who is this?"

The voice was fragile, breathy. "Li. . . ."

She froze.

"Help. . . ."

"Who is this?"

More breathing.

"Who is this?"

Another voice came on. "Hello, Ms. Harmon."

She went cold, instantly recognizing it. "What do you want?"

"It's not what I want. It's what your father wants."

She leaned more heavily against the dresser.

"He would like a little visit."

She swallowed, not trusting her voice.

"Are you there?"

"Where are you?" She winced at how weak she sounded. "Where is he?"

"Remember the river site you and Charles Madison visited?"

"Is he with you?"

"I think that would be appropriate, don't you?"

"Is Madison there with you?"

"I'm afraid he's no longer an issue."

Her gut tightened.

"Still, there's your father. And he would so very much like to see you."

She took a breath, forcing her voice to remain even. "When?"

"Why, now, Ms. Harmon. The sooner, the better."

She took another breath. "What assurance do I have that—"

"He'll be waiting in your brother's pickup."

Before she could respond, the line went dead.

Chapter Twenty-Two

In just moments, Charlie would have to remove his shirt again. He was not looking forward to that. Especially since he was dangerously close to hypothermia. But if Lisa and Quinn were right about a helicopter coming, there was no other way. With the chopper would come infrared equipment. And with infrared equipment, there would be no escape.

Unless they were drawn to the wrong place.

The loose change in his pocket had given him the idea. That, and the saltshaker. It took little effort to find the source of water, a small pool at the base of a rocky bluff. Here he emptied all but two tablespoons of the salt from the shaker and filled the rest with water.

Now he had what any high-school science geek knew to be an electrolyte.

Next he scrounged up dried leaves and twigs, about an armful. He placed them against the side of the bluff under a small outcropping of rock. A cave would be better, but this would do.

Now came the tricky part.

He emptied his pockets of the loose change from the arcade. The quarters and dimes were worthless, but not the nickels and pennies. He found half a dozen of each.

Next he slipped off his boots and removed his cotton socks. They would serve best to insulate. Carefully he reached into his pocket and pulled out the remains of the tracker—mostly a printed circuit, but some copper wire as well. For the last article, he removed the paper towel from his wound. The tape was far less sticky this time, and for that he was grateful. Still, there was enough adhesive for his needs.

He poured the saltwater from the shaker onto the paper towel, completely saturating it. Then he reached for the longest piece of copper wire. He taped its end to a nickel and lay it on the socks. With shaking hands, he tore a piece of the wet paper, making sure it was smaller than the nickel, and placed it on the coin. Next he set a penny on the paper and tore another piece of paper, setting it on the penny. Then he set a nickel on top of that.

He was making a battery, each layer producing roughly one-third of a volt. The higher the stack, the greater the power.

By the third or fourth layer, his shaking grew so bad that he toppled the entire stack and had to start over. It was frustrating, meticulous work, but there was no choice and very little time.

He ran out of pennies at the sixth layer and figured it would have to do. He taped another piece of copper wire to the top penny, then placed it on the last nickel with another piece of paper in between.

He took the ends of the two copper wires and touched

217

them together, creating a spark against a piece of one of the leaves. By the second spark, the leaf began glowing as a tiny ember. He carefully placed other leaves around it, blowing, cupping his trembling hands around them, until they also ignited. He graduated to small twigs until he'd built a fire. But not too big—about three hundred BTU for his weight and metabolism. After thirty seconds he put out the flames, allowing the leaves to glow and smolder.

But it was one thing to mimic the heat of the human body, quite another to duplicate its appearance.

Now, at last, he slipped off his shirt, though he was quick to put his coat back on. Crossing to the pool of water, he dipped the shirt into it and wrung it out until it was merely damp. He returned to the embers and arranged them into the rough shape of a human torso. Finally, he spread his shirt over them. This would diffuse the heat, giving the approximate signature of the top half of the body. They would suspect the bottom half was under the outcropping of rock.

He'd barely folded the arms and placed the M4 in the center to look like he was holding it, when he heard the chopper. He stood up and studied his handiwork. It wasn't perfect, but the decoy should occupy them long enough for him to get away.

†

Despite the sheriff's calmness over the phone, Lisa knew he was feeling the pressure. He was too good not to. "The pickup is a ruse," he insisted. "I doubt Kristof even has your father."

"But he said—"

"I know what he said, but we're tracking him. We've got him up on the screen in front of us."

Lisa pulled out of Cascade Valley Care's parking lot and turned east on 528, heading toward the mountains. "Why would he choose the same location where the kids meet? Where Will disappeared?"

Hutton gave no answer.

"Hello?" Deciding to give him a hand, she offered, "Could Jazmin be right? Could there be a connection between the two—Will's disappearance and Kristof?"

"I'm asking you to stay put. Let us handle this."

"No offense, Sheriff, but so far you've done diddly. If you want to join me up there, great. The more the merrier."

"Ms. Harmon?"

She hesitated a second, deciding how best to make her point.

"Lisa?"

She closed her cell and slipped it back into her pocket.

✝

Cindy hung up the secretary's phone.

Jaz asked, "What'd she say?"

"The same." Cindy did her best to look pleasant, but you could tell she was bothered, big-time. They were getting nowhere. "She has a big day at work. She said she needs her rest."

Jaz blew the hair out of her eyes. She wanted to swear but thought better of it, considering they were inside a church and all.

"She might be able to meet after work tomorrow."

"*Tomorrow?* Did it dawn on her that he'll be dead by then?"

"Maybe if we just told them it was a prayer meeting—maybe that would do it."

"But it was singing that stopped it. I got nothing against prayer, Charlie does it all the time. But it was the singing."

Cindy nodded.

"So where are we?" Jaz asked.

Cindy looked down at the list. "Sophia is coming down with a cold—bronchitis, she thinks. Bonnie has midterms. Jennifer can come in after she drops the kids off at school."

"In five hours, real helpful. And the guys?"

Cindy shook her head then added, "Rob might be able to get an extended lunch hour."

"We need to do it now! Don't these people know how important it is?"

"You have to admit, it does sound pretty far-fetched."

"It's in the Bible. You showed it to me."

Cindy glanced down at the desk.

Jaz sighed dramatically, "Doesn't anybody believe that stuff?"

By the way Cindy gave no answer, Jaz had hers.

Finally, the woman ventured, "There's always Lydia."

"Who?"

"Lydia Sanchez. She's a big advocate of worship. Tries out for the choir every year, but. . . ."

"But what?"

"She's eighty-one and can't carry a tune in a bucket."

"It never stopped me."

Cindy smiled. "And what she lacks in pitch, she more than makes up for in volume."

"Give her a call."

Cindy reached for the church directory and flipped through it. "There's also Phil Stewart."

"What's his deal?"

"We've had some good talks about worship. He loves to sing, and he's actually pretty good."

"I didn't see him up onstage."

"He was injured in the war. Left side of his face is all burned up."

"So?"

"So Pastor Thomas doesn't think it would be a good idea to platform him."

"Platform him?"

Cindy glanced away. "Put him up where everybody can see him."

This time Jaz did swear. And for whatever reason, Cindy didn't feel a need to correct her.

✝

Will continued to float or sit or lie—he wasn't sure what he was doing. All he knew was he touched nothing, felt nothing, and saw only darkness, if you could call it seeing.

But the emotions kept surfacing. Every minute his resentment toward God grew stronger, fed by memories of lies, betrayals, broken promises. It's not as though Will hadn't kept up his end of the bargain—prayer, church, Bible reading—and don't forget all the youth group junk.

And what did God give him in return?

Leftovers. While everybody else was partying, drinking, hooking up, what was he getting?

The scraps. That was his great reward for playing by God's rules.

As the betrayals swelled up inside him, he could feel the emotions of the voices also growing, so subtle that at first it was impossible to tell which were his and which were theirs. But, just as his anger toward his father had gradually shifted to anger at God, so his emotions gradually shifted to those of the voices.

Like a babbling brook, their chatter was impossible to understand. At first. But the more he opened up and allowed himself to feel with them, the stronger they grew until they solidified into specific thoughts, words.

Liar. . . . Betrayer. . . .

The similarity of their thoughts to his own surprised him. So did their growing clarity.

. . . loves not. . . .

Struggling to stay calm, Will tried to speak. He wasn't sure if he was moving his mouth, but his thoughts were as clear as theirs: *Who . . . are you?*

The reply came in gibberish. He opened up more, giving them greater access.

We saw truth. . . .

We? Will thought. *Who is we?*

Enlightened and liberated . . .

Who? What?

The banished.

Will continued releasing control. They were much clearer now. And as their voices grew, his own seemed to lessen.

What truth? he thought.

Tyrant . . . loves not.

Who's a tyrant? God? You're saying God is a tyrant? Just thinking the words gave Will a certain freedom, a thrill.

If love Him not . . . destroyed.

He tried putting together the thoughts. *If you don't love God, He destroys you?*

Lucifer's challenge: if not love, we are destroyed.

Will caught his breath. *Lucifer, like the Bible's Lucifer?*

Challenged God. Said it is not love but fear.

I don't understand.

Worship in fear is not worship in love.

Will tried again. *Lucifer challenged God. . . .*

Yes! The chorus answered, louder than ever.

And he said what?

If we do not worship in love, we will be destroyed.

But you aren't destroyed, Will thought. *I'm talking to you now.*

Banished. Not destroyed.

You're banished?

Quarantined so all creation will see.

You're quarantined . . . here?

Yes.

To show creation . . .

Not show, prove. To prove who speaks truth.

You or God?

No! No! No! Suddenly Will felt their fear. More like terror. *Lucifer. Not us. Lucifer, Lucifer. We are his servants.*

How . . . many of you are there?

There was no answer.

He strained to listen, giving up even more control. Again he asked, *How many are you?*

After a long moment, the answer came.

Legion. . . .

Chapter Twenty-Three

"Hey, bro."

Jason looked up from lighting the candles on the log altar. "'Sup, Troy? You bring the refreshments?"

The chubby senior held up two shopping bags, glass bottles clinking inside. "Beer and vodka for the boys, alcopops for the girls—strawberry, pineapple, or cherry." He set them on the ground beside the altar.

"And the dope?"

Troy motioned behind him as Elliott emerged from the woods, stocking cap over his ears, spike tattoo around his neck. He held out a plastic bag. "Hydroponics sensimilla—don't come any better, dog."

Troy and Elliott high-fived.

Jason gave a nod of approval and leaned past the chalice of cat blood to light the final group of candles. Underneath the chalice sat the old photo of the chick from the yearbook.

"You're really doing it up," Troy said.

Jason answered, "We're expecting company."

"Company? Who?"

"Not that vampire guy," Elliott groaned.

"The one with the cat-eye contacts and filed teeth?" Troy asked.

Elliott shook his head. "What a jerk."

"But the babes loved him. Speaking of which"—Troy turned to Jason—"you got any fresh 'talent' coming to-night?"

Jason ignored him.

"And what about the sky-cladding?" Elliott asked. "We haven't done that for, like, forever."

Troy gave him a push. "It's too cold, moron."

"But we got the refreshments to keep 'em warm."

"True," Troy agreed. "And if that don't do it, I know a couple, three studs who'll be happy to light their fires."

They laughed in agreement, and when Jason glanced up, he saw them grinning like idiots. Of course, peeling off clothes and worshiping God naked was always a possibility, and a huge drawing card—especially for the guys. The girls, on the other hand, saw it for what it was—an act of yielding and liberation. Not that Jason didn't enjoy imbibing from time to time. But tonight, sex was the last thing on his mind. And it should have been with these two as well. Luckily, he had just the cure to help them focus.

"Before we do anything, we have to set the proper ambiance," he said.

"Yeah, ambiance." Elliott nodded. "Like what do you have in mind?"

"Things may get pretty intense, so we're going to need all the protection we can get."

"I got protection." Troy snickered, slapping his back pocket. "Tucked right here in the ol' wallet."

Again the boys high-fived.

"I'm serious," Jason said. "Something heavy-duty is coming down tonight."

The guys looked at him. "So what do you want us to do?" Elliott asked.

"You're the man." Troy grinned. "Whatever you say, we're on it."

Jason looked from one to the other, fixing his gaze.

Elliott fidgeted. "Seriously, dude. Whatever you want."

He motioned to the giant star outlined on the ground of the clearing. It was made from sand Ashley was hauling up from the river's edge. "See that pentagram she's making?"

They turned to watch as the skinny red-head meticulously poured the final line from a large, plastic bucket.

"Make sure the group stays inside it. For the entire ceremony. It'll keep them safe."

They nodded.

"I'm serious. No matter what happens, keep them in it."

"Got it."

"That's all?" Elliott asked.

"Not quite. That bag there?" He nodded to the pillow-case beside the altar. "It's got our sacrifices for tonight."

"Sacrifices?" Troy asked. "As in plural?"

"Like I said, this is a big one." He motioned to the pentagram. "I want you to find the closest tree to each of the five points and nail one of the sacrifices there."

"Cool," Elliott said.

"No prob," Troy agreed.

Jason nodded for them to begin and they slouched toward the pillow case. He knew they'd think, *No prob-*

lem—until they saw the cute cuddlies inside. And after that? Well, the assignment would definitely help them take things a bit more seriously.

✝

> *All the saints in heaven adore Thee;*
> *We bow before Thy throne.*

Jaz sat cross-legged on the stage, her head against a boom box that rested on her shoulder. Three others sat in chairs singing with her: Cindy, some cranky old lady by the name of Lydia who had almost less hair than Charlie, and Phil, the guy in a wheelchair with the messed-up face. Jaz thought they were doing pretty good, until she saw Cindy flinch. For the most part, their leader was sweet and encouraging, though every so often Jaz caught her trying to hide a wince.

> *As Thine angels serve before Thee,*
> *So on earth Thy will be done.*

They came to the end with Lydia throwing in a long and heartfelt, "*Aaa-mennn . . .*"

When she was done, Cindy gave another one of her sweet smiles. "Great, that was just . . . great."

"How did you like my harmony?" the old lady asked.

Cindy nodded and pushed up her glasses. "Very imaginative."

"Yes," Phil added. "That was really something, Lydia."

The old woman beamed.

Cindy motioned to the boom box and asked Jazmin, "Is that loud enough? Can you feel the vibrations okay?"

"Why, aren't I singing the right notes?"

"Oh, no, you're fine, you're very close."

Jaz gave her a look.

Cindy smiled. "Sometimes."

Jaz blew at her hair and brought the boom box closer. She wasn't sure what Cindy heard, but what she felt sounded pretty good. Both Phil and the old lady were really into it, and she could definitely feel the little ripples of power and warmth around them.

"Okay." Cindy cranked up another smile. "Why don't we try something a little more . . . familiar? 'Amazing Grace.' Everybody knows that one, right?"

She began:

Amazing grace . . .

The others joined in.

How sweet the sound.

Once again Cindy did her best imitation of a smile.

That saved a wretch like . . .

She held up her hands. "I'm sorry, I—" She reached into her pocket and fumbled with her cell phone. "Sorry." She opened it and answered. "Hello?" She nodded. "I'll tell her." Another nod. "Yes, yes, we're worshiping right now. Yes. Good-bye."

She closed her phone.

"What's happening?" Jaz asked.

For a second, Cindy was lost in thought.

"Hello?"

She looked up. "Oh, sorry. That was Sharon. The killer"—she took a breath—"he's kidnapped Pastor Thomas's father."

The group traded looks of alarm.

"You're kidding," Phil said.

"That's horrible," Lydia exclaimed.

Cindy nodded. "They're heading up there to catch him now."

"Up where?" Jaz asked.

Cindy turned to her. "The same place where Will disappeared."

✝

Charlie leaned against the trunk of a big cedar, catching his breath. He'd pushed hard, not only to distance himself from the decoy, but to raise his body temperature. He was still shivering, but not like before. He could hear the chopper about a mile away, its engine droning, its blades pounding the air. But for the moment, he was safe.

He'd been careful to keep the North Star at two o'clock. This assured a north-by-northwest course, which allowed him to avoid his pursuers while still heading toward the coastal basin and civilization where he could clear his identity. Unfortunately, it involved climbing a ridge, which left him vulnerable to surveillance. He could circle around, but that would take time. Besides, a higher elevation would give him better bearings. So, gulping in another breath of sharp, cold air, he pushed off and continued his climb.

He arrived at the summit just in time to hear automatic rifle fire. He turned and saw the chopper's distant spotlight illuminating the woods, enabling the soldiers to better attack and kill his pile of leaves. The decoy had worked. But not for long. They'd soon discover his ploy and resume their search.

He looked west, searching for houses or roads. There were a handful of twinkling lights in the distance, but nothing of promise, except . . . three, maybe four miles away, he spotted two sets of headlights approaching, one following the other. Closer still, beside a dark band which could only be the river, he saw a faint, orange glow. Like fire. He squinted, trying to identify it. It wasn't a single light, but a series of smaller ones. Tiny specks clumped together. And just beyond them he spotted yet another car that had either stopped or was traveling very slowly.

The gunfire behind him ceased. He turned and heard faint shouting, no doubt angry oaths as they discovered the leaves. The helicopter began to rise and Charlie turned, racing down the hill toward the distant glow.

Chapter Twenty-Four

No one had to tell Lisa. As soon as her headlights caught the vehicles parked alongside the gravel road, she knew what was going on—another ceremony, another Black Mass. But as she slowed and searched the cars, there was no sign of her brother's pickup.

She peered into the forest where she knew the clearing to be and caught glimpses of candlelight. Maybe that was where Kristof and her father were.

No. "In the pickup," he had said. "He'll be waiting in your brother's pickup."

She stopped the car and looked back to see if she had somehow missed it.

Of course she hadn't.

Maybe she was early.

She knew better than that, too. Kristof was a pro. He'd be there in plenty of time before her to check out the place.

Then, up ahead, a hundred yards or so, just before the bridge, she spotted the red glow of a vehicle's reflector. She removed her foot from the brake and eased the car forward, careful to search the hill on her left and the woods sloping to the river on her right. As she drew closer, she saw it was indeed her brother's truck. It had been parked perpendicular to the road, the front facing the woods. From her position she could see the entire cab. And, though its windows were fogged, on the far side behind the wheel, she made out the dark form of someone sitting.

The knot in her stomach tightened.

At thirty yards, she pulled to a stop. She shifted into Park and left the motor running. Releasing her seat belt, she opened the door. She stepped into the cold and called out, "Kristof?"

No answer.

She unholstered Kristof's .45—the one she hadn't bothered to hand over at the nursing home, careful to keep it down at her side and out of sight.

"Kristof?"

Though he could be in the truck, she had her doubts. More likely he was staked out in the woods, his sights already trained on her. She listened intently, her body ready to spring at the slightest sound. There was nothing but the din of frogs.

She continued forward.

If Kristof had wanted to take her out, he'd had more than enough chances—the restaurant, the old folks' home. Like the other victims, she'd received her warning: 'Judgment without mercy to anyone who has not been merciful.' But it hadn't been the right time. He liked his irony, his poetic justice. And by the look of things, neither had been correct. With luck, she'd rescue her father before they were.

She focused on the shadow inside the truck. Most likely it was her father. Maybe he was already dead, his corpse propped behind the wheel. That would be hard, but not the end of the world.

White puffs of breath rose faster from her mouth—much to her frustration and, no doubt, to Kristof's satisfaction. The time had come to do what she'd vowed never to do, what the years of hatred and hurt and rage made impossible. She took a deep breath and called out to her father.

"Dad?"

There was no response. The form did not move. She looked up the hill to her left, the river to her right. Then back to the truck.

"Dad? Is that you?"

She was ten yards away now. "It's me. Lisa."

There was movement. Slight. The turning of a head. Her heart sank and soared.

"Are you okay?"

Five yards. Once again her pulse pounded in her ears.

"Dad?"

At last she arrived. She stared at the shape behind the fogged glass, knew it was staring back at her. She looked down at the door handle. She didn't have to do this. Let someone else rescue him. Hutton was on the way; let him do his job. And if he was too late, well—she pushed the thought out of her mind, but it returned—if he was too late, maybe the man would finally get what he deserved.

The thought filled her with guilt and shame. As much as she despised him, she could never allow that. Through some primordial, genetic link, she still thought of him as her father. She'd proved it earlier in the nursing home. She'd proved it in the drive out here.

And she hated him for it. And she hated her weakness. And she hated Kristof for playing it.

She reached for the door, her heart hammering. She felt the cold dampness of the metal against her fingers. She took another breath. And then she threw it open.

He sat behind the wheel and stared blankly at her. His cheeks were more sunken than she remembered, his skin blotched and paper-thin. But it was the eyes that sucked out her breath. She'd never seen them so sad.

His image blurred. Whether the tears were hatred or sorrow, she didn't know. She angrily swiped at them but more came. Her throat tightened, making it impossible to speak, difficult to breathe. The helplessness made her even angrier. How many ways did he still control her? She wiped her dripping nose and took another swipe at her eyes. Only then did she notice his hands. Each was hand-cuffed to the steering wheel.

✝

"Bread daily our day this us give."

Jason scanned the small group as they held their candles, repeating the prayer after him.

"Bread daily our day this us give."

Even though they were drunk or stoned or both, everyone knew the importance of the ritual. Word had gotten out. This was a big deal. The biggest.

"Name thy be hallowed."

He always knew it was possible. But for a manifestation

to actually occur—and at *his* beckoning—he couldn't be more pleased. Or excited.

They repeated: "Name thy be hallowed."

Of course he was also frightened. But to wield this much power, well, it didn't get any better.

"Heaven in art who father our."

At first he thought something would happen at the beginning of the ceremony, but as they approached its end, he understood. The climax of power could come only at the climax of the ritual.

"Heaven in art who father our."

That's why he waited until now to burn the woman's photo.

"Lord of light and Lord of darkness"—he turned to retrieve her picture from under the chalice—"we present to you—" He came to a stop. Another photo had been added. Not only was there the woman's photo, but now there was one of some old-timer, too. He spun around and searched the woods. In the time between the setup for the ceremony and now, someone had slipped the second photograph under the chalice.

But who would do such a thing? No one would challenge his authority like this. No one, except. . . .

He turned back to the group, trying to see under their hoods. Then he looked beyond them and into the night.

Kristof was there. Jason smiled. At last, the great Kristof had come to witness firsthand what he could do.

Louder, more empowered, he improvised. "We bring before you, not one sacrifice, O Lords, but two."

Some of the group looked up. A few exchanged glances.

"Two sacrifices. One for You, Jesus the Christ, and one

for you, Lucifer our Lord." He was making it up on the spot, but he liked it. More important, he knew Kristof would.

He pulled the photos out from under the chalice and reached for the largest of the black candles. "We purge them with the flame of your terrible and holy fire." He held the candle to the pictures, noticed the trembling of his hands.

The photographs blistered then caught fire—blue-green flames turning to red.

He looked up, breathing more heavily, searching the woods. Not for Kristof this time. But for glowing eyes, black mist, a glimpse of wings.

There was nothing.

The photos continued to burn.

He strained to hear any sound, a screech, rustling branches. Nothing. Just frogs and some kid coughing. He saw Troy raise his head and look up at him. Ashley was doing the same. He glanced down at the photos and saw the reason. A light had started to glow in the center of the flame. Not the color of the fire, but white. As pure and intense as a welding arc. He was so startled, he allowed the photos to slip from his fingers. But it didn't matter. The light remained, hovering where it first appeared . . . and growing larger.

Jason took a half step back, watching in fear and wonder.

Other kids were looking up, starting to murmur.

"It's okay!" Jason called to them. His voice was thinner than he intended. "It's what we expected." The light continued to grow until it was the size of a soccer ball. With it came the stench he had smelled before. Rotten eggs.

Suddenly, it exploded, lighting up the clearing with a flash brighter than any day. The kids screamed, and Jason staggered back to join Troy and the group.

Then it disappeared. It was over in a second, except for the smell.

And the creature.

The thing hovered in front of the altar. A thick, black vapor. And cradled in its arms was the preacher kid. Unconscious or dead.

As before, Jason felt the urge to look up into its eyes. But he knew better. He clearly remembered their power. "Don't look into its eyes!" he shouted. "Don't—"

The shriek stopped him cold. The thing extended its wings as wide as the altar. It dropped the preacher kid, his body falling to the ground with a dull thump. Then, without flapping its wings, it began to rise, growing denser.

Jason turned back to the group. By now everyone was staring at it, gazing up into its face.

"No!" he shouted. "Don't look at its eyes."

But no one heard. If they did, they refused to listen. Some started to sniff. A few began to cry.

"I'm sorry, man."

He turned to see Troy, staring up at the creature, tears welling in his eyes. "What are you doing?" Jason shouted. "Don't look at it! Don't look into the eyes!"

But, like the others, he paid no attention as the tears spilled onto his face. "I'm sorry." He swallowed hard and started backing away. "I'm so sorry. . . ."

✝

"Whoa!" Jaz raised her hands, bringing the song to a stop. "Do you feel that?"

Cindy frowned. "I'm sorry . . . feel what?"

She turned to Phil and Lydia, who were equally clueless.

"What do you feel?" Cindy gently repeated.

Jaz closed her eyes. It was gone. Sometimes when she tried too hard, she felt nothing. But what she had experienced just a moment ago. . . . "It's like what I felt in Will's room. And with that thing on the mountain. Coldness. A pressure." She opened her eyes and looked at Cindy. "Like you feel sometimes when you're worshiping."

"Here?" Cindy asked. She looked around the sanctuary. "I don't feel any—"

"No." Jaz shook her head. "Not here."

Phil motioned for her attention. "What do you mean, 'pressure'?"

"When we were singing just then, there was this, this vibration, this coldness pushing back."

"Pushing back?"

"Against our singing, yeah."

Phil didn't exactly look convinced. Not that Jaz blamed him.

Cindy tried to explain. "It's like there's this battle. Sometimes, when it's real intense, we can feel it. Jaz more than me. We can feel it; we just can't see it."

"A battle you can feel," Phil repeated.

Jaz nodded. "Yeah."

"But that's not visible."

Cindy glanced away, knowing how lame it sounded.

But suddenly the old lady spoke up, quoting, "For our

struggle is not against flesh and blood." Everyone turned to her as she continued, "But against the rulers, against the authorities, against the powers of this dark world and against the spiritual forces of evil in the heavenly realms."

No one said a word. Who could blame them?

She looked at them. "It's in the Bible."

More silence. But since silence was never one of Jazmin's specialties, she repeated herself. "Anyway, that's what I felt just now when we were singing."

"But now it's gone," Phil said.

She closed her eyes, feeling for something, anything. "I think so." She slowly turned until she felt the slightest brush of coolness against her face. "There." She opened her eyes. "It's real faint, but it's coming from that direction." She turned back to Cindy who looked a little concerned. "What?"

"That's the direction of the mountain."

"The mountain?" Phil asked. "The same mountain you saw that—whatever you saw?"

Jaz nodded.

He continued. "Which is also where Will disappeared?"

Cindy turned to him. "And where they're going to try and catch that serial killer."

The old lady must have said something, because everyone turned back to her as she finished. ". . . ask the obvious question?"

"Certainly," Cindy said.

"What are we doing here?"

Everyone looked puzzled.

She continued. "If all of the action is up on that mountain of yours, why are we sitting around down here?"

Cindy pushed up her glasses. "What do you mean?"

The old lady scoffed. "You know what I mean. Why aren't we up on that mountain, kicking butt in person?"

Cindy and Jaz traded looks.

✝

Thomas and Sharon had borrowed Aaron Buchanan's SUV and were following Sheriff Hutton back to the river. The sheriff had made it clear he didn't think they should, but there was no way he could stop Thomas. After all, his son, his sister, and now his father were all there. He'd be there, too, to help however he could.

They were only a couple minutes from the site when Sharon's cell phone rang. She pulled it from her coat pocket and answered. "Hello? Yes, we're almost there."

Thomas glanced at her from behind the wheel. "Who is it?"

She mouthed the name "Cindy," then returned to the phone. "Really?"

He took a breath and blew it out. Earlier, Sharon had confided in him about the "prayer meeting" she had sanctioned. He wasn't crazy about it, but there was little he could do. "Herding cats." That's what his father always said. "Pastoring is like herding cats."

"I see." Sharon nodded. "And you all agree?"

He looked to her. "Agree to what?"

She covered the phone and replied, "They're coming up to join us."

"No way." He shook his head. "Absolutely not."

She returned to the phone. "Are you really sure that's such a good idea?"

"Let me talk to them."

"Yes, I understand. No, that makes perfect—"

He reached for the phone. "Let me talk to them."

"Just a minute, dear, Pastor Thomas would like to speak to you."

She handed him the phone and whispered, "Be nice."

He nodded and took it. "Hello, Cindy?"

"Hi, Pastor." Her voice was as sweet as ever. "We took a vote and decided we're coming to join you."

"We?"

"Our little . . . prayer group."

"That's not a good idea. It's too dangerous. It's better if you and the others just stay—"

"Hello, Pastor? Are you there?"

"Yes. I was saying—"

"Can you hear me?"

"Yes, Cindy, I can hear you fine."

"Hello, Pastor?"

"I'm right here. I can hear you."

There was no response.

"Cindy? Cindy, can you hear me? Cindy?"

Nothing.

"Cindy?"

Sharon reached for the phone. "You must have lost connection."

He looked at the signal bars, trying to read them without his glasses. She relieved him of the phone before he had the chance. "It can happen," she said as she slipped it back into her coat. "Out here in the mountains."

"Yes," he said, eyeing her. "It can happen."

She turned to look out the window.

He watched her another moment before returning to the road. *Yes, sir, just like herding cats.*

Chapter Twenty-Five

Through her tears, Lisa saw the wavering form of her father staring back at her. She looked away and wiped her face, then turned back to the cab, searching. What was Kristof up to? What was his plan?

A six-inch strip of silver duct tape hung from the mirror. Near the end, stuck in the gumminess, were two small keys. One for each pair of handcuffs. Her cell vibrated and she ignored it. She looked to her dad. The dome light reflected shiny tracks of moisture running down both cheeks.

The phone vibrated again. She leaned into the cab, closer to the tape and keys—searching for a thread, any sign of a booby trap.

Again, the phone vibrated. She yanked it from her pocket. "What?"

"Hello, Lisa."

The voice stopped her.

"I can call you Lisa, can't I? Your father has spoken so much about you, I feel I know you intimately. And I do mean, *intimately.*"

Struggling to keep her voice even, she demanded, "What do you want?"

"Why, the same as you."

"What?"

"Justice, Lisa."

She glanced to her father.

"The day of the Lord is at hand. His justice will be poured out with swift and terrible fury."

She pulled her head from the cab and searched the hill above them. "I'm a big fan of leaving justice to the judicial system."

"The same judicial system that let him destroy you?"

It was supposed to be banter to keep him talking, but he'd already landed a blow. Referring to her father's broken health, she answered, "He got what he deserved."

"Did he, now? Look at him."

She continued searching the woods.

"Look at him!"

She turned back to the truck. Her father had not taken his eyes from her.

"Pampered. Surrounded by a loving family. He doesn't even remember what he did. But you, you live with it every day, don't you? Every day of your loveless life."

"What do you want?"

"To provide you the opportunity."

"Opportunity?"

"To carry out the Lord's justice."

"I thought *I* was the sinner. Isn't that what your card said?"

"In due time, Lisa. In due time. Do you see those keys hanging from the mirror?"

She ignored him and turned back to the woods. "Listen, I don't know what sick game you think you're playing, but—"

The window beside her exploded. She cried out and dropped to her knees, turning as she raised her gun, sweeping to the right, then left, then center.

There was no other movement. No other sound, except the frogs.

She spun back to her father. Pieces of glass covered his coat and lap. He was terrified and confused, but unharmed.

✝

The creature drifted toward the kids as they kept backing away, sniffing, crying.

"Dude," Elliott croaked. "Step back, man."

Jason turned to him.

Elliot's face was wet with tears. He motioned to the ground at their feet. "Stay inside the pentagram. Like you said, we're safe in here."

Jason frowned. By now the outer edge of the pentagram was ten feet in front of them, maybe more. Yet the group kept backing up like it was closing in on them. "What are you talking about?" he said.

Elliott gave no answer, and Jason held his ground until Troy's meaty hand grabbed his shoulder and pulled him back to join them.

"What are you doing?" Jason demanded.

"Don't mess," Troy choked out the words. He pointed to the ground. "Stay inside. It's moving to protect us."

"Moving?" Jason said. "It's not moving anywhere."

"Stay inside," Ashley repeated from behind him. He turned to see her with another girl. Both were looking up to the creature, their eyes full of tears as they continued backing up. "We're only safe if we stay inside."

He turned to the rest of the group. Everyone was crying and staring up at the thing. "What's going on?" he repeated.

No one answered as they continued backing up, pushed by a line they thought was moving and a creature whose spread wings were herding them back like cattle. The temptation for Jason to look into its eyes was fierce, but he was able to resist, keeping his vision focused on its body, its wings, noticing how they grew darker and darker, almost as if the kids were feeding it. He stayed with the group as they passed over the back edge of the pentagram, completely outside the symbol now. And *still* they continued moving backward. He felt sand under his feet, realized they reached the river's narrow beach. Then he heard rippling and splashing. Those behind him were entering the treacherous water.

"It's driving you into the river!" he shouted.

"Yes!" Elliott exclaimed. "We'll be clean. It's leading us to the water to clean us."

"That's right!" Ashley cried.

"Yes," another agreed.

"No!" Jason yelled. "It's a trick!"

"I can feel it!" a girl from the back cried. "I feel it cleaning me!"

"Keep going!" another shouted.

"Yes," others agreed, "yes!"

They continued deeper into the icy water. With an

oath, Jason turned and pushed his way through the kids to the rear of the group. The shorter members were up to their thighs, barely able to stand against the swift current.

"Stop!" he shouted. He waded toward the smallest, who was about to be swept away. "It's a trick! The river will kill you! It's a trick!"

"I am not in a habit of repeating myself. Now get up."

Lisa hesitated.

"I will not ask again."

Keeping the phone to her ear, she rose to her feet.

"Do you see the keys attached to the tape?"

"Yes."

"Do you know what they are for?"

Again she scanned the woods, eliminating areas that had no access to the shot-out window.

"Lisa?"

"They belong to the handcuffs."

"Two pairs of handcuffs, two keys. Now, the river lies sixteen yards in front of the truck."

She glanced down the bank, saw the reflection of the swift, dark water.

"Depending upon your speed and the Lord's favor, you will be able to release your father in approximately twenty to twenty-five seconds. Unfortunately, at an average velocity of three feet per second, that leaves you a bit short on time."

"I don't understand."

"Of course you do. It's your choice, Lisa Harmon. It has always been your choice."

Before she could respond, she heard movement at the front wheels. She ducked around the door and spotted a nearly invisible fishing line pulling a short log from the tire. She dropped, her eyes following the line into the darkness, and raised her gun. She fired four, five, six rounds, before she noticed the truck moving away from her, starting down the embankment.

She raced to it and leaped inside, undergrowth already scraping against the door. She grabbed the emergency brake and yanked. It offered no resistance.

The pickup's speed increased.

She looked at the gearshift, then at the floorboard. The clutch pedal told her it was manual, and she doubted her father could help. She reached for the duct tape, stripped the keys free, and scooted closer. Grabbing his right hand, she turned it over and found the lock. She inserted the first key but it didn't fit. Wrong one.

The truck dipped sharply. Looking out the windshield, she saw the river racing at them.

She fumbled with the second key, managing to drop the first. She'd worry about it later. She inserted the second key into the cuffs and turned, feeling their click and release as they gave way. She pulled her father's wrist free, then dropped to the floorboard, searching for the first key. It was difficult to find in the shadows—more so when her father's free hand fell on top of her head. An accident? A gesture? She didn't know. It still gave her the creeps.

She spotted a glint of metal on the rubber mat under his foot. She reached for it just as the truck lurched, slamming her head into the bottom of the dash. She may have lost consciousness, she wasn't sure. When she opened her eyes, she saw water flooding the floorboard.

She craned her neck, looking up. "Dad?"

He remained behind the wheel, staring out the windshield, terrified at what he saw.

She turned back to the floorboard, searching. The key was gone. The water had moved it. She dropped lower, rummaging under the seat, reaching into the wet darkness. She felt pieces of metal, the seat track, a crushed soda can. But no key. She pressed closer, her face against his leg, searching under his feet, fingers blindly groping. Nothing but trash and grit. She pressed closer still, icy water now up to her shoulder, until. . . .

There! Wedged under the gas pedal.

With fingers numbing from the cold, she pulled out the key and rose, just as the truck lunged violently and dropped. Water poured through the open door behind her.

"Li. . . ."

She was startled at his voice. "It's okay!" she shouted. "We're all right!"

She reached across his chest for his left hand. He watched, frightened and confused. She grabbed his wrist and turned it. His breath was hot against her bare neck.

Water churned about their chests now, icy cold, sucking out her air. It piled against his door and window. She heard the creak of metal, felt the passenger side rising. The dome light flickered once, twice, and went out as the truck continued tipping. Now there was only darkness and roiling water and bodies.

She searched his wrist and found the lock. She inserted the key and the cuffs gave way.

The water had risen to her shoulders.

"Liiii. . . ."

She felt her father's face. It was nearly submerged.

"Hang on, Dad."

She tugged, trying to pull him up and out, then remembered the seat belt.

"Liisss—" He gagged, then stopped as the turbulent waters covered him.

"Dad!"

It was time to cut her losses and get out. Time to turn and push through her door to safety.

But he was her father. The man who loved her, who gave her life . . . who crippled her and ruined her. There wasn't a day that she didn't hate him.

But he was her father.

She pressed her face to the roof of the cab, to the four-inch pocket of air that remained. There was still time. In this cold, even if his lungs filled with water, there was a chance she could revive him. She took a gulp of air and dropped back into the paralyzing coldness. She found the seat belt, followed it to the latch, and pressed the release. It gave way easily. She pulled, but his arm was tangled. She pulled one way, then the other, only making it worse.

Her lungs started crying for air.

She tried one last time with no success and surfaced to breathe. But instead of air, she slammed into the roof of the cab. The truck had rolled farther. She slid along the roof toward her door where she found two inches of remaining air in the corner. Splashing, trying not to panic, she gulped in a breath and then another, all the time knowing she should get out. *No!* She pushed the thought from her mind, took a third gulp, and dove back under. She found his arm and, this time working the belt instead of the arm, she succeeded. But the retractor was jammed. She had to keep pushing and pulling the strap away, reaching across his chest, insuring the other arm wouldn't tangle. Her lungs began burning for air, but she would not stop. His face floated before her—mouth open, eyes bulging and lifeless. She cried out, losing precious breath, but continued to struggle until he was finally free.

She grabbed his arm and pulled him toward her door. But the current had closed it. The cab was completely submerged. She pushed against the door. It would not give. Fighting the panic, she slammed her shoulder into it once, twice. Nothing.

Her head was growing light. She found the steering column with her feet. Using it for leverage, she smashed her back into the door again and again with no result. She had to breathe. Even if it was water. Anything to extinguish the fire in her lungs. One breath, maybe two and it would be over. No more fighting, no more panic. There were worse ways to—

No!

She thought of the windshield and turned to kick it out. The burning was unbearable. Just one breath. One cooling breath is all it would—

She saw a black shape dart by. The door shuddered. Someone pounded, then yanked. Suddenly, it gave way. An arm reached down, wrapping around her, tugging. She could help by letting go of her father, but she wouldn't.

A face came into view. Charlie!

More pulling, tugging. Her head hit the door frame and

a moment later she surfaced—coughing, gagging, gulping in air.

"Dad!" she gasped, "my—"

"You've got him!" Charlie shouted. "You've got him!"

She looked down and to her astonishment saw she was still clutching him. She had not let go.

Charlie circled around and grabbed her father's other arm. They pushed off from the pickup, holding his body between them. The current was strong, carrying them dozens of yards before they finally touched the riverbed and struggled to drag him to shore.

She barely noticed the nearby kids as she and Charlie pulled him out, as she laid him on the ground and began pounding the water from his lungs. Finally, she flipped him onto his back and began giving him mouth-to-mouth. Mouth-to-mouth to the one person who had destroyed her. Forcing life back into the man who had taken hers.

Chapter Twenty-Six

Jason turned to the commotion up the beach. Some man and woman hovered over an old dude they'd just dragged from the river. Suddenly the old timer started coughing and hurling. And as he coughed, the creature in front of the group screamed. But it wasn't like the other times. This scream was shriller, as if it was mad or in pain or something. It shook its head from side to side like it had been hit. As a result it broke its gaze with the kids and seemed to grow clearer—the solid blackness dissolving, becoming more like the misty vapor it had originally been.

"What the—how'd I get here?" Troy said.

Jason looked over at the boy, then to the rest of the group. Everyone was staring at each other, surprised and confused.

Elliott shook his head. "Too much pot."

One of the guys in the back shouted, "I'm freezing my tail off!"

"Get out of the water!" Jason ordered. "All of you, get out! And don't look at that thing! I'm telling you, don't look into its eyes!"

Puzzled and still very frightened, the kids sloshed back to shore. They spread out along the bank, keeping their distance from the creature and doing their best not to look at it. Some of the girls were still crying, but Jason figured it was more from fear than anything else.

Once again the thing screamed, puffing itself up, obviously trying to get their attention.

Troy joined Jason's side. "What is that thing, man?"

"I'm . . . not sure."

"I seen this picture once, where—"

"Shoot it!" a voice shouted from the woods.

They spun around to see Sheriff Hutton and a young deputy entering the clearing.

"Shoot it!" the deputy cried. "Shoot it!"

The creature pulled back within itself and faced them. Although the sheriff had drawn his gun, preparing to fire, he was unable to pull the trigger. Instead, it slipped from his hands as he stared up at the thing.

"Sheriff!"

He continued to stare.

The deputy prepared to fire his gun, but in an instant, the creature darted across the clearing, a blur of black mist. It grabbed the deputy's neck and lifted him off the ground. The man kicked and squirmed and yelled, until the thing flung him toward the altar. His cry was cut short as he slammed headfirst into the log. There was a crack of wood or vertebrae, or both, as his body dropped limp to the ground, just a few feet from the preacher kid.

Girls screamed and the group ran to one another, huddling in panic. The sheriff seemed unable to do anything as the creature turned back to face him. Instead of attacking, it simply held his gaze, paralyzing him, its darkness once again growing. The sheriff kept swallowing over and over again until he suddenly blurted out, "I'm sorry . . . I didn't. . . ." He swallowed again. "I. . . . " He shuddered. "I didn't know. . . ." He lowered his head and began to softly cry. "I didn't . . . I didn't know . . ."

The creature spread its wings as the sheriff slowly dropped to his knees, sobbing like a child.

Thomas slid the SUV to a stop behind the sheriff's car with its flashing red and blue lights. He hopped out and raced over to Sharon's side.

Reading his urgency, she waved him on. "Go on! I'll catch up! Go!"

He nodded and ran into the woods, barely seeing the path. He slipped once and then again, cracking his shin on a fallen tree, but he continued until he finally staggered into the clearing and slowed to a stop.

A giant, winged creature, right out of Dante's *Inferno*, stood near the center. It towered nearly ten feet high. Kneeling at its feet, with his head bowed, was Sheriff Hutton. Beyond him, at the river's edge, kids were standing in the moonlight. And to the right, at the foot of the altar, he saw his son.

"*Will!*"

It took a moment for Will to open his eyes. Longer than that to focus. He was lying on trampled ferns and grass.

"Will!"

Directly beside him, he saw a man sprawled out, his head twisted at an impossible angle.

"Will, can you hear me?"

He lifted his head and turned toward his father. A thick black mist shimmered between them. It was the thing, the creature.

"Will?" His father was terrified. "Can you hear me, son?"

"Don't look at the eyes!" somebody shouted.

Will turned to see a bunch of kids huddled by the river. One of them was Jason Ballard.

"Will!"

He turned back to his father. The man was trying to find a way around the mist.

"Stay back!" Will's voice was hoarse and raspy.

"Are you hurt? Are you—"

"I hate you!"

That brought his dad to a stop. Good. There was plenty more where that came from—Will had the memories, fresh and alive, to prove it.

"What?"

"I hate you."

The creature grew darker, more ominous. Will smiled. But instead of backing down, his father took a step toward them. Gutsy, Will gave him that. And, for whatever reason, the thing seemed to pull back.

"You don't mean what you're saying," his dad said. "You've been injured, you've been—"

"Stay back!" The shouting made him cough harder.

"Will?" his mom cried.

He turned to see her enter the clearing, her hand already to her mouth. Such a weak woman. She could have stood up to Dad. Demanded he be a real father. But she never did.

His dad took another step toward him. The thing countered and continued drifting back until it was at Will's side.

"Hypocrite!" The word came before Will even finished the thought.

"Wh—"

"Liar!"

"I don't. . . ." His father shook his head. "I don't understand."

"You preach love. . . ." Suddenly Will's eyes burned with tears, which made him all the more angry. "But you don't know the first thing about it!"

"Son, this isn't you talking."

"Oh, it's me talking, all right. For the first time in my life, it's me."

He felt an icy chill. Noticed the creature had lowered its hand onto his shoulder. He looked back to his father, delighted at the shock on the man's face.

"Can you move?" his dad asked. "Can you scoot away from that thing?"

"Why?"

"Because it hurt you."

"You're the one who hurt me! You and your God!" The words surprised Will, but they made perfect sense.

"I don't. . . ." His dad took another half step forward. "I don't understand."

"Look into its eyes," Will said with a sneer. "We'll be more than happy to show you."

"Don't do it!" Jason shouted.

His dad frowned, cocking his head.

"What's the matter?" Will taunted. "Don't you trust me?"

"Don't do it, man!" Jason yelled. "Don't do it!"

"You've never trusted me for anything, have you?" Hot tears spilled onto Will's cheeks. "Have you?"

"I trust you." His father's voice grew quiet.

"*Liar!*"

"I trust you, Will. You're my son. You wouldn't hurt me."

"Then look," Will demanded. "*Look!*"

His father held his gaze another moment. Will felt his jaw trembling but he would not back down—wasn't sure he could if he wanted to. Finally, slowly, the man raised his head and looked into the creature's eyes.

✝

Jaz shielded her vision from the flashing lights as the sheriff's car came into view. "Do you feel it?" she called to Cindy from the backseat. "The coldness, the heaviness?"

Cindy glanced at her in the mirror. "Yes."

Jaz's heart raced as they pulled to a stop behind Thomas's SUV.

"Are you frightened?" Cindy asked.

"Nah," she lied.

"Yeah," Cindy said with a nod, "me, too."

They opened their doors.

"What's that smell?" Lydia complained from the seat beside Jaz. "It's awful."

Jaz stepped from the car and turned to face the woods. "It's here," was all she said.

Fighting off a shudder, she crossed around to help the old lady out. Meanwhile, Cindy went to the trunk, removed Phil's wheelchair, and wheeled it up to the front. It was tricky, getting the big guy out of the passenger seat and into the chair. Even trickier easing the chair into the ditch and pushing it back up toward the woods. But they finally succeeded and were on their way.

Except for Lydia. She stood beside the car, not budging.

"Aren't you coming?" Cindy asked.

"Do I look like a fool?"

Cindy pushed up her glasses. "No, of course not."

"Then I suggest we do a little praying first."

"Praying?" Phil asked.

"It's what people do when they fight the devil. I'm all for your singing. But nothing beats some good old-fashioned prayer. And what about a Bible?"

"I'm sorry?" Cindy said.

"A Bible, 'The Sword of the Spirit'? Surely you brought a Bible."

"Uh," Phil said, trading looks with the others, "I don't think so."

"Amateurs." The woman sighed wearily. "Well, get over here and let's do some binding and loosening."

They stood staring.

"Prayer," she explained. "Let's do some praying."

More traded looks.

"Come on, we haven't got all night!"

Finally they turned and joined her.

"Dad?" The word felt strange in Lisa's throat, but it didn't stick in it as before. "How do you feel?"

The old man stared at her, shivering from the wet and cold.

"Here, let me help." With Charlie's assistance, she sat him up, leaning him against her. Then, as if seeing Charlie for the first time, she said, "You look like crap."

He nodded and stiffly rose. "Busy day at the office."

She spotted a large red stain on his shoulder. "Your wound's reopened."

He didn't answer but carefully scanned the woods behind them. "Keep your father warm."

She nodded and wrapped her arms around him. It felt awkward being this close to the man, embracing him, but it no longer disgusted and revolted her. Maybe it was because she had a task, to keep him warm. Maybe. But she suspected it was something else. Something that had happened inside the truck . . . and there on the beach when she was breathing life back into him. She was still angry and she was still afraid—but the cold, paralyzing hatred was no longer present.

She motioned to the clearing where the kids had gathered. "You going to check that out?"

He shook his head. "Sheriff's here. I saw his lights through the woods." He turned, searching the bluff above them.

"And Kristof?" she asked.

"He's close."

She nodded in silent agreement as he continued scanning the bluff.

Chapter Twenty-Seven

*L*iar . . . *failure* . . . *hypocrite.*

They were ravenous emotions, looking for something to latch onto. And, as Thomas stared into the creature's eyes, they found a home. Memories rapidly filled his head until they became as vivid as the first time he lived them. . . .

He is talking on the phone in their two-bedroom cracker box that always smells like wet wool. It is their first home. His first year as a pastor. "Yes," he says, "I appreciate the severity of her condition, but—"

The voice on the other end cuts him off. "It's your responsibility. It's your duty *to be here."*

"Who is it?" Sharon asks. With one hand she holds a suitcase; with the other she keeps the rambunctious three-year-old Will in tow.

Thomas covers the receiver and whispers, "Dr. Barington." She rolls her eyes.

He returns to the phone. "We were just heading out the door. We're taking a few days off, and—"

"She's dying. Do you understand me?"

"Yes, and I'm so terribly sorry."

"She's dying and you're taking a vacation?"

He watches Sharon watch him.

She searches his expression for clues.

"I'm sure one of the elders can—"

"Your father would never have done this."

Thomas runs his hand through his hair. It's always about his father. A week doesn't pass that he doesn't hear the comparison. "Yes, my father was a great—"

"You're our pastor now, and we're coming to you for help."

"I appreciate—"

"Just like you came to us for help on that new parking lot you're so proud of."

"Doctor Barington—"

"Or what is it now, some educational wing you think you need?"

He looks back to Sharon. She waits. He holds his ground. "Dr. Barington, we really need to take some time—"

"And we really need you here, Pastor. Now. You can take your vacation anytime. But my wife is dying now. Do you understand that?"

And as young Pastor Thomas struggles with the priorities, he sees his wife lowering their suitcase to the floor. She knows his answer before he gives it.

It was such a minor moment that he'd nearly forgotten. But not now. He couldn't shake her look of disappointment. He knew his real motive. He could disguise it all he wanted, talk about sacrifices for God until he was blue in the face. But there was only one word to describe his actions, one truth, and it stripped away all of his pious justifications: *ambition.*

The word barely surfaced before more failures appeared. Not complete memories—they didn't have to be—just sound bites, bits and pieces of lies and hypocrisy.

He is standing in the bathroom, insisting ten-year-old Will attend Sunday school, even with a fever. . . .

Now he's in the car, now the mall, now Will's bedroom, reminding his son he is an example, that everyone measures the pastor by the pastor's family.

Back in the woods, Thomas leaned over and choked out the words, "I'm sorry. . . ."

Now he is pursuing thirteen-year-old Will down the hall in any one of their dozen shouting matches. The boy turns on him, practically screaming. "It's like we live in some frickin' glass house!"

"Watch your language, young man."

"You're kidding? Frickin'? There's nothing wrong with frickin'!"

"You know where it can lead. And if someone in the church misunderstands—"

"That's exactly what I'm talking about!"

"A man is judged by his household!"

Suddenly, the meaning of the phrase flipped on him, carrying an irony more true than he ever imagined. He tried to catch his breath. Because it wasn't just Will. . . .

Now Sharon stands in the church lobby, the epitome of warmth and joy, despite the postpartum depression she endures for over a year behind closed doors.

Now she sits through one embarrassing sermon illustration after another as he parades their personal lives before the congregation for a laugh. . . .

A sob escaped from Thomas before he could catch it. And then another. And then—

Jessica. Her appearance in his mind is like a punch to his gut. Late twenties. So lovely. Not just physically. She is an incredible secretary who knows his every thought and mood, who understands more than any, the impossible burden he is under, the unbearable loneliness of leadership. They never consummate their relationship, but it's always there in the back of his mind. And hers.

Now they are in the copy room. Working late at night. Alone. The longing in her eyes. The hunger in his heart and loins. And she knows. They both know. Somehow he finds the strength to turn, to walk out of the room. He is trembling. He finds her resignation on his desk the following day. The emptiness after she is gone, that never entirely leaves.

"Thomas."

He heard Sharon's voice. It was far away but directly beside him in the clearing. "Please," he begged the eyes, "no more."

But there was more. Hundreds of memories rising, coming together into a parable, a metaphor, with more substance than any reality.

* * *

Sharon is upstairs and he is down in the den, holding a vibrant woman in his arms. It is impossible to explain how he knows, but this woman is his church, all of its attributes put into female form. This is his empire, with all of her strength and beauty and glory. Breathtaking. But even as she draws him to her, mouth desperate for his, the accusation screams:

Adulterer!

He knows it's true. Not with another woman, but he's as guilty and unclean as if it is.

Failure! Hypocrite! Adulterer!

Thomas could no longer stand. He sank to the forest floor, unable to stop the tears.

"Thomas!" Sharon called from beside him. But he couldn't answer. "Thomas!"

Paralyzed by his own selfishness, lies, and hypocrisy, he remained on his knees weeping in hopelessness.

†

Charlie's core temperature had dropped. The hours in the wilderness, the cold, the wet from the river, and now the intense shivering—there was little doubt that he'd entered the first stage of hypothermia. Nevertheless, he paused halfway up the bluff and tensed his body to stop shaking for two, three, four seconds. It was a trick he learned in the mountains of Syria, when he had not been there with the rest of his Special Ops unit that had not officially been there. In seconds his entire body would shudder in revolt. But during these precious moments, he held rock-steady, searching for the slightest movement of branch or bush on the ridge above him. Kristof had been at the river when he'd sent the pickup rolling into it. But he would not be there now. Odds were he'd moved to higher ground—at least that's what their training dictated.

Suddenly, Charlie spotted it. Seventy-five yards above, eleven o'clock, under a rock ledge. A glint of light—a reflection of the blue and red flashings from the sheriff's car. It lasted only a moment, but enough for Charlie to lock onto it and move forward. The only thing that could reflect light like that was glass—either the lens from a pair of binoculars, or the telescopic sight of a rifle.

Jaz was the first to race into the clearing and the first to stagger to a stop. Coldness struck her body and wrapped around her like an icy blanket. The creature hovered near the altar, Will on the ground beside it. He wasn't dead. She couldn't say the same about the deputy, the way his body was all twisted. Sheriff Hutton and the pastor were both on their knees, staring up at the thing. And Sharon knelt at her man's side, though she was careful to keep her face turned away from the creature.

"Don't look into its eyes!" she shouted to Jaz. "They said don't look into its eyes."

It seemed startled by Jazmin's presence and puffed itself up like it was trying to scare her. Not that it had to—she was about to pee her pants as it was. And that coldness, the way the waves kept hitting and wrapping about her. She could feel them closing around her head, forcing her to turn and look. She tried not to, but it was like she couldn't help herself. And when she finally gave in and did, she couldn't look away.

Emotions exploded in her head. And with them came awful memories, the ones she had tried so hard to forget. . . .

Suddenly she's back in her parents' home . . . crawling out her window, sneaking across the roof to be with Brad . . . wearing those low-cut jeans that make him crazy . . . her shirt snagging on the tree branch with him waiting below . . . them laughing so hard they almost get busted.

Now they're in his car making out, a real window-steamer . . . while her mom and dad are twelve blocks away doing what? Getting kidnapped because of that stupid Voice program. Getting kidnapped, when she could be helping them! Saving them! Instead, she's swapping spit with some Neanderthal, when they are . . . when they are. . . .

Emotion clutched her throat. She tried swallowing it back, but more memories poured in.

She is walking in the dusty Cairo airport holding Charlie's hand.

"Don't look back," he says, which of course means she has to, which of course tells the police something's wrong.

He yanks her forward, breaking into a run . . . but she slows him by wearing those stupid flip-flops he told her not to wear . . . until they are caught . . . hands and mouths taped . . . prisoners in that awful-smelling room . . . her mom just downstairs where she could be saved . . . if Jaz would have listened, if she would have stopped being so spoiled.

A faint warmth washed over her—not deep, barely brushing her skin. Like she felt at church. The creature's gaze faltered. Only a second, but enough for her to pull her eyes away. She glanced over and saw Cindy standing to her right, singing.

How sweet the sound.

But the emotions lingered. Hungry clumps of guilt urged her to look back into the eyes.

She sees Charlie's blood-covered face as the creeps beat him with pipes.
"Stop!" she begs them. "Stop it!"
But they don't stop. She can see his bones snapping, dislocating, poking through his skin. All because of her.

More heat rippled over her. Deeper. The creature shuddered, giving Jaz another opportunity to look away. When she did, she saw Phil and Lydia had joined Cindy in the song.

. . . that saved a wretch like me.

She felt another blast of cold. A single word exploded and repeated in her head:
Brat! Brat! Brat!
The desire to look intensified.

I once was lost, but . . .

Spoiled!
But she would not look.

Now I'm found.

Look at me!
It wasn't one voice, it was several.

Was blind. . .

Look at me!
Using all of her will, Jaz fixed her eyes on Cindy's mouth:

But now I see.

The group started again. This time she joined them:

Amazing grace, how sweet the sound.

The cold increased. The thing drew closer. But Jaz kept her eyes glued to Cindy. She sang louder until she felt heat coming from her throat. It immediately met resistance, icy pressure against her mouth, trying to stop her, but she would not.
Brat! Spoiled! Brat!
She wavered, started to look, then diverted her gaze to its wings. It had grown mistier, more transparent.
Selfish!
The voice was weaker.

That saved a wretch like me.

The heat of her singing joined with the warmth of the others, pushing back the cold, making the voice fade.

I once was lost. . . .

Spoiled!

She could barely hear it now. She looked at Cindy, who was opening and closing her fists like that first time back in church. Another word surfaced in her head, so feeble she could no longer make it out. There was nothing but the singing. And the heat.

The hold was broken.

But not just with Jaz. She saw Sheriff Hutton blinking, glancing around.

"Don't look into its eyes!" Sharon warned him.

He blinked again and nodded, then stiffly got to his feet.

Only Will and Thomas remained on the ground, Will shouting continuously at his dad, "You're such a fake!"

And staring at the creature, Thomas continued to take it, tears streaming down his face.

"Hypocrite!"

"Will!" Sharon started toward her son, but the thing moved to block her.

Slowly, the boy rose. He was a little wobbly but strong enough to keep attacking his dad. "There is no forgiveness. Not for you!"

"Stop it!" Sharon yelled. "Look what you're doing!"

But Will didn't stop. "You know better! You know better, and you just keep on doing it."

Thomas stayed on the ground, sobbing.

"Sweetheart," Sharon called to her husband. "Sweetheart, look at me."

"No." He tossed his head back and forth. "He's right. He's right, he's right. . . ."

Chapter Twenty-Eight

The violent shaking was a clear sign Charlie had entered the second phase of hypothermia. His feet and hands were already losing feeling. He stumbled, nearly falling, more than once. His outer extremities were shutting down. His ability to make sound judgments would soon follow. He had to reach Kristof before that happened.

Unfortunately, the closer he got, the slower he would have to move. Any sound, any snap of branch or twig, would bring deadly consequences—not only to him, but if that reflection had been a rifle scope, to the group below.

A trained shooter can hit a target from over a mile away. The top of the bluff was only two hundred yards from the clearing.

Since he could no longer trust his body, he had to think through every move before he made it. The snail's pace was even worse because he needed to circle Kristof from behind. Over the frogs, he heard the distant pounding of the chopper. If it came closer it would cover missteps, allowing him to move faster. Until then, his progress was one agonizing step at a time.

He crested the bluff where he and Lisa had been just thirty-six hours before and made his way toward the rocky overhang. Eventually he saw the flashing lights of the sheriff's car on the road below, then the clearing with the kids and their candles, and finally, the black winding river. He could no longer see Lisa or her father and figured they'd left the river's edge to join the kids.

He felt the sudden firmness of rock under his feet and knew it was the beginning of the overhang. He eased back. No way could he leap onto the man from above. Not only would his approach be heard, but the angle was too steep. They'd both tumble over the edge to their deaths. He headed to the right, planning to come at him from the side.

It took forever, but at last Kristof came into view. He was sprawled out just four yards ahead, his shape barely visible in the shadows of the overhang. His face was a pale green, illuminated by the night vision scope of his M4.

†

"Tommy?" Lisa called out. "Tommy, I'm talking to you."

As Lisa spoke, Cindy and her little choir came to a stop. They watched Lisa step from the group of kids and cautiously approach.

"Hey, bro?"

She'd seen a pattern. The way the thing grabbed hold of her brother and the others with its eyes, hypnotizing them with its mind games or whatever. But as Tommy's only sibling, Lisa knew a few mind games of her own.

The kids had been quick to help with her father, bundling him up and keeping him warm. Their breath reeked of booze, their eyes were red from dope, but they had definitely sobered up.

Keeping one eye on the creature, she continued her approach. "Tommy?"

He remained crumpled on the ground, weeping, Sharon at his side.

"He's a hypocrite!" Will shouted from behind the black vapor. "A liar!"

"Shut up!" Lisa yelled.

"Look at him!" the boy cried. "What a pathetic piece of—"

"I swear to God, Will, you keep talking and I'll—"

"Look at him! Look at what—"

She turned on him. "I don't care who your pal is. I'll come over there and shut your mouth myself, if I have to. You got it?"

The creature flared, seeming to grow darker.

"You got it?"

The boy swallowed, unsure how to respond.

Still very much aware of the thing, Lisa kneeled down to join her brother. "Hey."

He didn't respond.

"Tommy."

He seemed to know she was present, but was unable to look.

"What are you doing, man?"

No answer.

"Tommy."

He gulped back a sob, but that was all.

"Listen, we all mess up. You know that."

No response.

"Everyone makes mistakes." She forced a half smile. "Some of us specialize in them."

He opened his mouth, then closed it, then opened it again. "I knew. . . ." His voice was a ragged whisper.

She traded looks with Sharon, then replied. "And that makes you, what . . . more guilty?"

He didn't answer.

"Where's all that forgiveness crap you're always spouting off about?"

"I'm . . . a pastor."

She scoffed. "And that makes you, what, better than the rest of us?"

"Lisa," Sharon cautioned.

She ignored her. "I'm sorry, I'm a little confused."

"Lisa, please."

"Let me get this straight. Your Jesus, He can forgive anybody of anything. But not you, because you're, what, too special? Is that right? You're too holy for Him to forgive?"

Thomas swallowed.

"I'm sorry, brother." She leaned closer, whispering into his ear. "You ain't that special. If your God can forgive murderers, He just might be able to forgive you."

"I'm—" The word caught in his throat.

"You're what?"

"No different."

"Than what? Murderers?"

He didn't answer.

"What? What are you no different from?"

"Dad."

The answer stunned her. She glanced back at the kids

and her father. Recovering, she answered, "I don't know, he's pulled a few stunts you haven't gotten around to."

He shook his head. "My family, I . . . abuse them."

Sharon rubbed his arm. "Sweetheart. . . ."

"My son."

Lisa looked past the creature to Will, who was straining to hear. "Maybe you do. Maybe you do abuse him."

He swallowed back another sob, but she refused the self-pity.

"In your own way, you probably do."

Fresh tears spilled onto his face.

"But what's that verse you fellows are so fond of quoting? 'We're all screwups before God?' "

The creature flared its wings.

If it was an intimidation tactic, it worked. But Lisa was finally getting through to Thomas, she could see that, and she wasn't about to back down. "You, me, Dad . . . we're all pieces of work. When you get down to it, we're all losers, right?"

He continued to stare.

"And what does your Bible say about that?"

He didn't respond.

"Come on, don't be an idiot. What does your Bible say?"

He took a breath and swallowed. She gave him a nudge. Finally, haltingly, he quoted, "He came to seek and to save—"

Suddenly the creature hissed.

The sound made Lisa's blood grow cold. But something was happening to her brother. She could see it in his eyes.

He swallowed and repeated the phrase. "The Son came to seek and to save the lost."

"That's right," she repeated. "To seek and save the lost."

The creature began shaking its head.

Although weak and frightened, Tommy took another breath and continued to quote: "What a wretched man I am—"

It cut him off with a scream—part animal, part human.

But Thomas's resolve grew and he continued, "Who will rescue me . . . from this body of death?"

The scream became a shriek as the creature threw back its head in rage or agony or both. Whatever it was, it had been enough to break its hold over Thomas. He was finally free to look away. He turned to Lisa in shock and surprise, then slowly finished the verse in awe, as if it were the first time he heard it: "Thanks be to God—Jesus Christ our Lord."

The thing shuddered, pitching its head from side to side. Lisa grabbed her brother, figuring now was as good a time as any to get out of there. But suddenly he pulled her back down.

"Tom—"

He threw his arms around her in an embrace. It had been years since they'd done anything like that. Awkwardly, clumsily, she tried to return it, as she looked past him to the group of kids and her father . . . as a laser dot danced across the old man's face.

✝

With his eye to the scope, Kristof took a deep breath and exhaled. He was slowing his heart, preparing to fire.

Charlie had closed the distance between them to four yards. Two more and he could attack, leap onto the man, and drive his elbow into the back of his neck, just below the skull. At worst, it would stun him. At best, sever his spinal cord.

Kristof took another breath, blowing it half out, steadying himself for the shot.

There was no time. Charlie had to act now. He threw himself into the air. But his body betrayed him. He was too slow, and he tackled Kristof just as the man squeezed the trigger.

✝

Lisa's father gave a jerk, followed by a rifle report from the bluff that echoed through the forest. The kids around him looked confused until they spotted the hole in his vest, the fiberfill and blood on their bodies and faces. Then they began screaming.

Lisa scrambled to her feet and ran toward them. "Dad!" She expected to hear another shot, feel it slam into her own body, but it didn't happen. She reached the group and pushed the kids aside, fighting to reach her father, ignoring the blonde who stared at his blood on her arms, screaming over and over again.

"Dad!" she shouted.

He looked up at her, his face filled with astonishment as red liquid bubbled from his mouth. The hole in the front of his chest was barely noticeable. The exit wound was a gaping mass of fabric and flesh and blood. Hollow point.

And if that's what the exit looked like, she knew his insides were impossibly shredded.

She eased him down onto her lap. "It's okay, Dad, it's okay." She felt the hot wetness on her hands. All the time he kept his eyes on her. "You'll be okay," she lied, "you'll be fine."

He choked, gurgling more blood, starting to drown as it filled what was left of his lungs.

Charlie had missed Kristof's neck, landing a worthless blow to his right shoulder. Maybe he'd thrown him off target, maybe he hadn't. Either way, Kristof's reaction was swift and professional. In the instant it took Charlie to regroup, the man landed a powerful punch to his face, followed by the butt of his rifle.

For a moment, Charlie saw pinpoints of light. They were extinguished by another blow.

"Li . . ."

"Don't talk, Dad, don't talk."

He frowned.

"It won't hurt long, I promise."

He tried shaking his head.

"I'm right here. I won't leave you." Tears fell from her lashes, splattering onto her father's neck, mixing with his blood. "I promise, I won't leave."

"Lis . . ."

"Shh," she whispered. "It's going to be okay, everything's all right."

281

Angel of Wrath

But he was determined. "Lisss . . . a."

Her name. He had spoken her name. And the sound gripped her throat. "Yes, Daddy, it's Lisa." She took a trembling breath. "I'm right here. I'll take care of you now, just relax."

His eyes widened. He struggled to raise his arm.

"No, don't move."

He frowned, refusing to be put off. There was something else he was trying to say as his hand continued to rise.

"I love you," she whispered hoarsely. "You know, I love you."

Tears filled his eyes. His lips moved and still he continued stretching. She took his hand to press it against her cheek . . . until she saw the red laser dot shimmering across his fingers.

She ducked as a bullet whined past her ear and dug into the ground next to her. She turned toward a fallen tree and started dragging him to cover. A second shot kicked up leaves and fir needles. The third hit its mark, shattering her right thigh. Swallowing back a cry, she turned to her father. But he was already gone, eyes fixed. Oddly, his frown had given way to something else. Not exactly a smile. More a look of peace, even triumph. And she understood. He had just saved her life, returning in part, what he had taken so many years before.

Knowing he was gone, she forced herself to release him and rolled to the log for cover. The kids about her were shouting, some whimpering and crying. Most had hidden behind trees or boulders. The adults had also found safety. Only three remained in the open—Will, Thomas, and the sheriff, who had raced to his fallen deputy's side.

"Get down!" Thomas shouted at his son. "Will, get down!"

But the boy refused. He stood defiantly beside the misty creature.

Sheriff Hutton grabbed the deputy's gun and rose to search for the shooter on the bluff. The next shot threw back his head. He was dead before he hit the ground.

Five more pops rapidly rang from the cliff above them. They were lighter, smaller caliber. All around Lisa, the kids were screaming and crying, but as far as she could tell, no one else had been hit.

A sixth shot fired . . . followed only by the sound of the frogs and an approaching helicopter.

Chapter Twenty-Nine

Charlie woke to a searing pain in his left knee and the sound of Kristof's voice: "Highway 425, near the bridge. On the bluff overlooking the river."

He looked at his leg and saw his pants were wet with blackness, a handkerchief tied just above the knee.

"I've got him pinned down in the clearing. I think I winged him."

Charlie rolled his head to the side and spotted Kristof standing nearby, speaking on his cell phone. Their eyes met and Kristof gave him a nod.

"I don't know how many he shot!" Kristof shouted in mock impatience. "Two, three, four! Just get here as fast as you can!" He snapped the phone shut and motioned to Charlie's tourniquet. "You might want to check that. I was in a hurry."

Charlie coughed, looked again at his leg, then back at Kristof. "Why?" was all he said.

"Because you're a dangerous serial killer."

Charlie frowned, trying to think through the pain.

"Now if you'll excuse me, the fields are 'white already to harvest.'" With that, he turned and disappeared into the night.

Charlie rose on one elbow. As he looked about he realized he was in the middle of a clearing, not twenty yards from Kristof's hideaway. Apparently the man had dragged him up there and blew out his knee while he was unconscious. No doubt to keep him out of the way as he returned to complete his work.

But Charlie could still move. The pain was excruciating, nearly making him black out, but he could move.

He dug in and began dragging himself forward.

✝

"Tommy!" Lisa shouted. She had no reason to believe the shooting was finished, and now her brother was back on his feet, standing in the open like a fool. "Get down!"

But he had seldom listened to her before. Why would he start now? Instead, he began walking toward his son and the thing.

"Tommy!"

"Lisa's right," he said to Will. He motioned to the makeshift altar behind the boy. "Get behind there, where it's safe."

His son stood unmoving.

"Will!" she shouted. "Listen to him. Somebody's shooting at us!"

He did not respond.

She tried her brother. "Tommy!"

But he kept walking toward the boy and the creature.

"Stay away from us!" Will ordered. It was practically a snarl.

The intensity startled Thomas.

Will stepped behind the creature, keeping the black mist between them. Although the mist was less concentrated than before, Lisa could only imagine the terror her brother felt as he approached.

But that was his son.

"I hate you!" the boy screamed.

The thing darkened and hissed.

Thomas hesitated but continued, slower, cautious. "You're right. You have every reason to resent me."

"I don't resent you, I hate you!"

The creature grew even darker, more solid and menacing.

Thomas nodded. "You hate me because I love the church more than I love you. More than I love your mother."

The honesty must have surprised Will. For a moment he had no response.

Thomas kept approaching. "But that's not true, I don't love the church more than you or Mom."

"Liar!"

"No." Thomas shook his head. "I love *me* more than you two. *My* reputation, *my* accomplishments—that's what I love."

"Thomas." His wife stood near the edge of the clearing.

He turned to her. "It's true. I pretend it's about God. Most of the time, I even fool myself. But it's about me." He took a breath. "*My* life, *my* . . . kingdom." He turned back to Will. "And for that—for that, son, I'm very, very sorry."

Will raised his chin in defiance.

"To be honest, I don't even know if I can change—it's been who I am for so long." He continued forward, drawing closer, ten feet from the creature, an additional three from Will. "But if you would give me another chance—if you and Mom would help me. . . ." Thomas swallowed back the emotion.

Will watched in silence.

Thomas tried passing to the right of the creature, but it hissed and countered to block him. He tried moving to the left. It followed suit. Finally he came to a stop just eight feet away. He looked up but was careful to avoid its eyes. "That's my son."

It hissed, puffing itself up.

Thomas hesitated, took a breath for courage, then started toward it.

"Stay back!" Will shouted.

"I'm sorry." He continued forward. "There's no excuse for what I did to you."

"You ruined everything!"

"I know."

"Everybody thinks you're this great man of God." The boy's voice cracked with emotion. "But you're not. You ruin everything!"

"I know."

"Stay back!"

Lisa watched with fear and amazement. Thomas was calling its bluff. He was five feet away from the thing. It could easily attack, reach out and throw him aside as it had the deputy. And still Thomas continued.

"Stay away," Will croaked.

"You're my son."

"We'll hurt you!"

Thomas slowed to a stop directly in front of it, three feet away. "I don't know what type of control it has over you, but—"

"You don't know what we can do!"

"You're my son."

"I'm not kidding!"

"I'll do anything for you." He took a half step closer to the black vapor.

"Stop!"

"Anything." And then, without hesitating, he stepped toward his son and into the mist.

"Dad!"

The thing shuddered in surprise, throwing its head from side to side.

"Thomas!" Sharon cried.

Through the mist, Lisa could see Thomas's eyes wide with terror. She tried to rise, but her shattered leg wouldn't hold.

"Dad!" Will started forward.

"Will!" Sharon yelled.

But she was too late. Will ran into the mist.

The thing roared, convulsing and shaking. For a moment, both father and son were confused, lost, unable to see. Until their hands touched. They clutched one another, each pulling the other to himself, until they finally fell into an embrace. The thing roiled and writhed, but they hung on, refusing to let go.

"Will!" Sharon started for them until Cindy grabbed her arm, holding her back. "Thomas!"

Through the creature's screams, Lisa heard another voice—dry as paper, but shouting with authority: "In my name they will drive out demons—"

The creature staggered as if struck. It threw back its head and shrieked.

Lisa searched until she spotted the old lady Jaz had brought. She was on her feet, quoting: "I have given you authority to overcome the enemy's power. No one will harm you."

The shriek grew louder.

The woman took a step closer. Raising a wizened arm she shouted, "In the name of Jesus the Christ, I command you to go!"

It grew even louder, shriller.

"Now!"

Ear-splitting.

"Now!"

Suddenly, the thing exploded—blowing out and up into a fine, nearly invisible mist. As it drifted down, it condensed, turning into black, vaporous clumps—dozens of them, nearly three feet across. Within moments they were taking on strange, semihuman shapes, like the gargoyles perched atop old buildings. They no sooner touched the earth before they darted with lightning speed in every direction.

But not randomly.

Instead, each raced toward a specific child and adult.

Charlie had crawled less than eight yards before the helicopter rose up behind him. Its blinding light turned the night to day, its rotors deafening as they pounded the air and flattened the grass in the clearing around him.

He shielded his eyes with one arm and signaled with the other. "Over there!" He pointed toward the overhang where he knew Kristof was hiding. "He's over there!"

But the chopper remained, hovering above him, wasting valuable seconds.

"Over there!"

No response.

Angrily, he turned and resumed crawling. He'd lead them by the hand if he had to. There was the click of a PA system, then the words: "Do not move!"

He glared up into the light. "What?" Again he motioned toward Kristof. The overhang was twelve yards away.

"Throw down your weapon and do not move!"

Weapon? What were they talking about?

"Throw down your weapon!"

He raised one arm, then another, showing he was unarmed. "I've got no weapon!" In exaggeration, he pantomimed, patting himself down. "No weapon!"

"Throw down your gun."

He opened his coat. "See? No weap—"

And then he felt it. Extra weight in his left coat pocket. He slipped his hand inside and discovered the gun, its barrel warm from what must have been multiple firings. Warm enough to appear on infrared.

Kristof had thought of everything.

Reluctantly, Charlie pulled the Sig 228 from his pocket, holding it with two fingers and tossing it out of reach.

"Spread out on the ground."

His mind raced, searching for some solution.

"Spread out on the ground."

But there was none. He lay down on his belly, stretching out his arms and legs. He was played out. And yet, even as he lay on the ground, feeling the exhaustion overtake him, there was a spark that would not fade. It had nothing to do with refusing defeat. Nothing to do with Kristof winning. Instead, it had everything to do with Lisa. She was still down there. Hopefully still alive. And, as long as that hope remained, he would not give up.

He rose onto his good knee to resume crawling.

Lisa saw the darkness fly across the ground toward her. Because it was a thin vapor, it was impossible to discern any details, except a froglike snout and bulging eyes. She raised her arms to cover her face, but it made no difference. Suddenly a cold mist enveloped her. With the chill came a series of powerful emotions—feelings of guilt, disgust, self-loathing. They seeped into her, looking for memories to attach themselves to. And they found plenty. Fragments flickered through her mind. . . .

Boys in the backseats of cars . . . on sofas . . . floors. . . .

She winced and tried to push back the images, but they continued . . .

The frat parties . . . smells of beer and vomit . . . bedrooms she doesn't know . . . the stall of a men's bathroom.

She was aware of what was happening—they were the same attacks that struck her brother—but she could do nothing to stop them. Truth was truth. The acts could never be undone. Consequences never reversed. Not even—

"No!" she gasped.

She is lying on a gurney, staring at the little holes in the acoustic ceiling. A stranger is digging inside her . . . the sickening slurp of a suction hose.

"A few more minutes and you'll be good as new."

Painless, effortless . . . and she is done. Brand new and clean.

Except she will never be clean.

"Like a tiny tumor," he says.

But a tiny tumor that is a human, that would be Jazmin's age.

She gagged at the guilt and nearly vomited. She hadn't thought of this in years—or at least pretended she hadn't.

She's on the table again. Different doctor, same digging, disgusting slurps, and unbearable self-hatred.

Now she's in bed with another lover.

"Pretty expensive birth control," he jokes.

"Yeah. . . ."

This time she did vomit.

While all around, kids were covered in the same mist—weeping, sobbing, experiencing their own private hells.

Chapter Thirty

It felt good, Dad holding him like that. Better than good. As soon as the man wrapped his big arms around him, the rage inside Will started to fade. It's not that he forgot. It just didn't matter so much anymore. It was like his dad's embrace, his love, was greater than all his screwups. And as those arms surrounded him, the voices faded. The complaining, the accusing, the demands for justice, everything just sort of . . . evaporated.

Suddenly it was Will who felt the need to apologize. It was Will who was burying his face into his father's neck and croaking, "I'm sorry."

But Thomas didn't answer, at least not in words. Instead he just gripped his son all the tighter. And, to Will's surprise, he felt his father shudder.

"Dad?"

He tried to pull away to see the problem, but his father just kept holding him. He took a shaky breath and shuddered again. And again. He was crying! His dad was in his arms, crying. In a moment, Will was, too. Soon, both of them were standing out in the open, blubbering like a couple of babies in front of everybody.

And it didn't matter.

When they finally separated, they grinned stupidly at each other and looked away, wiping their eyes. Only then did Will notice the mist they'd been standing inside of was gone. The creature had vanished. So had the roaring and screaming. Now there was only the steady thump of a helicopter above their heads, just behind the ridge.

All around them, he saw people huddled on the ground. Some were sitting or hunched over on their knees, others were curled into little balls. And they were all crying. Everyone. Even his mother, who was kneeling fifteen feet away.

"Mom!" He started toward her and Thomas followed.

Her head was bowed and she was weeping softly. Will knelt beside her. Only then did he notice she was covered in a faint shadow.

"I'm sorry," she was sobbing, "I didn't—I should have done something, I—"

"It's okay." He reached out and hugged her. As he did, he felt the coldness of the shadow and, for the briefest moment, his own guilt seemed to return.

Thomas knelt down to join them. "Sharon?"

If she heard, she didn't answer.

"Sweetheart, listen to me."

He was interrupted by the sound of someone singing.

Amazing grace. . . .

Will glanced around until he spotted a young woman

with thick glasses. She was part of the worship team from church. She was on her knees beside Jazmin, her face wet with tears like everyone else's and, as weird as it was, she was singing.

How sweet the sound.

The words were forced, as if she was fighting to get them out. But she just kept on singing.

Charlie continued crawling toward the overhang. He was uncertain why Kristof hadn't resumed firing. Infrared couldn't pick him up under the ledge. Maybe he knew there was no rush. They had their man. Once they removed Charlie and left, he could take all the time he wanted, savoring each of the deaths as he picked them off, one by one.

Still, thanks to the chopper's relentless pounding, Charlie could now approach the ledge unheard. And once he arrived? The angle of descent had not changed. If he jumped, he would still land on Kristof, pulling them both over the edge and to their deaths.

But Lisa was there. If she hadn't been shot, she would be shortly. And that was not acceptable.

The helicopter remained twenty feet overhead. They could take him out anytime they wanted. Then again, he was unarmed. What harm could he do? Throw himself over the edge in attempted suicide? That would certainly save the government money for prosecution, not to mention hours of paperwork for the crew, the hearings, the unwanted media attention.

Charlie gambled the pilot was experienced enough to reach those same conclusions. Of course, that didn't stop the chopper's warnings. But verbal threats were the least of Charlie's concerns. Because, as he felt the needles of the forest floor give way to the harder rock of the ledge's ceiling, as he reached the edge, he saw Kristof preparing to take aim.

✝

. . . That saved a wretch like me.

Jaz felt the ripple of warmth and raised her head. Cindy was kneeling on the ground beside her, singing. It was probably a trick of the light or something, but she seemed to be getting brighter. Not just her, but everything around her. It was like Jaz had taken off a pair of sunglasses and could see everything more clearly. Not only see, but think. She'd been had. Hit by the guilt junk again. She wiped her eyes. Talk about stupid, falling for the same trick twice. But she didn't feel stupid. She felt . . . guilty. That was even sneakier, feeling guilty for feeling guilty? Smooth.

. . . but now am found . . .

She kept her eyes on Cindy's lips and started singing with her. Pretty soon they rose and looked around. Will stood beside his mom and dad. Apparently they'd made up. And the creature? She couldn't see it. She could still feel it, though. All around. The coldness, the waves—she just couldn't pinpoint it.

She watched as Cindy knelt beside Lydia, who was on the ground a few feet away. The woman took the old lady's hands into hers, all the time singing. And, as she sang, a filmy darkness started dissolving from Lydia. Jaz hadn't noticed it before, but as it left, she could see the difference. A difference Lydia must have felt. Because when she looked up to Cindy through her tears, she was smiling. A moment later, she joined them in song:

How sweet the sound.

There were three of them singing now, probably in different keys (old habits die hard), but it didn't matter. And when Jaz looked over at Phil, she saw him struggling to join in. It took a second, but once he did, the same shadowy junk evaporated from him, too.

I once was lost. . . .

But the coldness was still there. The kids were huddled all over the place, crying, covered in the shadowy stuff. Cindy and Lydia traded looks and started toward them, Cindy opening and closing her fists like she did at church. They began the second verse, which Jaz didn't know, so she just kept on singing the first. It probably sounded stupid, but she didn't care.

She joined them as they began walking among the kids. Sometimes they would stop at one, sometimes even kneel—whatever it took to get the creepy junk off them. Once in a while, the darkness would push back, shimmering a little, making her colder. That just meant they had to sing a little harder, concentrate more on the words until it disappeared.

Jaz noticed that even Will and his mom were getting into the act. Cooler still, so was his dad. He was already heading over to Lisa, who lay by a fallen log. But something wasn't right. She could see the mist evaporating from everyone and feel the coldness leaving. But it wasn't really gone. And when she looked up, she saw the reason. The darkness was leaving the people, all right, but it was forming back into the creature. Only bigger. And thinner. Its wings, almost transparent, stretched completely over their heads, covering the clearing.

Mustering the last of his adrenaline and with a final prayer, Charlie Madison threw himself over the stony ledge. He managed to catch Kristof's shoulders and wrap his arms around him, pulling him over the edge to join him in death. They bounced and tumbled down the rocky face, branches tearing exposed face and skin, rocks and boulders breaking bones.

But Charlie did not lose consciousness. Nor did he reach the bottom. Instead, they hit another outcropping of rock and rolled to a stop, just feet from its edge. Bracing himself for the pain that would hit, he lay staring up at the sky. All he could see was the blurred light of the helicopter, its glare somehow refracting into a dozen other lights, even brighter.

He tried to move but couldn't. The shadow of a man rising beside him said that Kristof could.

"Now what, Pastor?" There was no missing the irony in Lisa's voice.

But as Thomas turned from the mist, not twelve feet above their heads, to meet his sister's gaze, he also saw her sincerity. He looked over at the group. Their singing had come to a stop and, one by one, they were turning to him. *Him.* As if *he* could help. Didn't they get it? He had nothing to offer to them. He never had.

But that wasn't true. . . .

As he looked into their faces, he realized he did have something. He had his love for them. And his love for God. He turned to Sharon, Will, then to Lydia, Cindy, Phil. He had something else as well. He had them. Their faith, their talents, their experience. His gaze returned to Lydia, the oldest in the group, one of the oldest in his church. He said nothing. Whether she understood or not, he didn't know. But she gave a nod, ever so slight, and turned back to the creature. Clearing her voice, she raised her head and began to shout: "In my name shall they cast out devils!"

The thing turned to glare at her, but she would not back down. She lifted her frail arms, holding out her hands, and continued: "And he gave them power and authority over all devils."

The group listened and watched as the thing bristled, then shuddered. A few, like Sharon, bowed and began to silently pray.

Once again it started tossing its head from side to side.

Others in the group began praying out loud. To Thomas's surprise, a few of the kids began reciting the Lord's Prayer: "Our Father, who art in heaven. . . ."

More joined in. The creature convulsed, then threw back its head and let out a bone-chilling scream.

Amazing grace . . .

Thomas turned to see Cindy had resumed her singing.

How sweet the sound.

Jazmin, Phil, and a handful of others joined in.

The creature began to thrash, then to waver. With each undulation it grew smaller and darker, condensing.

Now everyone participated—Lydia shouting Scripture, adults joining in with additional Bible verses, kids praying, others singing . . . as the thing continued to shrink and solidify. Emboldened, they began circling it, frightened but encouraged by its reaction. Soon it was the size it had once been as it continued to writhe and convulse and scream.

And still it shrank.

They continued closing in until, suddenly, with a shriek that Thomas felt in his gut, the creature spread its wings and shot up into the sky.

✝

Against the bright lights of the chopper, Charlie saw Kristof's silhouette looming above him. With consciousness nearly gone, he focused all of his energy into his arm, dragging it across the ground, the pain unbearable.

Kristof shouted something he could no longer hear.

Charlie's hand found the man's boot. His fingers moved

up to the laces, to the ankle. He wrapped his hand around it as best he could.

Kristof laughed and kicked it aside like refuse.

Barely able to focus, Charlie saw Kristof raise a boulder high over his head. He could no longer keep his eyes open. They had to close. With luck he would be unconscious before it struck.

Unable to stand because of her leg, Lisa watched the creature streak up toward the sky. She feared it would attack the helicopter but before it cleared the bluff it suddenly stopped as if hitting a wall. It tossed its head, shaking off the blow, while dropping several dozen yards.

It tried to rise again and was blocked just as violently. This time, Lisa saw the reason. At first she thought the lights were some reflection from the helicopter's. But they couldn't be. They moved too independently. And each time the creature tried to rise, they countered, forming an invisible barrier.

Screaming in rage, it began to circle, searching for a way out. It spotted something halfway up the side of the cliff and shot toward it.

"With what judgment ye judge, ye shall be judged!"

Kristof spun around to the screaming voices. The creature of his dreams raced at him, wings spread, full of wrath and rage and justice.

"No!" he shouted. "I have obeyed!"

The hatred in its eyes was paralyzing.

"With what judgment ye judge, ye shall be judged!"

He could barely breathe, forcing out the words. "I . . . have done all you asked!"

It stretched its legs toward him, reached out its arms.

"With what judgment ye judge—"

"I am your servant! I—"

"Ye shall be judged."

The creature struck with fury, its talons piercing Kristof's stomach, its arms wrapping around his head. It veered to the left and pulled him off the cliff.

"No!" he screamed. *"Nooo. . . ."*

The cry forced Charlie's eyes open. He saw Kristof floating away, screaming, his arms and legs flailing. It was a strange hallucination, watching the man fly off into the darkness. Just as strange were the lights. Charlie had seen them earlier, an optical illusion from the helicopter. But now they were approaching. And to his astonishment, they began reaching out to him, touching him. He could feel the warmth of their hands.

Lights? Warmth? Hands? He was obviously in shock. Delirious. Which was okay. It would make the dying easier. And with that bittersweet thought, Charlie Madison once again closed his eyes.

Lisa watched the creature swerve from the bluff and circle back around.

But now it was clutching something. Some*one.* A man! He was kicking and screaming, too far away and too hysterical to understand. But his weight was more than the creature could bear and it began to drop, spiraling lower and lower.

Soon it was close enough to discern the man's words: "Help me! Somebody—"

Kristof! She recognized the voice.

The creature made one final pass before touching down directly in front of the altar, all the time holding the twisting, screaming man.

For a moment, everyone in the group was stunned. But only for a moment. Cindy and Phil were the closest. Without missing a beat, they resumed singing and started to close in.

When we've been there ten thousand years . . .

Others joined them, singing, praying, quoting Scripture.

The thing hissed and snarled, lunging at one, then another.

The group slowed, but they did not stop.

Bright shining as the sun . . .

It shook and shrieked.

"Help me!" the man screamed.

We've no less days to sing God's praise . . .

"In the name of God, somebody—"

*   *   *

The flash was blinding. No sound, just a burst of light above the altar—so intense that Lisa raised her arms to protect her eyes. And when the light faded, the creature was gone.

So was Kristof.

She looked up into the sky. The helicopter was still overhead, pounding the air and flooding the night with its brightness, but the creature was nowhere to be seen. The additional lights had also disappeared.

She turned to the group. They were searching the sky, the clearing, the forest. Gradually the singing and praying died out, giving way to exclamations, then high-fives and hugs. Some of the girls had started crying again, but it was more from nerves. The creature was gone and everyone knew it.

"Lisa!"

She turned to see Jaz running toward her.

"Was that cool or what?"

She nodded.

Spotting her leg, Jaz suddenly looked concerned. "Are you all right?"

Lisa tried not to wince. "No dance lessons for a while, if that's what you mean."

Jaz plopped on the ground to investigate. Of course, that didn't stop her from talking. "Did you see that?"

"Yes."

"I mean really see it?"

"Yes, I saw it, I really saw it."

"Talk about awesome! I mean, did we kick butt or what?"

"Yes." Lisa nodded. "We definitely kicked butt."

Suddenly Jaz looked up. "Where's Uncle Charlie?"

Lisa did not answer.

"I thought you two were together."

"We were." She nodded toward the bluff. "Until he went up there to find Kristof."

"That was the killer?" Jaz asked.

Lisa nodded.

"The guy that thing took—that was him, too?"

Again Lisa nodded.

"Cool." Then, giggling Jaz added, "Guess we could have saved Uncle Charlie the trouble, huh?"

Lisa continued staring up at the bluff. "Yeah. . . ." But already thoughts were returning. Memories of Charlie's weakened condition, of Kristof's expertise, and of the small-caliber shots she'd heard from the top of the bluff.

"You okay?"

Lisa tried to speak but couldn't.

"Hey, you all right?"

She nodded, then turned so the girl wouldn't see the tears filling her eyes.

"Lisa?"

And there, for the first time in years, Lisa Harmon began to pray.

Epilogue

The funeral wasn't as creepy as Jaz was afraid it would be. There was no dead body up front where all you did was stare at it in the coffin during the service. Actually, there wasn't even a coffin. When he was alive, Lisa's dad made a big deal about dead bodies being nothing but a shell you slipped out of to get a brand new one in heaven. Glancing down at her shapeless chest, Jaz hoped her luck would be better in eternity.

Instead of a funeral or even a graveside service, they just had a little memorial service—if you call "little" having more people jammed into the church than the Staples Center at a U2 concert. (Not that she'd been to either one, though both were on her list).

Charlie sat in a wheelchair beside her. He'd been banged up pretty bad. Actually, folks were surprised how he even managed to survive the fall. He said he had some theories but didn't feel like talking about them yet. What a surprise . . . Uncle Charlie not feeling like talking.

"So," Thomas said, looking out over the audience, "is there anyone else?"

He kept the service simple. No funny speeches, no production numbers. Instead, he just talked about how neat his dad was, then turned the mic over to anybody who wanted to say a few words. Unfortunately, more than a few people wanted to say more than a few words.

But now, at last, it was winding down.

"Anybody else?" he repeated.

Will sat on the other side of Jaz. He looked pretty cool, all dressed up. And he gave a pretty cool speech, too—about family and all that. Not that she entirely bought it, with all that had happened, but it sounded like he was at least trying. He was also trying to be nice around her, which was a first. They'd been hanging together more and more, and the truth was, he didn't even turn her stomach like he used to.

Thomas looked around the church one last time. "All right, then. For a closing song, I've asked Cindy Carlson and—"

He stopped as Lisa, who sat next to Sharon, fumbled with her crutches and slowly rose to her feet. You could tell she wasn't crazy about the idea. And by the way people were throwing looks around, you could tell they weren't, either.

She headed across the front of the church toward the stage steps.

Thomas took the mic to join her, saying there was no need for her to come all the way up. But she refused his offer and, after a little off-mic "discussion," she hobbled up the steps, to the center of the stage, and looked out over the crowd. You could feel the tension—hers and theirs. You could also see the California tan completely vanishing from her face.

"I, uh. . . ." She cleared her throat. "I just want to say a few things, if that's all right."

It was a stupid question. What were they going to do, yank the mic away from her?

"As you probably know, my father and I had some . . . difficulties. Things happened that neither one of us were proud about. Ugly things. Sick things."

Jaz glanced around the church. People were definitely listening.

"Perverted things."

Will shifted in his seat.

"My father . . . my father was not a well man."

Thomas looked like he wanted to take the mic back from her. Lisa's look made it clear that she'd break his hand if he tried.

"But he was also a great man. One of only a couple I have ever known." Her eyes landed on Charlie's. She held his look, and you could tell he was somehow giving her strength.

"I'm not sure where the sickness came from. Maybe it's because someone messed him up as a kid, like the shrinks say. Or maybe it's genetic. Or maybe it's just something he was responsible for all on his own. It doesn't matter. The point is, it was sin. Vile and degrading. It destroyed one life." She threw a glance at Thomas. "And crippled others."

He glanced away.

"But I'll tell you this. There's something greater than my father's sin. As sick and disgusting and destructive as it was, there's something greater."

Even in her deafness, Jaz knew you could hear a pin drop.

Lisa took a breath and continued. "You throw the idea around here like it's a Frisbee. I don't like your style, but it doesn't make it any less true. What Jesus Christ did on that cross is greater than any failure or perversion. The bloody death of God's Son is greater than anything you and I can ever do. Ever."

She turned to Thomas. "What's that verse he was so fond of quoting? 'If any of us . . . If we confess. . .' How's that go?"

Thomas leaned into the mic. "If we confess our sins, he is faithful and just and will forgive us our sins and purify us from all unrighteousness."

"Yeah," Lisa said. She nodded, taking a quick swipe at her eyes. " 'All unrighteousness.' Not some, not most—not the neat, tidy ones we like to talk about—but also the ugliest, cruelest, most embarrassing ones we can imagine. 'All unrighteousness.' "

She swallowed. "Now, I know lots of people abuse that—use it as a free ticket to sin. Dad talked about that all the time—how Christians treat Christ like a doormat, wiping the manure of their sins on His holy face, then just going off to merrily sin again. But that wasn't my father. You could see it in his eyes." Softer, she added, "Even during the worst times."

The words were really taking their toll on her, but in true Lisa fashion, she pushed on. "He knew the pain he was inflicting on us and on God . . . and it broke his heart. We"—again she looked to Thomas—"more times than I can count, we heard him at night, alone in his study, sobbing when he thought no one heard."

Thomas looked down.

"My father was a great man. He understood God's forgiveness more than most, because he was forgiven more than most." Her eyes brimmed with tears. "And he *is* forgiven. I'm as certain of that as I am standing before you. God paid too great of a price to let him slip through his hands." The tears spilled onto her cheeks. "He paid too great a price for all of us."

She stood there a moment. By now everybody's waterworks were going. Even Jazmin's. Finally she shoved the mic back at her brother, slipped her crutches under her arms, and started for the stairs. Charlie unlocked his wheels and practically rolled over Jaz to get to the bottom before she arrived. Not that he was much help, but you could tell Lisa appreciated the gesture.

As they moved back to their seats, Thomas asked Cindy and Phil to sing the closing song. Unfortunately, Jaz never really saw them, because Sharon was on her feet, hugging Lisa, then Lisa was hugging Will, and Jaz, feeling stupid for crying and not hugging anyone, knelt down and threw her arms around Charlie and, well, the whole thing turned into one giant hug-fest. How long it lasted, she didn't know. But by the time it was finally over, everybody was pretty much dehydrated.

<hr>

"What do you mean I can't accompany him?" Lisa said. "He's an invalid. He needs my help."

"We'll take it from here." The Sea-Tac security guard motioned to a nearby porter. Charlie watched the young man dash toward them as if he actually thought he'd get a tip.

"You don't understand," Lisa argued. "I'm . . . he's. . . ."

"Unless you have a ticket, this is where you say good-bye."

Lisa looked to Charlie for help, but there was nothing either of them could do. Which was okay with Charlie. Truth be told, he wasn't big on good-byes. Even less when they involved being schlepped around in a wheelchair. But the schlepping had been doctor's orders.

"Unless you'd like me to amputate," the physician had joked, "save you all the hassle of physical therapy."

Charlie wasn't crazy about his bedside manner. Or the idea that once he got back to L.A., there'd be plenty of downtime with reconstructive surgery, recovery, and therapy. Still, a gimpy leg was better than no leg.

He scanned the security area. "Where's Jazmin?"

Lisa looked around. "I don't know. She was here just a minute ago. Jaz?" she called. "Jazmin?"

Hearing her voice, Will emerged around the corner with the girl. He'd insisted on coming with them. "To keep Aunt Lisa company on the way back," he'd said. But his nonchalant swagger and the blush on Jaz's face indicated that wasn't the only reason. They'd gotten pretty chummy the past few days. Obviously, too chummy.

"You have your boarding pass?" Charlie asked as she arrived.

Jaz held it up.

He nodded. "Go on through. I'll be with you in a minute."

"I can wait," she said.

"That's okay, go on through."

"I said I can—"

"Go."

She gave him a glare that he pretended not to see. Then, blowing the hair out of her eyes, she turned back to Will, all soft and doe-eyed. She reached out to him for a final hug, which he nearly gave, until he saw Charlie and reconsidered.

Bright kid.

She turned to give Charlie another dagger look, then began dropping her stuff onto the conveyer belt with the usual melodrama.

Hiding her amusement, Lisa asked Charlie, "You sure you'll be okay?"

"I've got Jazmin."

"That's what I mean."

He grinned. "I'll have the dog test my food."

"Good idea."

"Okay, sir," the guard said. "You're next."

Charlie nodded and hoisted his bag onto the conveyer. Lisa knew enough not to help.

"You'll call me," she said. "Let me know how you're doing."

"Every chance I get."

She pushed back her hair. Not smiling, but not putting him off, either. As the porter prepared to wheel him away, he discreetly slipped his hand to the brake.

"I'll, uh. . . ." She cleared her throat. "I'll be here another two or three weeks. After that"—she glanced away—"after that I'll be home."

He thought of saying he'd be waiting but knew that was pushing it.

"Sir," the porter said, "you've got your hand on the brake."

He glanced down. "Oh, sorry." And when he looked back up, he was greeted by Lisa's lips. It wasn't a long kiss, and she rose back up so quickly, it was as if it never happened. She pushed back her hair again. "I'll see you then."

He nodded. "Yeah, I'll see you."

"Sir? The brake?"

"Oh, right." He moved his hand, and the porter pushed him around the gate, where Jaz waited with exaggerated impatience.

"You look after him," Lisa called.

Jaz sighed wearily. "As if I have a choice."

They shared another set of waves and started down the hall toward the elevators.

"So," Charlie said, touching Jaz's arm to get her attention, "is he a good kisser?"

"What?"

"You heard me."

"How should I know?" She nodded back to the security gate. "Apparently, you're the expert. Honestly, old people hooking up like that in public. Pretty racy, if you ask me."

"I didn't."

"But you're still in the running." She nodded with confidence. "Definitely in the running."

He ignored her and countered. "Speaking of racy, when did you get those jeans?"

"Lisa and I went shopping. I told you."

"No, you didn't."

"Sure, I did."

"No, you didn't."

"Well, maybe if you cared enough to ask, you would have known."

It was starting again—getting fast-talked into the world of teen schizophrenia. But he could handle it. He'd just helped put away a serial killer. "We have a dress code," he reminded her.

"*You* have a code."

"And I hope *you* have the receipt."

"You can be such a Nazi sometimes."

The elevator dinged. "And while we're at it," he said, "now would be a good time to button your shirt up a button . . . or two."

"What difference does it make? It's not like I have cleavage or anything."

"That's enough of that language."

"What? 'Cleavage'? There's nothing wrong with the word."

"Jaz—"

"What am I supposed to say? 'Brea—'"

"Jazmin."

The porter behind him snickered.

"I was going to say 'bosom.' What's wrong with saying 'bosom'? Or is that another Charlie Madison no-no word?"

"Jaz—"

"How 'bout 'mammary glands'? My 'mammary glands' have yet to begin develop—"

"That's enough!"

The elevator doors opened and they stepped inside. No more was said as they turned to face the front. The doors closed and they stood in silence. It felt good to finally have the last word, and Charlie actually found himself gloating . . . at least for a moment.

"Nazi."

About the Author

Bill Myers is an author/screenwriter/director who has sold over eight million books and videos, including *McGee and Me*, *My Life as . . .* , and the Soul Tracker series. His work has won over forty national and international awards. He holds a degree in theater arts from the University of Washington, studied filmmaking at the Italian State Institute for Cinema in Rome, and was awarded an honorary doctorate of theology from the Institute Theologique de Nimes in France, where he taught. When not writing and directing, he enjoys doing voice-over work (he's the voice of Jesus in the NIV Audio Bible), speaking at schools and campuses, and working with young adults in his church. You can visit him at www.Billmyers.com.